A Kingdom of Stars and Shadows

A Kingdom of Stars and Shadows

USA TODAY BESTSELLING AUTHOR

HOLLY RENEE

CONTENT WARNING

This book contains depictions of sexually explicit scenes, violence, assault, and sexual assault. It contains mature language, themes, and content that may not be suitable for all readers. Reader discretion is advised.

For Jayleigh Faye—
My love for you is endless.

.

A Kingdom of Stars and Shadows

ONE

I tried to swallow as the smoke from the burning embers encircled me in a cruel, slow torture. The royal army had been camped outside the cleave between our world and theirs for a total of three days. Three excruciatingly long days.

The grim tick of the clock echoed throughout the room, and my heart raced it before the next beat could sound.

My fingers trembled as I pulled my boot on my foot and tied up the laces. The room was as black as the starless night inside our home, but I didn't mind it. I welcomed it, honestly, because it was the only time I could do anything without everyone watching my every move.

"Where are you going?"

I clamped my eyes closed before quickly tucking my father's dagger into the side of my boot before she could see.

"I just need some air." I stood and pulled the hood of my worn-out cloak over my head. "Go back to sleep."

My mother wrapped her thin arms around herself and avoided my gaze. "Sleep alludes me." She shook her head. "You shouldn't be going out there tonight."

"I can take care of myself."

"I know that." Her dark brown eyes finally met my own. "But it won't be long now until they come, and…"

"And I should be able to enjoy my last few hours of freedom however I choose."

Her jaw clenched at my words. "They aren't taking you as a prisoner, Adara. Being the chosen Starblessed is a blessing from the gods."

"Of course." I bowed in front of her dramatically. "Look at the life it has afforded you."

She sucked in a shocked breath, but this wasn't a new argument. My fate had never been mine, and my mother had accepted many luxuries in exchange for her daughter. Luxuries that my father fought against. That he lost his life over.

I walked to the door and hesitated when my mother's trembling voice called back out to me. "Do not run. They will find you, and we will both pay the price for your treason."

I let her words skate over me and reminded myself of exactly who she was. My heart ached as dread filled me. My fate lay in the hands of the soldiers who waited for me outside the cleave, but I would mourn for no one that I left behind.

The cool night air danced along my skin as if it had been waiting for me to open the door and slide outside. I pulled my hood tighter around my face to hide my curse as I stepped onto the cobblestone street and headed directly toward the place I should have been avoiding.

The streets were bare and quiet. Even the small pub that was usually overflowing with ale and unfaithful husbands was locked down tightly and not a flicker of candlelight shone through the window.

A chill ran down my spine, but I wouldn't allow myself to be fearful like they were. The Achlys family was powerful, but they weren't gods. If they were, then they would have no need for me.

I had never seen a single one of them. Not the king, the queen, or the crowned prince to whom I was sworn to marry. All

I knew was that they were high fae and that the blood that coursed through my veins was somehow the key to unlocking their dormant power.

Lethal power they longed to possess.

To my knowledge, none of the royals had ever crossed over the cleave. They had men for that, and those low-ranked guards were the only ones I had encountered. If they had magic, I had never seen it.

My mother said they didn't use it here because they didn't have to, but part of me wondered if they still had any powers at all. If they didn't have magic, then I had no real reason to fear them. I could run, and my mother would be the one left to face the consequences.

Without powers, I doubted any of them would be able to find me. Only the twin moons knew my secrets as they watched me shift through the shadows. Everyone thought they knew exactly who I was, and that meant they all believed that I was the key to some blessing they thought the royals would bestow on them once I was sacrificed.

My fingers trailed across the bricks as I passed the last building and stepped onto the damp grass. I knew the path that led into the woods better than I knew my own home, and I let my feet lead the way as I looked around me for signs of anyone watching.

The edge of our town was only a few minutes' walk to the perimeter of the cleave, and I often liked to come here just to watch and imagine what life was like on the other side. It didn't look any different from the Starless realm.

The trees grew tall and heavy on both sides, and the only indication that the cleave existed was the thin veil that could hardly be seen at night. It reminded me of the mist that coated our land in the early morning hours, but the cleave never left. I crouched low and ran my fingers through the magic and a thrill of excitement rushed through me. I stared up as I watched the magic recoil from my touch, but it went on for as far as I could see.

It was hard to explain, but the divide between our worlds had felt more familiar to me than my own home. It felt like an old friend that I didn't even know. A familiar stranger that always greeted me.

Tonight, though, it felt different. Darker somehow as if it was warning me away. I pulled my hand back and searched through the gleam.

There were at least fifty soldiers camped in the woods about twenty yards from the cleave, and I watched the one who was standing guard at this edge of the camp.

His gaze was searching the tree line, looking for a threat, but he hadn't noticed me. I could easily cross the cleave and slit his throat if I dared. It would be far too effortless if he were only a man, but I didn't know what powers lay beneath his clueless stare.

My fingers edged toward my dagger as I looked past him and scanned the camp. There were several tents, all bearing the royal seal proudly, and a few soldiers sat by a large fire, laughing as they spoke to one another. I clenched my jaw as I watched them so at ease.

Soldiers sent here to take a human girl against her will, but that fate didn't seem to weigh heavily on any of them.

They were nothing but fools of a crooked kingdom, and my heart pounded in my chest as I watched them.

None of them sensed a threat. Not a single one of them worried about what the Starless could do to them.

But I wasn't Starless.

The twin moons shined brightly above me as my fingers traced over the rough metal handle of my dagger I had memorized years ago, but they tensed as my spine bristled. I turned to look behind me just as a gloved hand clamped down around my mouth.

Panic ensnared me as I searched the dark eyes behind me. His hand flexed against my mouth harder as if he was worried I would scream, but I wouldn't. None of these people would help me, and I didn't want to draw any attention from the fae soldiers.

They were already after me, and I didn't want them to know that I was watching them so closely.

"What the fuck are you doing?" his deep, sensual voice that I didn't recognize growled at me before he dropped his hand from my mouth and jerked my own away from my dagger and tugged it out of my boot.

"Give that back."

I reached out for my blade, but he quickly moved out of my reach. He opened his hand and my dagger was enveloped in black smoke that dripped from his fingers. It floated in the air as if nothing was holding it but his magic. My breath rushed out of me as my marks hummed against my skin. It was as if the stranger in front of me had roused them from a deep slumber that I hadn't realized they were in.

"That's not going to happen." He lowered his hood, and my face flushed with warmth as I looked up at him. His jaw was sharp and his cheekbones high. His hair was black as the night sky and cut short. And gods, he was beautiful. High fae, I was absolutely certain. His ears came to the slightest point that always gave the fae away, but it was his unnatural beauty that divulged what he was so easily. That and his domineering bold-ness. "What are you doing on the edge of the cleave with nothing but a dagger to protect you?"

"I can handle myself." I had become tired of repeating that sentiment, but I still said it regardless of the fact that I didn't owe this fae any explanation.

"Can you?" His hand shot out and wrenched me forward. I flinched and barely noticed his hand as he pulled my hood back with a harsh tug.

His head jerked back as his gaze flicked rapidly over my face, and I knew exactly what he was seeing.

"You're the Starblessed?" His hand tightened around my arm almost to the point of pain, and my pulse raced beneath his touch.

"Starcursed." I lifted my chin as I corrected him. "You are a fae soldier?"

He didn't look like the other soldiers I had seen walking around the camp. His clothes were all black and held no marking of the royal guard.

He hesitated for a second before a small smile appeared on his full lips. "You could say that."

I didn't trust him. Whoever this man was, I knew that he was someone I should stay far away from.

"Let me go." I jerked my arm out of his hold, and his smile widened until his teeth were bared.

"What is the Starblessed doing in the woods in the middle of the night by herself? Shouldn't you be getting rest to meet your new husband tomorrow?"

Tomorrow. I was going to meet the crowned prince of Citlali tomorrow.

"I have a name." I turned away from him and looked back toward the camp. The soldiers there seemed none the wiser that either one of us stood in the woods just outside their tents.

"Adara." My name sounded like a plea from his lips.

I spun back toward him and searched his face. "I seem to be at a disadvantage. You know me, but I have no damn clue who you are."

That only made him smile harder.

"I'm no one important."

His answer grated on my nerves. It was nothing more than a distraction. "So, you won't tell me your name then?"

His eyes narrowed and he cocked his head to the side as he studied me with a slow gaze over every inch of me. I wouldn't know the difference between the truth and a lie regardless of what he told me, but no matter who he was, he was strong. He screamed power without uttering a word. He could be the crowned prince standing in front of me, and I wouldn't know him.

"My name is Evren."

"Evren," I said his name aloud and savored the way it felt across my lips. "Are you going to be the one who escorts me to my prison?"

He jerked back as if I had slapped him. "You consider your betrothal to the crowned prince a prison?"

"I've never met the man, and yet my hand has been forced in marriage simply because he craves the power he believes my blood possesses. If that is not walking into a prison, what would you call it?"

He stepped forward, coming close enough to me that I could smell the hint of leather and something I couldn't quite put my finger on. I tensed as his eyes darkened and he clenched his jaw.

"You should watch the way you speak about the royal family."

Threatening. Everything about him felt like a threat.

"Or what?" I challenged and stared straight up at him as my breath rushed in and out of me. "They'll imprison me? They'll kill me? My blood is no good to them if it runs cold."

"You've lived a charmed life off the royal coin, have you not?" His tone was sharp and his gaze steady.

The urge to smack him was overwhelming, but I refused to let this fae see how badly his words affected me. "You know nothing of the life I've lived."

He was fae, and he couldn't possibly imagine the horrors that happened in our world. The Starless lived in poverty and fear. My family had been blessed by the starlight markings on my face and back, but we had also been cursed.

The royal favor had provided us with water and food to

ensure I didn't starve, a roof over our heads to keep me safe, but it also stole my father from me. It stole my fate.

My cheeks and nose were covered in what looked like freckles if it weren't for their unnatural light golden color that seemed to flow against my skin. But it was my back that always shocked people. Those same markings cascaded down my spine in row after row of starlight, and it shot out at the edges as if it couldn't be controlled. Some edges stayed tightly against my spine while others touched the curve of my ribs.

Markings that almost felt like nothing to me, but they meant the world to everyone else.

"Perhaps, I don't." He lifted his hand, and for a second, I thought he was going to touch the markings on my cheek, but his hand balled into a fist and dropped back to his side. "Perhaps you are nothing like I thought you would be."

"But you have thought of me?" I questioned, my curiosity eating at me.

"We have all thought of you, Adara." He took a step back, putting some space between us before clutching my dagger back in his hand and holding it in my direction. "You will determine the future of our world."

My heart raced at his words, and my fingers trembled as I took my weapon back from this stranger who so easily stole it. "And what if you're wrong about that? What if I am nothing like what you all thought I would be?"

He took another step back into the shadows of the trees, but I could feel his gaze still roaming over every inch of me. "I'm counting on that."

TWO

The sun blinked into my window, and I groaned. It was far too early to be awoken by the false promise of a bright new day. Especially when I had spent far too long into the night watching the army and imagining what today would bring.

I had watched Evren as he left my side and made his way back to the camp. He moved stealthily through the soldiers who waited there, and when I took my eyes off of him for only a moment, he disappeared. No matter how long I scoured those campgrounds, I was not able to find him again.

It didn't matter, though. Evren was nothing more than a soldier who was there to do his job, and it was a job I hated him for.

Because today I would be seized from my home and taken to Citlali.

I tugged on my quilt until it completely covered my head, and I pinched my eyes closed against the reality of the day. I just needed a few more minutes to dream. A few more moments to think about what life might have been like if I wasn't born with a few spots on my face and down my back.

Starblessed.

What a damn joke. The stars hadn't blessed me. They had cursed me and my future, and I wasn't prepared for what was to come.

Last night was my first experience with fae magic, but I knew they were capable of so much more. I had been told stories throughout my childhood, but every one felt like a dark fairy tale. I had been told of how they drank the blood of the Starblessed to fuel their powers. A custom they had adopted from the vampyres before they had been banished from their lands. None of it had ever felt real, but today I would find out the truth.

Evren hadn't looked like the monster I had imagined in my head. He looked nothing like I expected of the high fae at all.

"Adara, it's time to get up." My mother barged into my small room and jerked the blanket from my body. She was dressed in her finest pink dress that fell over her body as if it were made just for her. Her dark hair was pulled out of her face and showed off the gleam that lay in her eyes.

"Mother," I growled as I reached out for my quilt, but she was already ripping open my curtains.

"It's reported that the royal guards have already packed up camp and are soon to breach the cleave. You need to get up and get dressed. Today is your destiny."

My destiny. My mother was foolish if she truly believed that today was anything other than my death sentence. She was willingly handing me over to the fae, and she smiled as she moved about my room with no hesitation.

For a moment, I wondered what she would have done if it had been the vampyres who had come to claim me. She had told me many legends of the Blood Court that was beyond the kingdom of Citlali. Would she have given me over so willingly then too?

I knew deep down that she would have still sacrificed me for the life she now lived. The people of this town worshipped my mother. She had birthed the Starblessed with the largest mark in over a century.

She thought that made her special, blessed somehow, and I guess the reality of it was that she was right. Birthing me had afforded my mother a life she would never have been able to have on her own, and all that it cost her was her daughter and a husband she had supposedly loved.

"I'm up." I swung my legs over the side of my small bed and rubbed at my eyes. I was still wearing the same outfit from last night, and I figured my mother would complain about the dirt that I had managed to track into my bed.

But she didn't say a word.

Instead, she stared at me as she swallowed hard. "You need a bath, then I will do your hair. You can't arrive at the palace like this."

"I don't want to arrive at the palace at all." I pleaded with my eyes even as I felt my heartbeat pounding through me.

My mother shook her head, but I didn't feel like begging her to choose me. There was nothing I could say that would ever make her change her mind about the decision she was making. Even if I could, both of us knew that the royals would do the exact same thing to her that they did to my father when he had tried to deny them.

And my life wasn't worth losing hers.

I pushed past her and into the washroom. She already had a bath drawn for me, and I quickly stripped out of my clothes before sinking into the lukewarm water. Tension eased from my body, but it couldn't stop the way my heart raced in panic with every passing second.

I slipped under the water and drowned out the world for a few short moments. I tried to reach for that feeling I got when I stood at the edge of the cleave far above the town where no one could see me. There was a sense of freedom there that I never felt anywhere else, but that comfort eluded me today.

Instead, all I could imagine was Evren's face and the way his dark eyes had studied me.

You will determine the future of our world.

Damning words that I wasn't ready to face.

I pushed out of the water and gasped for breath. I didn't know what Evren thought of me, but whatever it was, he was wrong.

"Here." My mother handed me a bar of soap and gave no heed to giving me any privacy.

She didn't leave my side again. Not until after I was bathed and my tangled wet hair combed. She sat on my bed as we argued about the dress she had set out for me and how I decided to wear my pair of dark trousers instead.

She was angry when I tucked my black button-down shirt that had belonged to my father into the trousers, but I didn't care. She had made every choice for me, but I was going to wear what I wanted.

She offered to braid my hair and add a few flowers that she had picked from the field, and even though I wanted to argue, the anguish in her eyes made me sit down in front of her and bite my tongue until she was finished.

"You look beautiful." She tucked in the last flower, and I looked away from her before I did something foolish like begging her once again not to do this.

It was only a second later when a loud chime of the town bell rang out throughout the town and dread filled me.

"They're here," my mother whispered the thing no one needed to say. We all knew what today was, and we all knew what they came for.

I stood and grabbed my father's dagger from my dresser before tucking it down into my boot. My mother watched my every move, but she didn't dare say a word against it.

She led me back through our house, and I tried to take in every little detail as I followed her. The walls were worn and stained with years of life, and there were fresh flowers set on the small table only big enough for the two of us. I wouldn't particularly miss anything about it because it had never really felt like home to me, but it was the only real home I had ever had.

The place we lived before this, the home we had with my father, it was such a distant memory that I couldn't recall a single detail of it. It was nothing more than a feeling now, but it was stronger than anything I felt here.

My mother opened the front door, and I swallowed a deep breath as I heard whispers and some cheers from our neighbors. They had all been awarded just as handsomely as my mother for living with and protecting the Starblessed.

As if any one of them could ever protect me.

They were all filled with fear, and that fear had every last one of them bowing their heads as the royal guard rode along our dirt road that led to me.

I held up my head in defiance as I stared straight ahead. I would not bow to some fake royals who thought they were gods in our world because they possessed a bit of magic.

They would take from me as they saw fit, but they would do so against my will. I was Adara Cahira of Starless, and even though I feared them more than most, I refused to bend the knee to them.

I would rather die.

The royal guards stopped directly in front of us, and my mother fell to her knees before them. I swallowed down my disgust as I stared ahead at the guard who rode in the lead.

He watched me carefully, and his gaze dropped to my knees before his jaw clenched. He didn't reprimand me as he dismounted from his horse and moved around to stand in front of me.

"Adara Cahira." His gruff voice sounded as if he had spent far too many years with a pipe in his mouth.

I nodded my head once but didn't speak. My heart felt like it was lodged in my throat. I searched through the guards for Evren, but he wasn't anywhere to be seen.

"I am here on behalf of the house of Achlys to claim you for your betrothal to the crowned prince of Citlali."

I scoffed and looked down the line of the other royal guards. "They were too busy to come themselves?"

Shocked gasps rang out around me, but the guard's stern face carved into the slightest smile. "That they were, Starblessed."

I rolled my eyes at the name. I hated that name as much as the fate it damned me with.

"We are expected to arrive in Citlali by nightfall." He motioned toward the carriage that rode between the swarm of guards, and the dark black wood made me shudder with dread.

"How long is the trip?" I tried not to allow him to sense my fear.

"Several hours." He nodded toward my mother who still hadn't climbed from her knees. "You should say your goodbyes."

I looked down at her, and only after the guard took a step back did she rise. Emotion choked me as I stared at her, and I wasn't prepared for how affected I was by this moment. I had been angry with her for as long as I could remember, but I still wasn't ready to leave her.

I didn't want to say goodbye.

"Be smart, Adara." She reached out for me and gripped my hands in her own trembling ones. "Do what is expected of you."

I loathed her words. Every single one of them felt like a dagger to the chest, but I shouldn't have been surprised. That was all my mother ever wanted from me.

I nodded my head toward her once before pulling her into my arms. I didn't whisper words of love or fears of missing her because I didn't know if either were true. But she was all I had.

She clung to me before pulling away and tucking a stray hair behind my ear so nothing was out of place. Her dark brown eyes that were a mirror of my right one searched my face, but there were no more words to waste between us.

Part of me wondered if she regretted the decisions she had made as she looked up at me and saw the reminder of my father staring back at her in my ice-blue eye.

She had always told me that I was equal parts him and her. Half my father and half the woman who was so easily watching me leave, but she was wrong. I was nothing like her.

I stepped away and turned back to the guard who tilted his head in the direction of the carriage. I took the few short steps and ignored his hand when he held it out in my direction.

I climbed into the carriage and took a deep breath as the door closed behind me and surrounded me with the fear of my future. The interior was far nicer than anything I had ever seen in my entire life. The seat a supple black leather with satin red pillows against the wooden backrest.

I pressed against them before looking back out the open window. One of the guards was loading my small trunk onto the carriage while my mother gazed in longingly with unshed tears in her eyes.

The sight ripped at my chest until I noticed her hands clinging to a piece of parchment that was sealed with the blood-red royal crest.

I knew what that piece of parchment held without her even opening it. That was what she had traded me for. That was whatever she had been promised all those years ago when she had so willingly accepted my betrothal to our enemy.

The guards didn't linger, and they had no reason to. They had gotten what they came for, but I still clung to the seat as the horses lurched forward and the carriage began to move.

With panicked eyes, I looked back to my mother, but I could barely see her through the crowd of people that had gathered on the street. Most of them were waving at me with smiles on tired faces while others were tossing white wildflowers in my direction.

It was a sign of respect, something we usually only did to honor those who had passed to the gods, and dread filled me as I watched them hit the ground.

I traced the outline of my dagger as we began to pass by them in a blur. It was only a couple minutes' ride until we hit the cleave, and I anxiously watched my world fly by as I tried to steady my racing heart.

With every turn of the wooden wheels of our carriage, my fear spiked higher and higher.

I had never seen a single human pass through the cleave besides my father, and I was far too young to truly remember it. It is legend that passing through the cleave alters the Starless, changed forever by the magic that slumbered there, but there were very few stories about the Starblessed. The only thing I knew for sure was that it was said once you passed through, you shall never return.

It didn't matter how they were changed after they passed through the magic, because they were never going to return. I was never going to come back here after today.

I held my breath as we neared the edge of my world, and I slowly blinked them open once I knew we should have passed through. The horses didn't slow. They continued in their punishing rhythm.

I searched out the window, but the world around me didn't look much different from the one I had just given up. But it felt different. It was hard to explain, but it made me feel similar to the way I had with Evren the night before.

The smattering of marks across my cheeks and spine felt like they were alive, and my skin buzzed. It was as if the magic in this land sparked something inside of my curse to life. But it was duller than when Evren touched me. The magic of this world felt like a watered-down version of him.

I ran my fingers over my cheek as I tried to trace that feeling with my fingertips. It was foreign, but it also felt like it belonged.

I spent a long time tracing over those marks I had been born with before I switched over to staring out the window. The scenery that passed us was so like that back home, and I soon became bored of the lush fields and dense forests.

I hadn't even realized I had fallen asleep until I was awoken by the stopping of the carriage. My hand shot out to catch myself on the seat across from me, and my heart raced as I realized I had let down my guard so easily with these fae males.

It was already dark outside, and as I stepped outside of the carriage, I realized that the fae sky was as starless as my own.

Only the twin moons shined high in the sky and provided what little light that they allowed. We were still near the forest edge, and I saw no signs of Citlali City.

"Where are we?" I asked one of the passing guards as I wrapped my arms around myself. Nightfall brought a chill along with it. Another thing that hadn't changed between worlds.

"We're about an hour outside of the capital, ma'am." He tilted his head down as if he was showing me honor, as if I was one of the royals that he served. "We tried to make it the entire distance, but the horses require water."

I nodded in understanding before stepping away from him and looking down the line of guards. There were far too many guards for the task at hand, in my opinion, but I assumed giving up this many men was nothing to the royals.

I stepped into the line of the dark forest and a chill ran down my back. The moonlight seemed to disappear with that one simple step, and I searched the line of black trees as my mark felt like it was flaring against my skin.

"Whoa there." A strong arm wrapped around my middle and jerked me back against his hard body and a step outside of the forest.

Evren.

My curse knew it was him before I could manage to put even an inch between us.

"The Onyx Forest is no place for a Starblessed. Especially not alone."

I looked back at him over my shoulder, and my stomach fluttered under his hold. "I didn't see you."

"That's because you were staring out into the trees."

"No." I shook my head softly. "Before."

"Were you looking for me?" A half smile formed on his lips.

"No." I told a lie we could both easily see through.

His hand tightened around me, almost involuntarily, as he stared down at me, and for a moment, we said nothing.

Evren had given me no reason to, but something deep inside me told me that I should fear this male. Everything inside of me felt tense and my heart hammered against my chest. But I couldn't bring myself to look away from his dark eyes even as that feeling sank into my gut.

"Don't go near the forest again without someone accompanying you." His voice was a hard warning.

"Why?" My gaze finally flicked away from him to look back to the quiet woods. "What's in there? Why are the leaves black? Are the vampyres this close to Citlali?"

My spine straightened at the thought. As much as I hated the fae, I was far more fearful of the vampyres. Every story I had ever been told of them had been of their cruelty. While the highest of fae fed from the Starblessed to garner their powers, the vampyres fed from anyone they chose.

For food, for power, for pleasure.

"You have no reason to fear the vampyres here." Evren spoke softly above me and brought my attention back to him. "There are far worse things that lurk in those trees."

A chill coursed through me at his words.

"I am surrounded by enemies then?" I took a step out of his hold and tried to clear my head.

"You are surrounded by threats." He nodded his head once as if in warning and took a small step closer to me. He searched my eyes for a long moment before he lowered his tone. "You shouldn't trust anyone here."

"Even you?"

"Especially me." His eyes darkened and my stomach became heavy with yearning that made me feel like a traitor. This man was no different from the rest of them, and I would do well to remember that.

"Captain!" one of the guards called out, and Evren's jaw tensed. "We're ready to push on."

He looked over his shoulder toward the guard, and I watched as the young guard flinched. I wasn't sure if it was from respect or true fear, but my hands trembled as I watched the guard lower his head.

I couldn't trust him. He had just warned me of that himself.

"The future queen needs a moment." His voice was pure power, and it sent shivers down my spine.

It took a moment for his words to really hit me. I had known almost my entire life that I was betrothed to the future king of Citlali, but I had never imagined myself as anything other than his property. To hear someone call me the future queen, it messed with my head.

"Of course, Captain." The guard quickly backed away from where we stood, and Evren brought his attention back to me.

His gaze was still dark and domineering, but I couldn't bring myself to look away.

"We'll arrive at the Achlys palace shortly. You should prepare yourself."

"And how am I supposed to do that?" I asked breathlessly. "How am I supposed to prepare myself for what lies inside that castle?"

I didn't know why I was asking him these questions. Evren was one of them. He was a high fae and loyal to the house of Achlys. But part of me was still desperate for his answer.

"You are the future queen of Citlali. Those who reside behind those castle walls will fall to their knees when they see you, as will all of Citlali."

"You didn't." I lifted my chin as I stared up at him.

A small smile played on his lips as he searched my face, and I could see his gaze roaming over every inch of the starlight that marked my face. "Trust me, princess. It took everything inside of me not to fall to my knees before you."

He slipped his hands into his pockets, and even though I knew I should have retreated, his words made me fall impossibly closer to him.

"Don't call me that."

He lifted his fingers until they were only an inch away from my jaw before he slowly pulled them away. "You should get back to your carriage. The night is still young, and as the chosen Starblessed, you have much to face."

THREE

"Welcome to Citlali," one of the guards said next to my window just before riding ahead of the carriage.

I scrambled to the side of the carriage so I could see the city that I had heard about since I was a child. Cobblestones thrummed beneath the carriage wheels as we hit the city streets. It should have been shrouded in darkness, but it was alive with bright lanterns that hung from the stone townhouses and candlelight that adorned almost every doorstep.

The residents of the capital city stood at their doorsteps and along the street as they watched our procession pass them by. Some waved while others simply tried to peer inside the carriage to look at me.

Some tossed flowers in the path that we took, but instead of white flowers of honor like those of the Starless realm, the Citlali people tossed red poppies as they cheered.

And that reaction shocked me.

Almost all of the faces staring back at me were fae, but I noticed one man who bore the markings of starlight on his left shoulder. The marking was much smaller than my own, but he was the only other Starblessed I had ever seen.

And he currently had his arms wrapped around the fae woman in front of him.

He looked nothing like me. His skin was much darker than mine and his mark was so light that it almost looked white. My markings reminded me of the soft glow of the sun as it fell below the hills near my village.

Both of his eyes a light blue that matched my father's.

We were so different yet the same.

But he looked like he was happy to be here. Like he was in love.

I didn't take my eyes off him as the carriage continued through the city, and his gaze stared back at me as well. He had a gentle smile on his face, but I didn't return it. I didn't even know this man, but for some reason, I had the overwhelming urge to call him a traitor.

He was nothing to me, a complete stranger, but I still felt betrayed by the way he fit in so well with our enemies. I couldn't stop the deep ache in my chest even as the carriage turned the corner and the man disappeared from my view.

I had always imagined how the Achlys palace would look in my head, but my imagination hadn't done it justice. Even at night, the large building was striking, yet daunting.

The dark towers loomed over the town below, but most of the castle was hidden behind an imposing stone wall that reached higher than anyone could climb.

The carriage slowed as we approached the black iron gate, and my heart raced as the loud grating of metal rang out around us. I watched as the gate slowly opened to allow us through, and the urge to run hit me full force.

I knew once I passed beyond that wall that there would be no turning back. This was my fate, the fate decided my men and fae, not the gods. Only I could change it.

I could run, but I knew that they would find me. I shivered at the thought of what fate would wait for me then.

The fae soldiers I had met so far hadn't been what I expected, but I knew better than to provoke the fae of my childhood fairy tales. Evil, lethal, venomous. I didn't know if I had the courage to face those nightmares.

But the carriage moved forward again before I could truly consider it.

I was on edge, and I couldn't believe that it had only been this morning when I was taken from my home.

It had already felt like a lifetime ago.

The gate closed behind us with a loud clang, and my fingers edged toward my dagger as I searched out the window. The palace grounds were grand and beautiful, even though I had expected it to look like something else entirely.

The dark stones rose high into the sky, but glass windows were intricately weaved into the structure in a way that made it feel almost dazzling in the lanterns that hung within. Flowers caressed every inch of dirt that remained inside the stone grounds. Splashes of white and red everywhere to be seen.

The carriage stopped before a set of grand stairs that led up to the even more imposing set of doors. I quickly checked my boot for my dagger before pushing my hair out of my face. I wished I had thought to bring my cloak. I felt desperate for the solace and privacy a simple piece of fabric could bring me.

The guard opened the carriage door, the same guard who had first approached me in Starless, and he once again held his hand out to help me. This time I took it. My hand trembled in his as I climbed out of the carriage and pressed my back against the smooth dark wood.

"Welcome to the Achlys palace." He bowed his head, but I wasn't really looking at him. I was too busy searching down the line of guards in the red and white uniforms, and I was only looking for black.

But Evren was nowhere to be seen.

The door to the palace opened with a deep groan that spoke

of its age, and three fae women stepped outside. The youngest one with blonde curls that were thrown into a mess on top of her head, hurried down the stairs and kneeled before me.

I jerked back at her action, but my body was still pressed against the carriage.

Her brown eyes peered up at me, and I could see the confusion on her face. "Welcome, Starblessed. I'm Eletta, your lady-in-waiting."

I had no idea what that meant, but I was more than ready for the girl to get up off her knees. "Please call me Adara." I reached my hand out for her, but her cheeks reddened, and she quickly stood on her own.

"You must be tired from your trip. I have prepared your rooms where you can rest until the king and queen are ready for you." She motioned up the stairs, and I quickly looked back in search of Evren one last time.

He still wasn't there, and I scolded myself for caring. He was a fae, a captain of a royal guard, and he would be no help to me here.

"I just need to grab my trunk." I started toward the back of the carriage, but the guard stopped me.

"It will be taken to your rooms."

My rooms. As if this was to become my home. I knew the reality of it was the truth, but it felt like the closest thing to a lie.

This palace would never be my home. It didn't matter what waited for me inside.

"Okay." I nodded and started up the stairs after Eletta.

She watched me with every step I took, but she didn't speak. We walked through the large doors, and I was instantly hit with the heat of a large hearth that sat at the base of the room. The fire was roaring inside as if it was trying to heat the entire palace, and I shuddered as I watched the large flames lick up the sides of the stone.

"Your room is in the north wing." Eletta nodded in that direction, and I followed behind her.

Everything we passed was gilded in gold or marble or beautifully aged stone. I had never seen anything like it in my entire life.

"How old is the Achlys palace?" I asked, and my voice echoed throughout the empty hall.

"It is said that the palace was built by the first fae king, Novak, more than three millennia ago." Eletta absently ran her finger along the wall as she passed.

There was no way that could be right.

We finally reached my room, and Eletta opened the door before standing aside to allow me through. I did so hesitantly.

There was another small hearth at the edge of the room, and a much smaller fire danced inside and warmed the space. A large bed sat across from it covered in rich fabrics that draped to the floor in the softest shade of rouge.

As much as I hated it, my muscles begged for me to lie against it and feel if it was as welcoming as it appeared. There was a small desk perched next to the single window in the room, and atop it was blank parchment and ink along with a gold mirror that spanned the width of the dark wood.

"The washroom is this way." She stood near the only other door in the room, and I quickly followed her inside.

I couldn't stop the sigh from passing my lips as I spotted the large copper tub that took up most of the space. Eletta smiled.

"I shall prepare a bath for you so we can get you ready to be presented to the royal family. They should call upon you within the next couple hours."

"Okay." I nodded my head even though I was wholly unprepared for what was to come.

Eletta lifted her fingers and turned them in the smallest pivot, and water began pouring out of the stone wall into the tub. I shot backward and clung to the door as I watched her magic. The tub steamed with the heat of the water, and I couldn't speak a word as she lifted a small bottle and dropped oil against the surface.

The smell of jasmine hit me just as she turned to face me.

"Are you all right?" She looked around quickly, reassuring herself that no one else was there.

"You used magic." It was a question and an accusation.

"Of course, I did." Her brows lowered, and she stuttered over her words. "Everyone here uses magic."

I stared at her because I wasn't sure what to say. Of course, I knew that the high fae would possess powers, but Eletta wasn't high fae. She was my lady-in-waiting, and I couldn't wrap my head around what I had just seen.

If Eletta could do that, what was Evren capable of?

"All fae have magic?" I finally managed the words as my hands tightened on the door.

"Most do." She nodded. "It's very rare for a fae not to possess any magic even if it is the simplest enchantments."

I was dying to know more. "And the royals, they possess a lot more magic than others?"

Her eyes flicked to the doorway, then back to me. I could see her hesitancy staring back at me, but she still spoke even though her voice was barely a whisper. "The Achlys family has passed down a potent magical line for the hundreds of years that they have been in power, but some worry that power may be waning."

I stepped forward, closer to her. "What does that mean?"

"I don't like to speak of this." She looked back toward the doorway.

"Please," I begged, and her eyes flew up to meet mine.

"It is said that the magic that lies within you will determine the fate of the Achlys family and all of Citlali. You will either be the key to their rise or the catalyst to their fall."

My heart hammered in my chest at her words. "I don't have that kind of power." I shook my head. "I don't have any power."

"Every Starblessed is born with the ability to awaken the dormant and lethal magic that hides within a fae. From what we've been told for years, you are the key to guaranteeing our safety." Eletta fidgeted with her dress.

Safety. "Safety from what? What if you're all wrong?" I clenched my fists at my sides as the weight of her words hit me.

Her eyes flashed with fear. "We should really get you into the bath, Starblessed."

"What if you're wrong?" I asked my question more firmly. If I was the one who was supposed to be such a vital role in the future of this kingdom, then I deserved to know the truth. Everything I had ever been told about my betrothal had been minimal and useless.

Never had I been told anything like this.

"If Prince Gavril feeds from you and he doesn't gain the power that is prophesied, then I fear that the kingdom will be truly vulnerable to Queen Veda for the first time in millennia." Her voice shook and fueled my unease.

I had never heard that name in my entire life. I had never heard of any other queen besides the one I was to serve. "Who is Queen Veda?"

Eletta turned and ran her hand over the rim of the tub. "She is the ruling monarch of the Blood Court, the vampyres, and it is told that she is ruthless in her power and her hatred."

A chill ran down my spine. I had heard legend after legend of the vampyres, and none of them were good. But I had never heard of their queen. "And she wants what?"

"To rule all." Eletta grabbed a towel from a small gold hook on the wall that looked softer than any fabric I had ever felt and set it beside the tub. "Queen Veda has wanted to overthrow Citlali for as long as I can remember, but this is the first time her threats have any real chance of coming true."

She nodded toward the tub, and I slowly slipped off my boots and set them directly beside the tub where I could reach them.

Eletta's eyes widened as she watched me slide my dagger inside my boot, but she didn't say a word. I started to undress as my mind raced. "And you all think that I am going to be the one to stop her?"

I stepped inside the tub, and even the heat from the water couldn't cure the chill across my skin. I didn't know what these fae had been told of me, but I wasn't what they thought. I didn't possess the power to stop a vampyre queen. I didn't possess the power to stop anything.

"We pray to the gods that you are." She dipped a cloth into the water before lathering it with soap while I hid my breasts with my arms. "If the foretelling is wrong, then I hope the gods are truly watching over us."

For the first time in a long time, I prayed that they were too.

FOUR

I stared into the mirror and hardly recognized myself. My dark hair was pulled back and twisted on the top of my head in an elaborate design that was already starting to give me a headache, and Eletta had painted on a thick line of coal along my eyes that somehow made me look so different from myself.

But none of that was the issue. It was the white dress that fell from my shoulders and shined like stars cascaded down the fabric. I hadn't known where to look when Eletta had slipped it over my head, but my astonishment quickly slipped away when I realized that the back of the dress fell to just below the small of my back.

The markings on my back were fully exposed, and even though I tried to argue against the dress, she warned me that the queen had demanded I wear a garment that showed off exactly what they were after.

They didn't care about the woman who was about to be standing in front of them. They cared about one thing and one thing only, and that was on full display even as I tremored from the chill of the night.

I longed for bed, but I didn't have a choice. I was standing with Eletta right outside the great hall, and she was still fidgeting with my dress as I tried to breathe. I refused to allow the royals to see how badly they affected me.

My fear was their power, and they would yield it against me if only I gave them the chance.

These were the people who had murdered my father when he had tried to deny them his only child, and I would not dare to let them see that fear in my eyes.

"Are you ready?" Eletta spoke softly in front of me, and I let my eyes meet hers. She was fae just like the rest of them, but something told me this girl wasn't anything like them at all. She had treated me with nothing but kindness and respect since I had arrived.

"I'm not sure I will ever be ready." I was honest with her, and I watched as the small smile fell from her lovely face.

But she didn't have time to respond. The doors to the great hall opened, a royal guard on each side, and she quickly moved behind me. I could hardly see inside the hall, but it felt like hundreds of faces were staring back at me.

I was looking at each and every one of them, and I hated that I was searching for a guard who I had met only today.

A guard who was completely inconsequential.

I passed through the doorway, and I straightened my exposed spine as I noted the rows and rows of people who stood in the space. They were all watching me with wonder and want in their eyes, but none of them met my gaze. They looked upon my cheeks before their gazes fell upon my shoulders, hungry to see my back.

A curse to me, yet a blessing to them. A savior.

I looked away from all of them and let my gaze fall upon the three fae that were seated upon a low dais. The queen was the first to catch my eye, and it was no wonder. She was dressed in a long red gown that stood out among everyone else's, and the crown that sat atop her head matched. Spires of gold topped with large rubies that should have made it impossible for her to stare down at anyone.

But she managed it just the same.

She looked down at me with a severe and calculating gaze, and it took everything inside of me not to cower. She was beautiful, there was no doubt about that, but she considered me carefully as her eyes narrowed.

She was the power. She was far more than a face to be looked upon.

Even with two men sitting at her sides, the queen of Citlali was the one who ruled, and I feared her far more than I ever thought I would.

I let my gaze slide away from her to the king at her side. He wore a similar crown, much smaller in size, and he looked regal in his deep blue surcoat adorned only with a royal crest in gold and red.

His gaze roamed over my body as if he was trying to calculate every inch of me that could be used. I hated the look in his eyes, as if I was prized cattle being brought to the highest bidder.

I jerked my gaze away from him, and I stopped short when it slammed into the only other who stood upon the dais. He was much younger than the king and queen, and the crown that fell upon his head was much less grandiose.

But he didn't need the crown upon his head to catch my attention. He was strikingly handsome, in a way that I had only felt with one other, and there was a soft smile upon his lips as he looked down at me.

I stopped in front of the three of them, and I refused to let my head fall as I stared up at them. This was the royal family, the family that would take from me, the family I was to be married into, and I refused to bend the knee even as they shook beneath me.

A hush fell over the crowd as the queen stood. "So, you are

the Starblessed that has been promised?" Her voice was unyielding, and every head turned to face her as she spoke.

I didn't know how to answer her, so I didn't say a word in
return. I simply held her gaze as she assessed me.

"You're the girl with the power of the stars?" She clenched
her jaw, and I knew she wasn't used to repeating herself.

"I hold no power."

"Ah, but you do." She stepped down from her dais, and one
of the guards rushed to hold his hand out to her. "I can feel it
from here."

The queen dropped the guard's hand and stepped toward me,
and my breath rushed out of me. She stopped in front of me,
within arm's reach, and I couldn't help noticing how vastly we
differed. Her skin was pale and free of any signs of a hard life,
and her hair was so light it was almost white.

She reached forward, her finger dipping below my chin and
causing me to flinch before she tilted my face back and forth to
examine me. "Your face is remarkable." Her fingers flexed
against my chin. "But I would like to gaze upon your back."

I didn't want to turn around. I was already so exposed, and I
could already feel the stares of those who stood behind me. But I
was given no choice.

The queen's eyes darkened, and the floor beneath my feet
began to move.

I reached out to grab ahold of something to stop myself from
falling, but she was the only one within reach. I refused to use
her help against her own power.

I hadn't seen her lift her hand or mouth in any sort of spell, but
the marble floor where I stood spun easily as if her power didn't
require such things. It didn't stop until I was facing the doors in
which I had arrived, and I heard her gasp along with others.

A cold finger ran down the length of my spine, and I shuddered under her touch. "Are you pure?"

Her question snapped me to attention, and I had no idea what she meant. "Excuse me?"

"Your blood. The blood of the stars. Is it pure, or have you been fed from before?"

A knot settled in my stomach at her insolence.

"Mother." I heard the crown prince's voice growl from the stage, and I balled my hands into fists at my sides.

"I am as pure as you demanded." I tried not to let my voice waver. "No one has ever fed from me."

Not in the way she was asking and not in the way I had wished for before. No one in my town dared to touch me. I was the Starblessed, and I belonged to the royals. The boys of my town had taken that as literally as they could.

Anyone who tainted me would be cursed. Anyone who harmed me, ill-fated.

"Good," the queen spoke from behind me. "My son will be the only one to taste your powers and unite with them. You will be his and his alone."

I hated her words. I despised how effortlessly she referred to me as an object to be devoured.

"Come, Gavril. Look upon her."

I tensed as I waited with my back turned to the dais. I could hear movement, but I could see nothing but the faces of those who still watched the spectacle in front of them. But none of them were looking at me, not truly.

I knew the moment the crowned prince stood behind me. I could feel him along my marks like a buzz of power coming to life. It reminded me of Evren, and I quickly searched the faces around me for his familiar one.

"She is exquisite." The crowned prince spoke before slowly moving around me. He stopped when he faced me fully, and he dipped his head in the slightest of bows. "It is a pleasure to finally meet you, Starblessed."

"Adara." I couldn't stop myself from saying. "My name is Adara Cahira."

"Adara." He purred my name, and a chill ran down my mark. "It is a pleasure to meet you, Adara."

I didn't know what to say back to him because I didn't share the sentiment. He was handsome and had been respectful thus far, but I was still sent here to be claimed as his belonging.

"And what am I to call you?" I asked, and I heard murmurs from those around me. But the crowned prince grinned.

"I go by many names, but as my future wife, I shall like it if you will call me Gavril."

He watched me as I took in his words, and that small smile didn't fall from his lips. "Would you honor me in a dance?" He held his hand out to me, and I faltered before slipping mine into his hold.

Music began playing the moment he drew me toward him, and my palm fell upon his chest as he slowly lifted my other in his hand.

I didn't miss the way his hand fell upon the small of my back or the way his fingers clenched as they came in contact with my mark. That buzz of power from earlier only amplified under his touch.

"I'm sorry about my mother." He spoke softly as he began spinning me around the floor. "I know she can be a bit over-bearing."

I glanced up at him. Overbearing didn't feel like the correct word to describe the queen. My gut told me she was ruthless, cunning, unyielding.

I had no allies in this palace. I was wary of everyone here, but she was my true opponent in this palace. She was the one who I needed to watch at all times, but even knowing that I couldn't look away from the prince as he spoke.

"She means well."

"Means well for who?" My hand tightened on his shoulder.

"I don't believe the queen has any interest in me other than what I can provide for you."

Gavril had the gall to look embarrassed by my words, but I didn't know how he thought I could possibly think otherwise. "You are to be my wife, Adara. You are more than the blood that runs through your veins."

His words were like a whisper over my skin. A whisper that captivated me.

"And how exactly do you feed from me?"

I knew this hall wasn't the right place for that kind of question, but I had to know. The lores I had been told stated that the fae fed from a Starblessed like we are warned of vampyres. But as I looked up at Gavril, I saw no signs of sharp teeth for him to puncture my skin. I saw no signs of the monster that I feared lay beneath.

"You have time before you are to worry about that." He cleared his throat before his fingers gently trailed over my skin. "I will not feed from you until we are wed. Until you are mine."

That both calmed me and filled me with unease simultaneously. "And when are we to wed?"

"In a month's time." He drew me closer to him absently. "You will become a princess of Citlali before the twin moons meet in the starless sky."

A princess. The thought was absurd to me.

I was no more fit to be a princess than I was to be a queen.

"I know this isn't what you wanted, but you will learn to love it here, Adara." He sounded so sincere, but I didn't trust him. How could I learn to love something my father had died to try to prevent?

"But this is what you wanted?"

He didn't answer me immediately. His gaze fell over every inch of my face as he thought about my question. "What I want is to fulfill my duties as the crowned prince of Citlali. I can't expect you to understand that."

His words felt like a whip.

"I think I understand more than most, considering my duty was to give up my entire life."

He jolted backward like my words hit their mark.

"So it is your duty that causes you to long to feed from me? None of that comes from your own thirst of power?"

He leaned in closer to me, and I stiffened in his hold as his mouth pressed in close to my ear. "My thirst, as you put it, will be quenched soon enough, and we shall see what I long for after I have my first taste."

He pulled back and his dark blue eyes stared down at me.

"Have you fed from another?" The question felt so intimate, but they had paid no mind when they asked the same of me.

"I have." He nodded. "But none that have awoken my true power. None that feel the same as you." His hand skimmed up the length of my back, and the touch felt indecent with all of these people watching. But I would be a fool to deny the thrill that ran through me with his touch.

It was unlike anything I had ever sensed before. It was a persuasion and a cautioning all at once.

The song came to an end, and Gavril wavered as he finally removed his hand from my back. He dipped into a small bow as he let my hand fall between us. There were several others dancing around us, others that I had barely even noticed, but I looked up toward the dais to find the queen's eyes directly on me.

"Thank you for the dance, Adara." Gavril stood back to his full height before he lifted his hand as if he wished to touch my face. I took a step back before I allowed him to do so.

Gavril searched my face, but I just needed to get away. I needed to escape his touch and their watchful eyes.

I turned toward the doors, and no one stopped me as I quickly made my way back to them. I could feel my heart hammering in my chest and my breath rushing out of me as I tried to calm my mind. This was too much. It was all too much.

I grabbed my long skirt in my hand as I finally made it to the doors, and I looked back to see the queen still following my every move with cold, calculated eyes.

I turned down the hall, desperate to get back to my room, when my chest slammed into another and my breath fell from my lips in a rush.

Evren's fingers dug into the skin of my upper arms as he steadied me, and that feeling of electricity from earlier intensified. "What happened?" His dark gaze searched mine before he quickly glanced over my head. "Are you okay?"

He was still dressed in solid black, a uniform which I had yet to see him out of, but the fabrics that were currently draped across his skin were much finer than earlier. They reminded me of the prince's if it weren't for the lack of the royal crest along his chest.

"Adara." His hands shook me slightly to get my attention.

I stared back up at his face as I tried to calm myself.

"Are you all right?"

It should have been a simple question, but I didn't feel all right at all. Not really.

"I don't want to go back into that hall." I didn't need to glance behind me. The voices of the many patrons and the echoes of revelry fell out of the doorway as if it couldn't contain it.

"We don't have to." His fingers tensed on my arms, and he once again looked over my head before nodding once. To one of the other guards, I presumed. "I'd like to show you something."

Evren reached for my hand, slowly linking his with my own before he pulled me in the opposite direction of the great hall. With every step we took away, my breathing eased. I didn't think of where Evren was taking me, I simply allowed him to pull me along behind him, and when the cool night air hit me and danced along my exposed skin, I shivered.

The gardens. Evren pulled me farther away from the palace and into the lush gardens that were covered in flowers of a hundred different varieties. I was sure it was breathtaking during the day, but at night it gleamed under the many lanterns that hung from iron posts.

"I tend to come out to these gardens when I need a moment of solace." Evren hummed as he turned toward me. "It is a nice reprieve from what goes on inside those walls."

"I was not prepared." I gently shook my head. "The queen."

I couldn't get the way she spoke to me, the way she looked at me, out of my mind.

"The queen is..." He pondered before looking back down at me. "Difficult."

"Yet you serve her?"

He swallowed hard and shook his head gently as he thought over my question. It weighed heavily on him, but what I didn't know was why. "You look beautiful." His gaze trailed down the length of me, and it felt like a slow caress. "Has anyone told you that tonight?"

I shook my head gently. The things the crowned prince had said, they weren't about me, not really.

"That's a fucking shame." He stepped closer to me, and the smell of him was overwhelming. "I shouldn't be the one to tell you."

"And why not?" I tilted my head up to look at him.

"We both know why not. My..." Evren looked over my head before quickly looking back down at me. It was a foolish thought, but I could have sworn that his gaze darkened as he did so. "The crowned prince is a fool if he doesn't see how beautiful you are, nevertheless, you are his."

"I am no one's." My voice was firmer than I intended, and the slight smile on Evren's lips frustrated me even more.

"But you are." He moved his hand along the backside of my forearm, and my stomach tightened as I watched his skin against mine. "And soon you'll be his in marriage and in flesh."

My gaze snapped back to his. "In a month's time," I repeated the words that had felt like my doom. "I will become the princess of Citlali and my blood taken from me in a month's time."

"I have been told that the experience is quite pleasurable."

"What?" My arm recoiled in his touch, and he lowered his voice even further.

"The act of being fed from." His dark eyes ran over every inch of me. "I have been told that some can hardly control themselves from the type of frenzy it causes inside of you." His thumb ran along his bottom lip, and for a moment, I couldn't help wondering what it would be like to have Evren to be the one to feed from me instead.

Would I still be so fearful?

"And have you?" I looked away from him before I could finish my question. "Have you fed from a Starblessed before?"

His fingers lifted and touched my chin gently before he forced me to look back at him. "I have not, but I could only imagine what it would be like." Every word was like a stroke along my starving skin. "I could only dream of what one would feel to taste you."

Evren was barely touching me. Only his finger remained at the base of my chin, but he was stripping me bare with his words. I did not know this man, and I knew that I shouldn't want to. But my body craved the way he was speaking to me now with his hushed voice and his lips only a whisper away from mine.

Every part of me felt alive, my mark stirring along my skin, and I couldn't stop myself as I leaned farther into him.

"Adara."

"Yes?" I blinked up at him, and my hand ached to reach up

and push away his dark hair that was falling into his handsome face.

"I should escort you to your room."

"Of course." I nodded, but neither of us moved. I was too mesmerized by the way he was looking at me. At me and not the mark on my skin. He was nothing more than a captain of the royal guard, but I was more intrigued by him than I had been with anyone I saw in that gilded hall.

Evren was staring at my mouth, and I could hardly breathe as he did so. I dug my fingers into my palms to keep myself from reaching out for him and demanding him to close the distance between us. My body begged for him to do so, but I wouldn't dare allow my words to do the same.

His gaze ran over my face before he cleared his throat and stepped back from me. My center of gravity was thrown off with that one small step, and I avoided meeting his eyes as I straightened myself.

"Please allow me to make sure you get back safely to your rooms." His voice held an edge to it that it had lacked only moments before, but I simply nodded my head once before turning back in the direction of the palace.

I barely noticed the flowers as I walked in front of him and desperately wished for the comforts of a room I did not know.

I didn't wait for him to open the heavy door that was an inlay of glass and iron. I headed back into the hallway, the warmth of the palace once again overwhelming me, before he could reach for the door.

"Adara, please wait," he called behind me, but I didn't stop. I was being foolish, and I had only been gone from my home for one day. I needed sleep and to clear my head.

I needed...

"There you are." I stopped in my tracks at the sound of Gavril's voice and watched as he strolled out of a small room with an amber glass in his hand.

Evren almost ran into my back as I stopped so suddenly, and Gavril's gaze quickly flicked to meet his captain's.

"I see you finally met my brother." Gavril's words felt wrong, and my body stiffened as the truth of who the man I had almost just begged to kiss me hit me. "Who decided that tonight wasn't important enough to grace us with his presence."

"Someone has to man the borders." His voice was much calmer than I felt. "Not all of us can simply host balls and send someone else to fetch their betrothed."

I watched as Gavril narrowed his eyes at his brother, and I quickly took a step away from the man at my back. I turned to look at him, and it was as if I was seeing him for the first time.

Evren was a high fae, he was a royal, and he was a liar.

He pulled his gaze away from his brother to look at me, and I could have sworn I saw a moment of remorse flash in his dark eyes before it was quickly replaced.

"And how are the borders?"

"Quiet." Evren didn't pull his gaze away from me. "I'm not sure where the rumors of the threats are coming from, but we didn't see any signs of what's to come."

What did that mean? Evren was manning the border between Citlali and the human lands?

"But maybe this isn't the best place to discuss it." Evren nodded his head in my direction, and I hated how easily he had just dismissed me.

"You're right, brother." Gavril moved forward and clapped his hand on Evren's shoulder.

I searched the two of them for similarities I might have missed, but they looked so different from one another. So in opposition. And I had been easily fooled.

"I was just escorting Ms. Cahira to her room." Evren bowed his head to his brother. "I will make sure that she gets there safely."

I didn't want to go anywhere with him, but I didn't say those words. I just stared ahead as the two of them discussed me like I wasn't even there.

"I will handle it from here." Gavril held out his arm to me, and my hand trembled as I wavered in my choice. But I finally slipped my hand upon his arm and avoided looking at Evren altogether. "She is my betrothed, after all."

"Of course." Evren bowed deeper this time, and I absently wondered what such a powerful man would look like on his knees. He had said that the kingdom of Citlali would fall to their knees in front of me, but I wasn't interested in them.

Suddenly, I felt so angry with this man that I couldn't spare an ounce of concern for anyone else.

Gavril started forward, and I looked over my shoulder just as Evren stood back to his full height. He didn't meet my eyes, though. He was staring directly at the spot where his brother was touching me.

I watched as his fist clenched at his side, and my own hand tightened against his brother. Evren's gaze flew up to meet mine, but I quickly looked away and followed the crowned prince where he led me.

He was quiet for a long moment as my heart raced. I simply wished to get back to my room so I could put the entire day behind me. I had a month's time in this palace. A month to figure out what exactly I planned to do with the role my fate had handed me.

"I'm sorry you had to hear all that talk of borders and threats." Gavril gave me a tight smile. "I fear my brother is equal parts brute and royal, and he sometimes forgets his place in this family."

"That's all right, Your Highness." I faltered over my words because I was unsure of how to address him.

"Please, call me Gavril. Especially when there are no watchful eyes."

Would that mean the expectation would be different when there was?

We arrived at my door, and I let my hand fall from his arm. "Good night, Gavril."

"Good night." He smiled again, this time with much less tension. "I shall see you again tomorrow."

I nodded because he had summoned me here. I had no other choice. I opened my door, but I hesitated before walking through it fully when he called my name.

"You looked absolutely beautiful tonight."

FIVE

I awoke with a gasp before I realized where I was. Eletta was already in my room busying herself with what looked like my breakfast against the small desk.

"Are you all right?"

"Yes, sorry." I sat up in the bed and pushed my wayward hair out of my face. "I had forgotten where I was for a moment."

I could see the pity in her eyes, and I swallowed it down quickly before I allowed myself to drown in it. Her pity would be no use to either of us.

"He is a great man, you know." She lifted a lid off the tray before setting it aside. The smell of warm pastries and fruit hit me instantly and caused my stomach to growl.

Her words angered me because I had lost countless hours of sleep last night thinking of how he was no such thing.

"I do not believe him to be so." I swung my legs off the bed and stood before grabbing the small throw and wrapping it around myself.

"But you hardly know him." She softly shook her head. "I have worked in the palace for several years, and I have always known him to be noble even when situations require him to be ruthless."

I couldn't stop the small scoff that fell from my lips. Her gaze flew up to meet mine, and I actually felt bad.

"I do not mean to insult you, Eletta, as I have only known the prince since he arrived in Starless yesterday, but he seems to lack the decorum that you speak of."

Her brows scrunched together as I made my way toward the desk. "The crowned prince came to Starless?"

Shit. She was talking of that prince. "Oh. No." I quickly shook my head. "I thought you were referring to his brother."

"You met Prince Evren?" Her voice held a touch of alarm.

"I did. He was the first fae I met at the cleave."

She looked away from me, and her fingers clenched tightly against her skirts as she adjusted them.

"Please, Eletta. Tell me what you're thinking. If this"—I motioned my hand back and forth between us—"is to work, then I need us to trust one another."

"Of course, ma'am." Her eyes slid to the door. "It's only that I do not wish to speak ill of the Achlys family."

I stepped closer to her and lowered my voice. "It's just us here."

She nodded even though she didn't owe me an ounce of her trust. "You should stay away from Prince Evren."

A chill ran down my spine at her warning.

"He is everything that his brother is not. Brutal and merciless. I hadn't realized that he had yet come back from the Sidra border."

"The Sidra border? The Achlyses send their prince to patrol the vampyre border?"

"We shouldn't speak of this." She pulled out the chair from the desk and motioned me forward. "You should eat. I'm not sure what the day holds for you."

I sat even though my mind was racing with the information

she had just given me. The way she described Evren was the opposite of what he had shown me yesterday. That was until I realized who he truly was.

"Am I to see the royal family today?" I took a bite of a sweet melon and moaned as the flavor hit my tongue. I hadn't tasted fruit with such sweetness in years.

"They haven't called upon you yet, but I would presume so." Her voice shook, and she fidgeted behind me.

"Until then, could you give me a tour?" I hated how helpless I felt here, and not knowing the palace grounds only intensified that.

"Of course, ma'am." She smiled, and I quickly ate my breakfast before she could change her mind.

She helped me dress in a long silk dress that was as beautiful as it was impractical, but she had balked when I had suggested wearing something of my own. She had at least allowed me to wear my hair down when she had seen how uncomfortable I was with even a sliver of my back exposed.

She led me from the room, and I followed her every step as she explained every room that we passed.

"This is the Hall of Kings." She was droning on about history I hardly cared about. Instead, I was mentally mapping every turn, every room.

Portraits hung along the wall, all of them men who looked like they thirsted for power almost more than the one before them. Until we came to the current king of Citlali. It should have been his wife's face who stared down at me from that wall.

"This is where Prince Gavril's portrait will hang once he is crowned king."

She glanced back at me, but I was still staring up at the blank wall. I was overwhelmed with the thought of the future king of Citlali's portrait would hang there. My future husband.

"He'll make a handsome king. Don't you think?"

"Yes. Of course." There was no denying it. Gavril Achlys

was beyond handsome. Everything about him felt regal and impressive. He was nothing as I thought he would be.

"The library is just this way." We turned down the hallway and through an arched door that led to the low-lit space.

Rows and rows of books reached from floor to ceiling, and the room seemed to break off even more as the books continued.

"This is beautiful." I ran my hand over a few spines as I explored. I had read my fair share of books, but I had never seen anything like this. There were more books here than I could read in a lifetime.

"It is. This library holds all of our histories including your own," Eletta said so absently, but my gaze slammed into hers.

"There are histories of the Starblessed here?"

She nodded before fidgeting with her dress. "I have seen Prince Evren reading them before."

That news shocked me. What did he care about the history of my people?

"Can you leave me here, Eletta?" I looked around me and tried to give her a convincing smile. "I would like to read for a bit. You can retrieve me if I am called upon."

"Certainly." She bowed her head before quickly departing and leaving me with my thoughts.

The only history I had ever been told of the Starblessed was what those in my town had known. Legends passed down from one generation to the other, and most of the information was lacking.

My heart raced as I skimmed through the titles on the shelves. There were books of kings and fae legends. Tales of past wars and alliances.

But I stopped when I read the gold words along a black leather-bound book. *The Rise and Fall of Sidra.* I slid the book from the shelf and flipped it open quickly.

This was where Evren had been stationed. A prince of Citlali occupying the border of his enemy.

And from what I had been told, they were a formidable enemy indeed.

I dropped into a chair near the small fireplace and flipped through the fading pages. There were drawings depicting the vampyres of Sidra. But to me, they looked so similar to the fae; the lack of sharp ears the only real difference I noted.

But then I came to the page that told of the way a vampyre fed. My eyes prowled over the words quickly as I took in every bit of information I could. The legends I had been told and that of this text were differing.

I had thought a vampyre must feed daily, but according to the book in front of me, they could go years without tasting blood on their lips. But a lack of blood also meant lack of power. With every day they abstained, their power grew weaker.

But it was the drawing on the next page that made my breath leave me in a rush. It depicted a male vampyre with his teeth exposed and ready to sink into the neck of the woman in front of him. She didn't look frightened from the drawing. She looked euphoric. She looked...

"I hadn't realized you had such an interest in the vampyres of Sidra."

I slammed the book closed as I heard his voice and brought my trembling hand to my chest. "You startled me."

Evren was leaning against the doorway, his shoulder pressed into the wood and his legs crossed at the ankles. I had no idea how long he had been there.

"I didn't mean to." He ran his hand absently over his bare forearm where his shirt was rolled up. "You were enraptured in that text."

I pressed the book into my chest as if that would save me from him knowing exactly what I was reading. "Am I not allowed to read it?"

"Of course, you are. I just find your interest in them curious."

"From what I've overheard, my curiosity is a mere necessity. You yourself guard the border. Do you not?"

"I do." He was watching me so closely, and I hated the way it made me feel. I shifted in my seat and pressed my thighs together to stop the small ache that started there at the sight of him. His gaze immediately tracked the movement.

"You lied to me."

I expected him to look back up at me defensively, but he didn't. Instead, he did a slow perusal of my body before his eyes finally met mine again. "When did I lie?"

My fingers tightened around the book, and I stood angrily. "When you told me that you were one of the royal guards."

I walked back to the shelf and gently placed the book back into its place.

"I am a royal guard."

His words made me press my eyes closed before I turned back to face him. "You are a prince."

"And what?" He cocked his head to the side as he pushed off the wall. "If you had known, you would have kneeled before me to show your loyalty?"

My chest heaved as he closed the space between us. "No." I shook my head and tried to remind myself of who he was. "I will never get on my knees for you."

"Ah, princess." He stepped into my space, closer than was proper. He reached forward, slipping a piece of my hair between his fingers before he slowly twisted it in his hold. "I would give just about anything to see you on your knees."

"That will never happen." I sounded breathless, and Evren knew. His mouth lifted in a wicked smile as he stared down at my mouth.

"I wouldn't dare insinuate that the future queen of Citlali would ever do such a thing." He pushed forward again, and his hands moved to the bookshelves on either side of my head. He leaned down until I had no option but to look at him. "But gods,

I can imagine it. The way you would look staring up at me, the way I would make you beg."

My breath rushed out of me as my stomach tightened with his depraved words, and I knew he could feel it against his lips.

"My brother's betrothed on her knees before me, ready to pledge her allegiance with her perfect mouth."

I jolted away from him, and my back hit the bookcase. That only made him smile harder.

"I would…"

"You would what, princess?" His gaze darkened as he leaned forward and ran his nose along the shell of my ear. I shuddered against him, my mark sparking to life in a way that consumed me. "You would beg the brother of the future king to give you exactly what you crave? The things he couldn't dare give you."

"Evren." I said his name in warning, but it came out as a plea.

He breathed me in slowly before finally pulling away. "Prince Evren. Until you are queen, you should address me as such."

"You're an ass." My voice shook with anger and need.

"As I've been told." He ran his hand across his jaw as he looked at me, and I wasn't foolish enough to miss the hunger in his eyes. And that one glimpse of his desire made me feel as if I was starving. "My brother has asked for you to meet him for a lunch in the gardens."

I swallowed hard at the mention of the crowned prince. "And you're just now telling me this?"

"My apologies, Starblessed." He dipped into a deep bow. "It seemed to slip my mind."

SIX

I couldn't do this. About that one fact I was absolutely certain.

It was the only thing I could think of as I followed Evren back down the hallway and out into the gardens where I stood with him just last night.

Evren opened the door and then motioned for me to pass. I did so with my head held high and not a word muttered from my lips. I had no idea what his motives were, but Evren was far worse than I had initially thought. Gavril sat at a table set for two, and he was looking over some parchments that were spread in front of him.

"Adara," Evren said my name so softly that I worried I imagined it, but I quickly looked back at him to be sure. There was something in his eyes, something he wasn't telling me, but I knew better than to expect the truth out of him.

"You're here." Gavril stood from his chair, and a servant quickly moved behind him to pull it out of his way. "I was worried you had gotten lost in this maze of a castle."

"No." I smiled softly. "I just lost track of time exploring. My apologies."

"No need to apologize." Gavril reached out for me, and I allowed him to take my hand in his. "Thank you, brother."

Evren was already walking back into the palace, his back turned to us, and he didn't answer the crowned prince before disappearing out of sight.

Gavril pulled out my chair, and I took my seat before looking over the display in front of me. There was an array of food and wine covering every inch of the table that hadn't been out here the night before, and I absently thought of all the people this amount of food could feed.

People were starving, and here we sat with more than enough food to waste.

"Are you hungry?" Gavril sat back down across from me, and his servant quickly jumped into action, pouring me a glass of wine.

"Yes. Thank you." I reached out for a piece of crusty bread but simply held it in my hands as a million thoughts ran through my mind.

"Is everything okay?"

"What am I to become?" The question blurted out of me before I could stop myself.

"I'm sorry?" Gavril laughed softly, but I was serious.

"After I marry you, what am I to become?"

"Happy, I hope." He reached for his own food before laying some out on his plate. "Isn't that all anyone could hope for in a marriage?"

"A normal marriage, yes, but this isn't normal. I was brought here to be a vessel that holds the blood you seek. Nothing more."

Gavril's hands steadied and the smile dropped from his face. "I do not need to marry you to take your blood, Starblessed. I simply need to take my dagger and make the smallest slice in your skin before I press my mouth upon it. Your blood will flow beautifully whether you are the future queen of Citlali or not."

Fear, pure and unrelenting anger flowed through me. "Then why go through with this betrothal at all?"

"Because, Adara." He lifted his knife, and I watched as he slowly buttered a piece of bread before drizzling it with honey. "No one else shall feed from what's mine, and there are only two ways to assure that. I can either marry you and everyone will fear touching what's mine, or I can lock you in the dungeon and visit you when I need to taste your power. Which would you prefer?"

He leaned back in his chair and stared at me as he lifted his bread and took a bite. He licked the sticky honey from his full lips without taking his eyes off me for a second, and I wanted to run.

Every part of me was screaming for me to get up from this table now and run. But he would catch me.

There was nowhere in his world or mine that I would be able to hide from them. Especially now that Gavril was looking at me in the same way their mother had only the night before.

"Obviously, I would prefer not to be locked in a dungeon." My voice shook, and I hated it.

"That's a smart choice." He smiled before plucking a grape from a platter and pressing it into his mouth. "Our marriage will strengthen this kingdom along with its king. Together, we will be unstoppable."

That thought almost scared me more than his threat of the dungeon.

"And the vampyres?"

"What of them?" He narrowed his eyes, and I knew I had to tread carefully.

"I have heard rumors of their threats." I swallowed hard and tried not to allow him to see the fear in my eyes. "Do you truly believe that my blood is strong enough to fight them off?"

He chuckled, the sound cynical and bitter. "I believe that my blood is strong enough. What runs in your veins means nothing without me."

I bit my tongue as I stared at him. No. I wouldn't survive running from him, but I knew I couldn't endure a life at his side either.

I had a decision to make. One that I wouldn't take lightly, but I couldn't sit here and stare at this man, my future husband, my future king, and accept his word as if he was one of the gods.

He was fae, but that didn't make him deathless.

"Don't worry yourself about the Blood Court." He leaned forward and pressed his elbows into the table as he watched me. "Your focus should be on serving me and my kingdom alone. You are my Starblessed, and fear of creatures who don't dare cross our border are not your concern. Now eat."

I lifted the bread I was still holding to my mouth and slowly took a small bite like the dutiful intended that I was, and as I stared at him, everything became clear.

I was to escape Citlali and run as far as I possibly could, or I was going to have to kill the crowned prince. I was going to take the son from the very people who stole my father.

Neither of those choices would end well, but they were better than the fate that was laid before me.

SEVEN

G avril hadn't called on me last night.
  After our lunch, he left me in the garden, and I hurried back to my room where I had locked myself away until now.

Thoughts of fate plagued me through the night, and I tossed and turned and searched the starless sky outside my window for more hours than I was able to sleep. It was torturous. The thought that what lay in front of me could be simply changed with only one decision. A decision that wouldn't be easy, but it would be fate-altering just the same.

"It will just be you and the royal family tonight." Eletta was braiding my hair into a thick plait over my shoulder. "The king may have his counsel present, but otherwise this is a family dinner."

I snorted at her insinuation that I was a part of this family. Even if I was to marry the crowned prince and go forward with my dealt fate, these people would never be my family.

I would become one of them in name only.

I would become Evren's sister in marriage and his queen in duty.

I would be his brother's wife, and everything about it would be agonizing.

I was dressed in another white gown, this one much simpler than the one before, but my back was still on full display. It was as if the queen was dressing me so that she may see my mark and nothing else.

The fabric was beautiful and chaste, but it felt obscene against my skin. The queen had wanted to know if I was pure, but she also wanted to put me on display in a way that made me feel exposed.

Eletta stood at my side the entire walk through the palace. I was to dine with the Achlys family in their private hall, and the room we walked to hadn't been a part of the tour yesterday.

There were guards standing outside the doors, and I absently wondered if any of them ever went anywhere without one of their royal escorts. One of them motioned me forward, and I lifted my chin as I passed through the door and into the room.

A large wooden table was centered in the room beneath a monstrous chandelier, and the king and queen were seated at opposite ends. Two men I didn't recognize sat to one side while the two men that I was trying not to think about sat at the other.

"Ah, Starblessed." The king lifted his wine goblet in my direction before motioning me forward. "Please join us."

Evren stood before any servant could head in my direction, and I tried not to look at him as I slid by him and into the chair he had just pulled out for me. Gavril was sitting to my right, at the hand of the queen, and as soon as I was settled into my seat, Evren took the seat to my left.

I didn't know what to do or say, so I simply sat there and looked ahead of me at the grand tapestry that draped down the wall. It held the gold emblem of the royal crest, and the deep red of the fabric unsettled me in some way.

It reminded me of what this kingdom desired of me.

"Starblessed, these are my advisors, Draven and Erebus.

They both wished to have a better look at you than they were able to get the other night." Both the name he called me and the words the king spoke begged of me to recoil.

Instead, I simply nodded my head once in their direction before looking back to the tapestry.

"Adara." My name slipped from the queen's lips like a curse. "How are you finding the palace thus far? Is it to your standards?"

I looked at her, and I could feel her watching, assessing.

"I have never seen another palace before, so compared to the home I grew up in it is quite grand."

"I'm sure it is, but I hope what we provided for your family before you were summoned kept you comfortable." She drank from her wineglass slowly, but her gaze never fell from mine.

"What you provided for my mother and me, you mean?" My hands tightened into fists in my lap. "My family was ruined the moment you all stole my father and slayed him for trying to fight against this betrothal."

A hand skimmed across my knee, and I flinched. Evren's fingers gripped my leg in his hold and tightened. A warning.

I knew why.

The queen's eyes had darkened with venom and the words she spoke felt like they were laced with poison, eager to destroy me. "Your father sealed his fate, my dear. Not the crown. If he had been loyal, then he would still be with his family. If he were loyal, he wouldn't have died a traitor."

My chest heaved, and I opened my mouth to speak, but Evren's hand tightened again, stopping me.

"The blood that runs through your veins strengthens our kingdom and the human lands. Without your fealty, we could easily allow the Blood Court to move into Starless as they please." She cocked her head and narrowed her eyes as she studied the way her words were affecting me. "Who would be there to protect your mother when the vampyres decided to feast upon her flesh?"

I didn't answer her because I could hardly breathe, let alone speak.

"No one, my dear. You and your mother have been protected because we offered you that protection. Your father couldn't see that, and he wouldn't have been able to provide you with the life that we so graciously did. You should remember that."

My hands trembled in my lap, and I could feel tears burning in my eyes as she spoke of my father. But I wouldn't dare allow them to fall in front of her.

I barely knew him, too young to even remember the look of his face, but he had fought for me when no one else had. He showed me more love in that one act than anyone else ever had.

"Have some wine." Gavril lifted the decanter and poured the red liquid into the glass that laid before me.

I looked at him for the first time since I had arrived at the table, and I hated how his mother's words had felt like nothing to him.

"Please." His whispered word had me searching his face, and his gaze softened as he stared down at me.

Evren's hand slipped away from my leg in that moment, and even though I felt desperate to look back at him, I didn't. I wrapped my hand around the glass and slowly brought it to my lips. I welcomed the bitter liquid, drinking more than I should have, as the king began speaking to his advisors.

I wasn't listening to a word he said. I was too busy trying to calm the rage that was consuming me.

Food was laid on the table by the servants as the king laughed at something that was said, and Gavril spooned something onto the plate in front of me.

The queen answered the king, and my gaze flew back to her at the sound of her voice, but Gavril blocked my view. He leaned forward, his fingers touching my braid, and he whispered, "Eat," low enough for only me to hear.

The tenderness in his voice caught me off guard and made me even angrier. He had acted just like his mother at lunch yesterday, but tonight? The look he was giving me felt like he was taking pity on me for things she had said.

I didn't need his sympathy. It made me feel weak, and I refused to show any fragility to them.

I lifted my fork and took a bite of food as he had directed me to. The warm potatoes tasted divine, so I quickly dove into the meat that Gavril had just served.

"Son, when do you head back to the border?" The king drew my attention to him.

"In a week's time." Evren said it so calmly, and I couldn't stop myself from looking at him. "I will be back in plenty of time for the ceremony, though."

"Good." The king clapped his son on the back before taking a large pull from his wineglass. "We need to make sure the border is secure to ensure our future."

Evren nodded his head in understanding before he glanced over at me. His gaze was cold and harsh, but somehow it still made me feel like I was burning inside. "Nothing will stop the joining of Gavril and the Starblessed."

He said the words like a promise, but they sounded bitter on his tongue. I had no idea what Evren wanted from me, but that want felt like it was in contention with the way he had looked at me and spoken to me before.

"You are correct about that, Evren." The queen barely looked at him. "And we have much to plan before the nuptials take place and Gavril is blessed with the powers he has been carrying all along."

Part of me wondered if that was true. Would my blood simply be awakening a power inside Gavril, or would he be taking from me something I didn't truly wish to give?

"The people of Citlali will gather from afar to watch the crowned prince marry the Starblessed, and they will bow before his power."

I heard her words, and I knew that they should have been what I was focused on. But all I could think about was the fact that Evren was going to be leaving.

This man was the son of my enemies and the brother of my betrothed, but I knew I didn't want to be in this palace without him. It was a thought that was both foolish and reckless.

"You may be the Starblessed, Adara, but there are many things you must be taught before you can become the princess of Citlali. Things I have no doubt your Starless upbringing will leave lacking."

I set my fork down against my plate as my stomach rolled. This woman hated me. She had wanted me here so badly, but she hated me just the same. And her venom was lethal.

"May I be excused?" I looked away from her and directly up at the king. If the queen wasn't going to show me even an ounce of respect, then neither was I.

The king faltered and looked to the queen before glancing back at me. "Of course." He nodded once, and I quickly stood before anyone could reach for my seat to help me out of it. I didn't need their help. I didn't want it.

I didn't offer any of them any sort of pleasantries as I walked away from the table and pushed out of the doors that were still guarded heavily.

I wanted to escape their judgment and superiority. I felt like I was drowning in it. I pushed through the hall, one foot after another, as I tried to calm my racing heart.

I rounded the corner to my room when I felt someone's hand slide over mine and jerk me to a stop.

"What are you doing?" I searched over my shoulder and tried to pull my hand away from Evren's touch, but he refused to let go.

"Are you okay?" He practically growled the words at me, and the sound infuriated me.

"Am I okay?" I laughed. "Why in the gods would you care if I am okay?"

He stepped closer to me, and I retreated. "I didn't know."

"Didn't know what?" I jerked away from him again, and this time he let my hand fall from his. But that didn't stop him. He pushed forward until I had no choice but to press my back against the wall.

"About your father. I had no idea."

I swallowed hard as he searched my face. I didn't want to talk about my father with him. Not when his parents were the ones who took him from me so ruthlessly.

"It doesn't matter." I shook my head and looked away from him.

"It does." He lifted his hand as if he was going to force me to turn back to him, but the markings on his fingers caught my attention.

"What happened?" I reached for his hand and turned it over in my own. The tips of his fingers were solid black, and the color seemed to be bleeding up his skin. I had no idea how I hadn't noticed it earlier. I pressed my fingertip to his dark one and a flare of power shot through me.

"Nothing." He pulled away from me and slid his hands into his pockets as if I could forget what I had just seen.

"Something happened." I pointed toward him. "Were you hurt?"

A grin slid across his lips. "Are you worried about me, princess?"

"Of course not." My chest felt heavy under my lie.

"You're not a very good liar." His voice was low, and his gaze dropped to my mouth as he spoke. The combination was deadly.

"I'm not lying."

"You know that I face far worse every day than what lies behind the walls of this castle. I can handle myself."

"Do you?" I blinked up at him. "Your mother seems pretty terrible to me."

"The queen is not my mother."

I shot back, my back slamming harder into the wall, and searched his face for the truth. "What?"

He pulled his hand from his pocket, and I could barely focus on the stain of his skin. He touched the bottom of my braid, exactly where Gavril had earlier, and he twisted it around his dark finger.

"I am the bastard son of King Riven. I was born a month after his wedding to the queen, and I was brought to the castle shortly after." His muscles tightened as he spoke, and I felt dizzy as I watched him.

"Where's your mother?"

He shook his head, but I felt desperate to know the truth of his words.

"Is she alive?"

"From what I know, she is." His gaze darkened as he looked down at my braid which he was still toying with. "I am forbidden to see her."

"Why?"

He bit down on his bottom lip as his jaw clenched. I should have respected his privacy. But Evren was such a mystery to me, and regrettably, he was one that I was desperate to figure out.

"Why, Evren? Because of the queen?" I practically begged for his answer.

"Because my mother resides in the Blood Court."

My mind raced over what he had just said. I had never heard of a fae living in the Blood Court. "How can she? Is she safe?"

His hand tightened against my hair. "She is."

"How? I don't understand." I shook my head as I tried to make sense of what he was saying.

"My mother isn't fae, Adara. She is of Sidra."

"What?" I jerked back and my braid fell from his touch as fear ran down my spine. "That's impossible."

He watched me for a long moment before he answered. "It's rare, but it's not impossible."

In all the history and legends I had ever heard, no one had ever spoken of such a thing. Fae and vampyres were enemies and had been for centuries.

"So, you're…" I trailed off as I searched his face, but he refused to finish my sentence. He didn't move a single inch as he stared at me. "You're of the Blood Court."

"I am born of blood and magic," he corrected me with a voice that was resolute. "I am neither of the Blood Court nor the Fae Court fully. But I choose to serve my father."

"But you're still—" My voice trembled.

"Yes, Adara," he cut me off. "I am half vampyre."

Even though I could see the seriousness in his eyes, I didn't want to believe him.

He was a prince. A member of the royal family, and I didn't want what he was saying to be true.

"You're older than Gavril?"

"I am." He nodded, and I noticed that he inched closer to me still.

"But you aren't the crowned prince?"

He studied me before smirking. "Is that what you would have preferred?" He closed the gap between us again, and this time I didn't retreat. Fear coursed through every inch of me, mixed with a lust that I didn't understand. "Have you been dreaming of what it would be like if you were betrothed to me instead of him?"

"Why would I ever do that?" I whispered, but gods, he was right.

"Because, princess…"

I watched his dark fingers as they ran across his jaw.

"I think we both know that I could do things to you that my brother would never dream of."

My stomach tightened at his words, and I reminded myself that I was to be fearful of him. He was everything I had ever been warned about, a mirror image of my nightmares, but I couldn't stop myself from wishing that he'd close the distance between us and press his lips to mine.

"I'm not your betrothed because they wouldn't dare put that precious crown on the head of the king's half-blood bastard son."

He slid his hand along my side and inhaled sharply when his fingertips met the bare skin of my back.

"What happened to your hands?" I searched his face. "Did the queen do that to you?"

"I just told you that I am a half-breed, and you're worried about the color of my fingers?" Those fingers in question pushed against me, and his touch thrummed with a barely controlled power.

I didn't answer him because I didn't know what he wanted me to say. I was more fearful of him than ever, but even that fear couldn't stop my eagerness to understand him.

"It's a consequence of my magic." He lifted the hand that wasn't clinging to me and held it up between us. "All magic leaves a mark whether it's on the soul or on the skin, and dark magic leaves a notably more grim scar. Though it does fade."

"You've been using dark magic?"

I didn't truly understand what that meant, but I knew that it wasn't good. Magic itself already felt so unthinkable to me, but dark magic? I couldn't fathom the things Evren could have done to leave such a mark on his skin.

"One of the many costs of being a captain in my father's army." He clenched his hand into a fist before dropping it back to his side.

"And are there any advantages to it?"

His fingers tensed against me, and I almost lost my train of thought.

"Bastard son or not, you are the son of the king."

A smile danced along his lips as he looked down at me and his voice felt so rough as he spoke the next words to me. "I was the first to find you just outside the cleave, was I not?"

"And that is an advantage?"

"That was an honor." He stepped closer to me, and his knee pressed between mine. "I may not be the Achlys that gets to claim you, but I was the first to look upon you. The first to dream of your star-marked face and imagine what it would look like beneath me."

"You cannot say things like that to me." I looked away from him as my stomach hardened, but he lifted his hand and quickly brought my face back to meet his.

"Why not? Because you are betrothed to my brother or because your thighs just tightened around mine as you imagined it yourself."

I opened my mouth to argue, but he wasn't finished.

"It doesn't matter that you are destined to be his. Every part of you is begging to be mine." His hand lowered, and I so easily allowed him to tug my hips forward until they met his. I was lost in the way he was looking at me, lost in the way his body felt against mine. "Tell me that isn't true?" he whispered against my neck.

"It's not." I shook my head and my chest brushed against his. It was a lie, and we both knew it. Here he stood against me, the embodiment of my enemy, and he was right. I was ready to beg him for things I didn't fully understand.

It suddenly didn't matter to me what he was or how easily he could harm me. I was willing to beg him just the same.

"You're really not a very good liar, princess." He ran his nose along my neck, and I shivered as he took in a deep breath. "You smell fucking divine."

I turned toward him, my lips so close to his, and I opened my mouth to say anything to make him do something that would stop the deep ache that began in my lower stomach.

"Evren." His name was a plea, and he gently pressed his lips to the skin of my sensitive neck with a sigh.

I was shocked when I felt his teeth follow. Not hard enough to puncture my skin, but enough pressure to give me a mix of pleasure and pain that caused me to gasp at the sensation. I clamped my eyes closed and pressed my hips harder against his. His hand stiffened and his breath rushed out against me.

"Oh my!" I heard Eletta's soft gasp just as Evren jerked away from me.

"Eletta." Panic consumed me as I called out her name, and she stopped in her tracks in the direction in which she was trying to retreat.

"I'm sorry, Starblessed." She shook her head gently, and I moved away from Evren as quickly as I could. "I didn't mean…"

"You have nothing to be sorry for." I pushed my hair out of my face as I made my way toward her. Evren's hand slid against mine as I passed, and I couldn't force myself to keep walking. Instead, I stopped and looked at the prince who didn't belong to me.

His face was hard and unreadable, the opposite of who he had been only moments before, but it didn't lessen the way I wanted him.

He didn't say anything. His eyes simply slid past me to where Eletta stood with her back now turned to us, and when he looked back to me, his gaze delved into me like a warning. *Of Eletta?*

I felt like I could trust her more than anyone else in the palace. She had been the most forthcoming out of everyone thus far, but something in my gut told me to trust Evren.

I let my hand slide away from his, and I continued in the

direction of my lady-in-waiting. She glanced up at me with embarrassment marring her lovely face when I got to her side, but she didn't say a word about what she had just seen.

"Would you like to head back to your room, my lady? I can draw you a bath."

"Thank you, Eletta." I looked back over my shoulder, but Evren was already gone. "But I think I would like to spend some time in the library tonight."

"Of course." She bowed her head gently before leading the way.

EIGHT

E letta followed behind me quickly as I made my way toward the Achlyses' private hall the next morning. The sun was high in the sky and shining through the glass of the palace in a million dazzling spectrums.

"This isn't a good idea, my lady," Eletta whispered just as I passed by a guard and made my way into the room.

Gavril was sitting at the table with a half dozen parchments spread out in front of him. Several guards and men who looked to be of nobility stood around the table as he worked.

He glanced up just as I made my way toward him, and a gentle smile graced his lips. "Adara." He stood from his chair. "How are you this morning?"

"I'm fine." I nodded and adjusted the long skirt of my light blue dress. "I was hoping to speak with you for a moment."

"Of course." He moved from the table until he was standing directly in front of me, but he didn't dismiss any of his men. They all stood there within earshot of where we spoke, and I hated the feeling of them all watching and listening.

"It's a beautiful day, and I would love to get outside the palace." I felt like a child having to ask his permission, but Eletta assured me that there was no way the guards would allow me outside the gate without his or the queen's approval.

"Would you like to go out to the gardens?" He looked back toward the table. "I have a bit of work left, then I could join you."

"No." I quickly shook my head and winced at the trace of hurt that crossed his face. "I was actually hoping to go into the city. I would have Eletta with me, and I would like to see the kingdom at which I am to serve."

He looked back to one of his men, and I watched as the one closest to us softly shook his head no. Gavril wasn't even the one making the decision. He had a room full of men who were so willing to keep me trapped for him, and I did feel trapped.

After walking away from Evren last night, I went to the library and spent several hours reading about the vampyres of Sidra. I had every intention of looking into my own history, but I couldn't bring myself to walk past the book that had interested me just a couple days ago. Especially not after I found out the truth about Evren.

A truth that not even the history books told. I saw no reference to any half-breed. No legends of the bastard son of King Riven. All I had was Evren's word and Eletta's warnings when I told her that I had found out the truth about him.

She told me that even the fae people of Citlali feared their prince for what he was. They feared and distrusted him, regardless of his noble lineage.

I should have shared in that distrust, but I found that all I could think about as I flipped the pages and flopped in my bed was the way he had spoken to me and touched me in that hall. Distrust did not equal distaste, and even though I knew it was bad for me, I found the allure of the dark prince to be too hard to not want.

And that want made me feel more trapped than anything else.

"Please, Your Highness."

Gavril's gaze slammed back into mine.

"I would just like to walk and see the city. No harm will come from me leaving the palace for a few hours. Your people would never harm something that belongs to you."

"You're right." He nodded because my words had struck the exact chord of his ego I was aiming for. "But I will send a couple of my guards with you."

"That's not necessary."

"It is." He looked beyond the men who stood around his table to one of the guards along the wall. "Jorah, gather my brother. The two of you will escort Adara into the city."

"I'm sure that they have much more important things to do," I quickly argued. I needed to get away from Evren, not be thrust into the city alone with the prince who haunted my every thought.

"Nonsense." He looked back at me. "I trust my brother above all others with you. He will assure your safety."

Jorah walked up to us and gave a deep bow before he addressed me. "The captain and I shall ready a carriage, Starblessed." His skin was a deep brown that looked absolutely lovely against his uniform, but his deep brown eyes were what caused my breath to catch in my throat.

"Please don't." I shook my head. "I would prefer to walk."

Jorah looked to his crowned prince who gave a quick nod of his head. "Of course. We shall meet you at the grand entrance when you are ready."

"Thank you." I looked to both of them before turning on my heel to head back to my room.

"Adara."

I stopped as Gavril called my name. "Yes?"

"I hope you enjoy your time in town. Next time I will try to join you." He smiled, and even though the gesture didn't meet his eyes, part of me wondered if Gavril was genuine.

He was the one letting me out when everyone else seemed content with keeping me in.

"I would like that." I nodded before he made his way back to the table where his men were waiting for him.

Eletta helped me back to my room and into a silk cape that would do little against the chill in the air and a pair of black gloves. She refused to allow me to slip on my own trousers and shirt, and I decided that getting to leave the palace was enough of a battle won for the day.

Even if Evren was to be my escort through the city.

We made our way to the grand entrance of the palace, and I tried to avoid looking at Evren as much as I could when he and Jorah came into view standing by the door. Evren was dressed in his usual black attire, and I noticed he had minimal weapons strapped to his body unlike most of the other guards.

"Are you all ready?" Evren asked, and I finally looked up at him.

"We are." I reached for the door, but he quickly knocked my hand away and pushed the door open for all of us. It would have almost been chivalrous if I didn't already know him to be otherwise.

The sun beamed down against my skin, and for a long moment, I simply closed my eyes and allowed my face to bask in the warmth it provided. My skin tingled under its touch, and I took a deep breath.

"This way, my lady." Jorah motioned me forward, and I followed him dutifully.

Evren and Eletta both walked behind me, but I didn't pay either of them any attention as I passed through the gate with Jorah and out onto the busy street of Citlali. I slid my cape over my head before anyone was to look upon my face, and Jorah watched wordlessly.

"You are to stay at my side." Evren's rough voice growled from beside me. "If you stray, we will return immediately."

"You're grouchy today." I adjusted my glove just as Jorah laughed.

"I am not joking, princess." Evren moved closer to me. "You stay at my side or you will be brought back to the castle."

"I heard you the first time, *prince*." I enunciated his title, and his lips slipped into a smirk.

"And where exactly would you like to go?"

"I don't yet know." I shrugged my shoulders, and he grinned harder. "Surely, one of you knows of something in this city that is worth showing me."

"Right this way." He bowed playfully and motioned for me to walk ahead of him. I did so quickly and began walking down the cobblestone street with him at my back.

There were a multitude of vendors out on the street selling everything from spices to wool to pastries. The smell of it was divine and made my stomach growl in hunger.

"Which one do you want?" Evren pulled a coin from his pocket and nodded toward the pastry cart.

"Oh." I shook my head. "I'm fine." I took a step back from the cart, but Evren quickly caught my arm in his hand.

"I can buy you a pastry, Adara." He handed the coin to the older woman who ran the cart, and she looked back and forth between us. "Now tell her which one you want before I decide for you."

I narrowed my eyes at him, but he wasn't budging. "The lemon, please."

She nodded before wiping her hands on her flour-covered apron. She wrapped my pastry in a small cloth before handing it to me.

The smell of lemon and sugar hit me the moment it was in my hand, and I wasted no time biting into it. A small moan slipped from my lips as the flavor hit my tongue. The palace was full of food, but nothing had tasted like this.

"That good?"

I looked up at Evren and he was watching me so intently as I licked the lemon glaze from my lips. "It is. Would you like to try?"

"I would love to." How did he manage to make such a simple phrase feel so erotic?

I held the pastry out to him, but instead of taking it from me, he gripped my wrist in his hand before bringing the treat to his mouth. He didn't take his eyes off me as he bit into it, and I couldn't force myself to look away.

I knew that others could see us, I was absolutely certain that Eletta was probably watching us after the way she had walked in on us last night, but nothing mattered when he was looking at me like that. Everything beyond him seemed to fall away, and he was all I could see.

It didn't matter that the prince I wasn't betrothed to eating from my hand was inappropriate at that moment. I would think of it later when I couldn't sleep. But right now, all I could think about was the trace of sugar that clung to his lips and how desperately I wanted to lean forward and see if it tasted differently on his skin.

"Let me show you my favorite place in the city." He wiped his mouth with his thumb, and I pulled my pastry back to me before bringing it to my lips. "I think you'll like it."

"Evren," Jorah said his name in warning, and it caused Evren to grin unabashedly.

"Calm down, Jorah." Evren laughed. "I think you'll find your future queen is much more daring than you'd think."

"And the future king will have our heads if either of us let anything happen to her."

"Nothing's going to happen to her." Evren held his hand out in my direction. "Do you trust me, princess?"

The answer was no. Irrevocably and absolutely no, but I still slid my hand into his. He smiled before pulling me toward him and through the crowds of people that seemed to barely notice me. Instead, they were all looking at him.

I watched as they watched him. If they feared him as Eletta said, I couldn't tell. Instead, they looked upon him with an air of respect. Many nodding their heads in his direction, but none bowed.

"Do they know you're a prince?" I whispered as we passed, and Evren's hand tightened against mine.

"Who?"

"Your people." I waved ahead of me before pulling my silk cape tighter against myself.

"Of course, they do." He chuckled and turned suddenly as we passed an old tavern. He pulled me up to the door where loud music was pouring out, and I quickly looked behind me to see Jorah and Eletta following us, both with a frown on their faces.

"Then why don't they bow to you?" I searched the dark tavern as we entered before one of the men stood and clapped Evren on his back.

Evren didn't answer me at first. He found us a small round table and pulled out a seat for me before doing the same for Eletta at my side. He then waved to the bartender before sitting beside me.

"As you said, princess, these are my people. I don't treat them as if they are beneath me, so they don't feel as such. I am not my brother."

"So, your brother does treat them as if they are beneath him?"

He studied my face for a long moment before answering. He leaned closer to me so only I could hear. "Gavril is my brother, and as such, I won't speak badly about him. But open your eyes, princess. The truth is right there in front of you."

"Stop calling me princess."

"Why?" He slowly ran his fingers over my cape. "You'll be

one soon enough. You should get used to it. Now take off this ridiculous cape."

I slowly lowered the hood just as the bartender sat four large ales on our table, some of the liquid splashing over the sides. "Evren. Jorah." He nodded to both. "It's been a minute."

"It has." Evren laughed before sliding an ale in front of me and Eletta. I almost joined him in laughter at the look on her face. "Duty calls and I typically need a few days' recovery when I walk out of these doors."

"Ah. It's not so bad." The man chuckled before looking down at me. "Who's this?"

"Jean, this is Adara Cahira, my brother's betrothed. Adara, this is Jean."

"It's nice to meet you." I held out my hand to the man, and he smiled before slipping it into his much larger one.

"You too, girl. Although I'm a little shocked that you're in my tavern. You trying to get the queen to take your head, Evren?"

"That's what I said." Jorah sighed before taking a long pull from his ale.

"She's fine." Evren chuckled before tugging my seat closer to him. "She's got the best guards this kingdom has to offer."

"When they aren't full of ale." Jean laughed before looking back toward his bar. "I have to go serve someone else, Your Highness. Don't break anything."

Evren saluted him with a laugh just as Eletta reached for my hand under the table.

"I think we should head back to the palace," she whispered as her gaze jumped around the room, attempting to keep an eye on everyone.

"Just try a drink." I lifted my ale and brought it to my lips. It was cold and bitter, but I much preferred the taste to the wine they served in the palace. "We'll be back at the palace shortly."

I looked around the tavern as I took another long sip of the cold liquid, and everyone seemed to be lost in their own worlds. No one was paying a bit of attention to us, and when someone's gaze did collide with mine, they simply nodded their head in my direction before going back to their conversations.

"How many other Starblessed are in Citlali?" I looked over at Evren, and he was already watching me.

"At least a dozen, I'd say." He still hadn't touched his drink. "Most of them live within the city. Some are married, others are not."

"Where are the Starblessed that Gavril has fed from?"

Evren's eyes darkened at my question, and his voice was much lower when he answered me. "Gavril has fed from them all. Along with the king and queen."

"What?" I shook my head as I tried to wrap my head around what he had just said. I had always been told that as a Starblessed I would belong to the future king and him alone. It had never crossed my mind that another could feed from me. I had never even considered that the lives of other Starblessed would be any different.

"They crave power, Adara, and the Starblessed are the way to gain that power within."

"And what about you?" I narrowed my eyes at him. "You say that you have never fed from a Starblessed, so what is it that you crave?"

He stared at me for a long moment before his gaze dropped to my lips. "I think we both know what it is that I hunger for."

I glanced over at Eletta, but she was too busy watching those around her with a careful eye.

"Enlighten me, prince." I lifted my glass and took another drink. "I couldn't be more uncertain about anything."

"You should slow down on the ale." He looked at the glass in my hand, but I didn't want to change the subject.

The ale was making me feel brave, and I knew that he was probably right. "Answer my question."

.

"I don't think you really want to know my answer."

"And why is that?" I stared up at him, and it hit me how easy this was. Sitting here talking to Evren, fighting with him. It was far easier than it should have been.

"Because if I tell you the truth, then you'll know what you're imagining between us isn't simply in your head, and you'll feel guilty for betraying a man to whom you're betrothed."

"I'm not betraying anyone."

He searched my face before finally reaching for his own ale and bringing it to his lips. "Not yet, you aren't."

He stood suddenly, his chair scraping across the floor, and I turned away from where he was retreating. Jorah was watching me. His eyes were narrowed and his brow wrinkled. I wasn't sure if he didn't like what he was seeing with me and his captain or if he simply didn't care for me. But either way, he didn't approve.

I lifted my mug and drained the remainder of the ale before looking back over my shoulder. Evren was at the bar with a few other men, and they were all laughing as if they had no cares in the world.

I turned back and avoided looking at Jorah's disapproving gaze as I nudged Eletta. "Have you ever been here before?"

"No," she answered quickly. "And this place isn't suitable for you, my lady."

"Eletta, please call me Adara," I grumbled, and her cheeks blushed pink. "I see nothing wrong with this place. It's fun. Try your ale."

"Absolutely not." Her voice wavered as her hand pressed against her chest.

"Fine." I lifted her cup in my hand. "Mind if I drink it then?"

"I don't, but you should be careful. Fae ale is not for the weak of heart." She scrunched her nose and looked around the tavern with trepidation pouring off her.

"It's a good thing that I'm not weak of heart then." I smiled and took another sip. My head did feel light, but so did my chest. It was a feeling I craved at that moment, a pleasure I hadn't known for a long time. "What about you, Eletta? Are you betrothed to anyone? Anyone in here that's catching your eye?"

If I thought she was blushing before, I was wrong. Eletta looked at me like I was crazy. "Of course not. I will get married when the queen deems it so."

"Bummer," I muttered around my drink before setting it on the table and clasping her hand in mine. "We should dance."

"That is a bad idea," she argued, but she still stood as I pulled her along behind me.

"Everything seems like a bad idea, Eletta. We should at least enjoy a few bad ideas while we're able to."

She laughed softly and the sound caught me off guard.

"One dance." She held up a finger.

"To start." I winked at her before reaching out for her other hand and spinning us in a small circle.

The music blared from the musician's instruments and coursed through my body with each beat. Eletta was stiff in my arms for a long moment before she finally gave in and spun around the old wooden floor with me in a fit of laughter.

I pulled her toward me, wrapping my arms around her shoulders, and we laughed as I leaned my head back and closed my eyes. For a second, I imagined there was no one else in this place but the two of us. I imagined what it would be like for her to not be my lady-in-waiting, but my friend.

I felt euphoric from the fantasy.

But then as the beat of the music slowed and our dancing slowed with it, all I could think of was Evren and what it would be like to be here with him and him alone. Would he have danced with me if I wasn't the Starblessed? If I didn't belong to another?

If I ran, Evren would more than likely be the one to find me. He may have hungered for me now, but I would force him to feel otherwise. My head spun as I considered running or the alternative. If I took the life of his brother, everything he felt for me now would turn to hate.

And I should have been happy about that.

I hated the people that surrounded me, and it was all the better if they hated me too. Even if my chest ached at the thought.

"May I cut in here?" I blinked my eyes open, half expecting Evren to be standing in front of me, but it was Jorah who held his hand out in my direction.

I slid my hand from Eletta's neck and let him pull me away from her and against his body. He danced slowly and efficiently to the beat, and when I glanced over his shoulder to where I knew Evren stood, his eyes were on his guard and me.

"You shouldn't be looking to him," Jorah muttered above me, and I pulled my gaze away from Evren to look back at him.

"I wasn't." I shook my head softly.

"You were, and it's a dangerous game you're playing, Starblessed."

I tried to pull away from him, but he held on to me tightly, so I had no choice but to follow him in the dance. "I'm not playing any game."

"Then you're a fool," he growled and his hands stiffened against me. "The queen is watching your every move whether you realize it or not, and she will not be happy to know that the savior of our kingdom prefers the company of a half-breed to that of her son."

I stopped completely and jerked out of his hold. His shocked gaze flew to meet mine, but I had too much ale to care.

"Do not call him that."

"Why not? That's what he is."

My hand shook with the urge to slap him, but I knew that assaulting one of the king's guards would do me no favors.

Jorah stepped closer to me as if he could sense my thoughts.

"Evren is my dearest friend, Adara. I know who he is just as he knows me, and I also know that what you two are doing will mess up…"

He shook his head to stop what he was saying, but I was desperate for him to finish his sentence.

"Mess up what?" *Please answer.*

"The plans the kingdom has for you. You can't save the people when you are too focused on only one of its patrons."

"And what if I have no interest in saving these people?"

Jorah gripped my arm, pulling me closer to him, and when he spoke again, he did so directly next to my ear. "Then you should learn to pretend. Show your love for these people and your future king before the queen drains every bit of your precious blood from your body and Evren's."

A chill ran down my spine as his words hit me. As I looked up at Jorah, every part of me believed he was speaking the truth. Whatever it was that he knew, he was telling me this to protect me. Or possibly to protect his friend.

Either way, my head spun with the truth of his words, a truth that I had known all along. I was to do exactly as the queen wished, or she would make me beg for a life I dreaded.

"Are you all ready to go?" Evren stood next to Jorah, and I blinked up at him as panic hit me. Here I was dancing in a tavern and dreaming about this man who I couldn't have when I should have been back at the palace figuring out my next move.

I was a fool.

"I need to return to the palace."

"Okay." Evren laughed, but I was already turning on my heel and running for the door.

My shoulder knocked into someone else's, and I tried to apologize as my cape was stepped on and pulled from around my shoulders. A few gasps filled the space around me, but I didn't stick around to listen. I sprinted for the door and out onto the cobblestone street as I gasped for breath.

The alcohol coursed through me as I spun in place and searched for the direction at which we came. The palace. I spotted the towering building ahead and took off in that direction before any of my escorts could catch up to me.

The sun was setting behind the palace, the gleam of its rays reflecting off the dark surface, and I raced in its direction.

"Adara!" I heard Evren shout from behind me, but I didn't stop. Fear coursed through me at how foolish I had been.

I tripped on the long skirt of my dress, almost falling forward, but I caught myself against the old brick of someone's home. I could feel people watching me, but it didn't matter. Jorah said the queen was watching me, the queen that I feared above all others, and I knew that she was the one who held the power to make my life everything I had ever feared.

She wanted her son to grow powerful at my expense, and she would do whatever it took to assure that happened. Even if that meant locking me away. Away from Evren, away from everyone.

"Adara, wait!" Evren grasped my forearm in his hand and stopped me from pushing forward. "What the hell is wrong with you?"

"I need to get back to the palace." I tried to pull away from him, but he stopped me with his firm grip.

"What happened? Did someone say something?"

"The queen is probably watching us," I whispered my fear, and I watched as his face morphed into anger.

"Jorah warned you of the queen." He said it so simply, as if it was something everyone had been thinking but no one thought to share with me. "Adara." He shook his head before pushing forward, my arm still in his hand, as he made his way to the castle.

"Please don't call me that."

"Your name?" He laughed as if I was joking. "What would

you prefer I call you if I can't call you by your given name or princess?"

"Starblessed," I answered him quickly just as we arrived at the gate.

His jaw clenched and his hand hardened against my arm. He didn't stop as the gate opened. He simply pulled me through and marched forward up the steps of the palace. I saw no one as we entered the palace and Evren pulled me toward my room.

We made it to my door quickly, and he jerked the door open before pushing me inside and following behind me.

"You can't be in here." I pulled away from his touch and put as much space between he and I as possible.

"I am a prince of Citlali, Starblessed." He spat my name. "I will do as I please."

I wrapped my arms around my chest and looked to the window. The setting sun was leaving room for nothing but darkness, and it was falling over the sky like a curse.

"Please leave."

"I am not leaving you alone while you are panicking over whatever Jorah said to you. He is my best friend in this world, but he's also an idiot. He scared you when he shouldn't have."

"No." I shook my head. "He was right. I have spent my entire life preparing for my betrothal to the crowned prince, and I am a fool to allow the queen to think I am loyal to anything but that."

A dark smile graced his lips as he shook his head. "You are loyal to my brother?"

"I am." I lifted my trembling chin as I answered him.

"He is what you want?" He moved closer to me as his dark eyes pierced through me.

"He is my destiny," I corrected him and took a step back as he moved forward.

"A destiny that makes you wish you were anywhere else." He

chuckled softly just as he moved in front of me. "Tell me, Starb-lessed. Is it your want for me that makes your breath catch in your throat when I am near or your boredom? If you simply need a man to cure your temptation, then please allow me the pleasure."

"You can't say things like that to me."

His smile deepened as he watched me, and I knew that he wasn't going to leave unless I made him.

"Your brother can satisfy my temptation just fine."

His smile dropped as he stepped closer to me still. "I think we both know that is a lie. Unless you close your eyes and imagine that his fingers are mine, I think the only thing my brother will leave you is wanting."

"The queen is watching me," I whispered, and Evren simply lifted his stained fingers and ran one over the other before my room was clouded in darkness. Every lamp and the glow of the fire had completely disappeared, and I grasped the post of my bed as I tried to see in front of me.

"What did you do?" My voice trembled with fear and antic-ipation.

"The queen can only see what I allow her, princess. I may be the bastard prince, but I still have power."

I could hear him talking, but I couldn't see him. I lifted my hand in front of me, and I couldn't make out the simple shape of my fingers.

"What happens in my darkness only comes to light if I choose."

His fingers grazed my elbow, and I jumped at his touch. "Evren," I whispered his name and reached out for him, but my hands couldn't find him.

"I'm right here." He spoke softly at my side. His breath rushing out against my neck.

"I can't see you."

"You don't need to see me to feel me." His lips pressed

against my bare shoulder, and my heart shuddered as I still tried to look around me.

His fingers grazed over my neck gently before he ever so slowly ran his fingertips along the curve of my back. Everything inside me awoke at his touch. The mark along my spine felt like it was aflame.

"Fuck." His one simple word made my stomach flip, and I wondered if his touch had felt as strongly to him as it did to me. "You're so damn gorgeous."

"You can't even see me." I reached behind me, and my hand met his hard thigh.

"Gods, but I can." He pressed his torso against my back, closing the space between us completely, and I closed my eyes as I felt how harshly his breath fell from his lips. "Tell me what you want, princess."

"I... I don't..." I shook my head because I couldn't make sense of what I wanted in my own head. There was no way for me to proclaim something I didn't understand.

His hand moved around my body and pressed against my lower stomach. The move forced my body harder against him, and I could feel how much he desired me. He didn't require words to make me feel his need.

"I could simply show you what you want." His fingers lowered minutely, and even through the layers of my dress, I felt completely exposed to him. "I can smell how badly you need me. I bet you're soaked between your perfect thighs."

I swallowed hard as I tried to catch my breath. No one had ever spoken to me this way before. I should have been embarrassed by his words, but they simply made me want him more. Because he was right.

His hand moved down the front of me and down my thigh until he gathered my dress into his hand. His fingertips met the bare skin of my leg, and a whimper I couldn't control passed through my lips.

"Gods, you're perfect." His other hand snaked around my chest, and he pressed his hand against my neck before his thumb forced my chin to turn in his direction. His breath passed over my lips, and I felt desperate for him to close the distance between us. "Take it," he growled, and his hands tightened against my throat and my thigh. "If you want me, take it, princess."

This was my chance. He was giving me this moment to walk away. If I didn't want this to go any further, I simply needed to stop. But I knew I wasn't capable of doing so. Not when he was so close and the smell of him surrounded me.

I pushed forward, closing the space between us, and he moaned at the first meeting of my lips to his. I was hesitant and unsure, but once Evren got the first taste of me, he left no room for my uncertainty. His hand pressed hard against my throat as his mouth opened and begged entrance into my own.

I didn't have the power to stop him even if I wanted to. I opened for him, and he kissed me like he hungered for nothing else in the world. He kissed me as if every bit of the power that was prophesied to flow through my body fueled him with every swipe of his tongue.

And it felt that way to me too. My marks buzzed along my skin, craving his touch with as much ache as the spot between my thighs, and that ache was unbearable.

"Please, Evren," I begged against his lips, but I had no idea what I was asking him for. I just simply needed him to do some-thing, anything, that would satisfy the need that was eating at me.

His fingers spasmed against my thigh, and he rose them higher and higher as my breath rushed out of me and into him.

"Tell me that you're mine, princess. Even if it isn't true, I need to hear you say it."

My stomach fluttered, and I knew this was dangerous. The way I craved Evren wasn't simply going to go away after he touched me. I feared that it would only make everything worse. But still I did as he asked. "I'm yours."

His fingers slid over my undergarment, a whisper of a touch, but it was enough to make my knees feel like they may buckle beneath me. He ran his fingers up and down, barely grazing over the fabric, and I lifted my hand behind me and buried it in his hair to keep him against me.

His mouth pressed against my shoulder, just at the base of my neck, and his fingers toyed with the top of my undergarment. "Gods, I'm dying to taste you." His teeth grazed over my skin just as his fingers sank beneath the fabric.

His teeth felt sharp and lethal, like the vampyre I knew him to be, but I was far too lost in my lust to have any room for fear. I held my breath as his fingers slid against my wetness, and a shock wave of pleasure shot through me as he pressed harder against my flesh.

"Oh gods." I tightened my hand in his hair, and Evren only took the sound for encouragement.

His fingers moved faster against me as his mouth continued to lick, suck, and graze over my skin. He pushed two fingers inside me, and I whimpered as his palm continued to work against the spot that was begging for him.

My legs trembled beneath me, but Evren's hold on my neck refused to let me fall. There was a deep ache building and building in my lower stomach, and I felt like I was about to lose myself in him. My hand tightened against him, and I clamped my thighs down around his hand.

"Let go, princess," he growled against me before his fingers curled inside me and his teeth scraped over my spine.

I had no choice after that, no control left in my body. I was thrown over the edge, pleasure unlike anything I had ever known surging through me, and Evren held me against him as I fell apart.

It took me long moments to catch my breath and for the

reality of what we had just done to truly hit me. Evren slid his hand away from my body before he pressed a gentle kiss against my spine, and I tensed beneath his touch.

He felt it, of course he had, and as if it were possible, the room seemed to darken even more.

"Adara," he called my name, but I stepped out of his touch before I could let myself get lost in him again.

He chuckled soft yet deafening, and I blinked when the shroud of darkness lifted and my room appeared as if the light had been there all along.

I looked to the door, and I knew that my next words were the wrong thing to say the moment they passed through my lips. "You should leave."

"Of course, Starblessed." Evren bowed deeply before standing back to his full height and sinking two of his dark fingers into his mouth. Two fingers that had just been buried inside of me. I watched as his tongue lapped at the evidence of me on his skin, and I couldn't look away from his canine teeth that gleamed on either side of his fingers.

"Your dark magic has a cost." I nodded toward his hands that were far darker than they had been earlier just as he let his fingers slip from his mouth.

"That it does." He nodded before slipping his hands into his pockets. "As it appears, so does your loyalty."

"Evren, please." I shook my head, but I didn't truly know what to say. I felt so confused, so lost in between what I wanted and what was demanded of me.

"No need to beg now, princess." He grinned, and I could see the darkness hiding behind his smile. "You've already got what you needed from me."

"You know that this is dangerous," I whispered, but he was already passing me by and heading toward the door.

"Don't worry, Starblessed. My magic-stained fingers didn't leave a single trace between your thighs. My brother will never know that you just came so hard for me while not even thinking once about him."

"Is this a game to you?"

My question caused him to stop with his hand already resting on my door handle. He didn't turn back to face me, and I hated that he didn't. He spoke as if what had just happened didn't matter at all. "Of course it's a fucking game. Now maybe you should think twice before you tell the queen how pure you are for my brother."

He opened the door and disappeared before I had a chance to answer. Before I even had a chance to catch my breath from the impact of his words.

NINE

It had been three days since I last saw Evren. He left my
room so swiftly after his cruel words, and I hadn't seen him
since.

And every part of me was yearning to see him, to feel him.

But I couldn't think about Evren and the sinful way he had
touched me when I was standing across from Gavril and the
queen.

"The ball is in two days' time," the queen barked at the seamstress who was pinning fabric along my body. Her hands trembled as she worked, and I didn't blame her. I had barely been
able to look the queen in the eye for fear that she would know
what I had done. "Everyone who matters in our kingdom will be
here, and the Starblessed must be the most desirable person in
the room. We want everyone to want what belongs to us and
know that our family will be the ones to strengthen our
kingdom."

My gaze met Gavril's in the mirror, but he didn't say a word.
He was simply looking upon me as if he knew what his mother
said was right. I doubted Gavril ever spoke against the woman.

I wouldn't have either if it wasn't for the lack of fabric of the dress. "Couldn't we add a bit more fabric?" I kept my gaze on Gavril. "While the dress is beautiful, I feel completely exposed."

The dress was fitted against my body in pure white silk that left little to the imagination. Thin straps caressed each shoulder and slid down my back to meet the fabric where it hung just above the curve of my backside. A piece of chiffon that was covered in small clear gemstones wrapped around my chest and fell over my upper arms and upper back.

It did very little to cover and only seemed to draw more attention to my body that was exposed.

And I knew that was exactly what the queen wanted.

"That's not an option, Starblessed. It is imperative that everyone sees your mark." She didn't even look up at me as she spoke. She was staring straight at my back.

I nodded once and clenched my fists at my sides. It didn't matter what I said or what I thought. I was only here to be viewed and to be used for a power I wasn't even sure I possessed.

"Can we have a moment, please?"

I searched for Gavril in the mirror, and he was still staring straight at me.

"This dress must be finished." The queen was still fussing over the fabric, but she stopped when Gavril spoke again.

"My betrothed and I require a moment alone." He finally looked away from me to focus on his mother. "Surely the dress can spare a few minutes."

I watched as anger flashed across her face, but she hid it quickly.

"Of course." She headed toward the door with the seamstress behind her, and I held my breath until the click of the door proved that Gavril and I were alone. And even then, it almost felt impossible to breathe.

"I'm sorry." The prince was still watching me through the

mirror as he spoke. "I know that my mother can be overwhelming."

"It's okay." I looked away from him and back toward the door. "To be honest, everything about this is overwhelming."

He stood and slowly made his way behind me, and I tensed as he got within arm's reach from me. He noticed the movement immediately.

"I'm not going to hurt you, Adara." He stared at me over my shoulder before slowly lifting his hand and pressing his fingers to my bare shoulder.

My mark sparked to life under his touch, but it felt dull in comparison to what I had experienced with Evren. I wondered if he knew, if he could sense his brother's touch against my skin that was supposed to belong to him and him alone.

"Do you trust me?"

His brother had asked the same of me just days ago, and my chest ached with how much more I trusted Evren. His dark blue eyes were soft and pleading, and I knew that in another life, I could have easily fallen for this man. But fate was cruel, and I craved another.

"I don't trust anyone, Gavril."

His gaze dropped to my back, and he stared at it for a long time before his hand slowly moved from my shoulder and down my spine. It felt like he was appraising every inch of me as his hand slid down my skin.

"You really are amazing." His touch was a whisper, a promise of what was to happen between us, and I couldn't stop the dread that filled me as thoughts of his brother flashed through my mind.

"I'm simply a girl born with a mark on her skin that everyone worships. I have done nothing to be called amazing."

He looked back up at me in the mirror before he let his hand drop from my skin. "I disagree."

He slowly moved around me, and I held my breath until the

crowned prince was standing directly in front of me. I stared up at him and waited for whatever it was he needed to say.

"It isn't your mark that makes you so exquisite, Adara. There is just something about you that I can't look away from."

I swallowed as his words washed over me, and my stomach dipped as his gaze slid to my lips. The man that stood in front of me was so different from the crowned prince he became under his mother's thumb.

I didn't know which version of him was real.

I didn't want to like either one.

"When they had told me I was betrothed to the Starblessed, I hadn't expected you." He lifted a piece of my hair in his fingers and watched as it slipped through his hand.

"What did you expect?"

"Someone who I would be bound to in law and blood only. I didn't imagine that I would want you in the way that I do."

"You want what my blood is supposed to hold for you." I straightened my shoulders and tried not to let his words affect me. He was the future king and my future husband, but even as his words made my stomach tighten, I wished it were Evren standing before me.

"No, Adara." He shook his head gently before his eyes met mine. "I want you. I lie in my room at night thinking of you and you alone. I fantasize about what it will be like to truly touch you, for you to call my name out to the gods."

"Gavril," I whispered his name, and it sounded far too intimate.

I wanted to tell him to stop, but I saw the pleasure in his gaze as he watched me. He took a step closer to me, eliminating any bit of space that I had been clinging to, and his chest pressed against mine. My breathing rushed in and out of me, and my breasts pressed against him with each deep pull into my lungs.

"Gods, I wish not to leave an inch of your body undiscovered. It will be for me to worship, and I will worship you,

Adara." He lifted his hand and buried his fingers into my hair at the base of my scalp. "You will want for nothing once you belong to me."

He pressed his nose against my jaw and inhaled deeply. I turned away from him as I tried to catch my breath, and I hated that I wasn't pushing him away. I didn't have a choice, but there was also a part of me that didn't want to.

I felt desperate to want Gavril in the way I yearned for his brother. If I had, then thoughts of running away would have slipped through my fingers easily. The overwhelming longing to hurt the people who destroyed my family would have been washed away and replaced by my guilt for wanting my enemy.

But I felt neither of those things when he pressed a soft kiss to my neck. His skin against mine only seemed to strengthen my resolve that this wasn't the life I was meant for. Even if Gavril was handsome and the scent of him alluring. There was a vast difference between the way he was making me feel right now and the way my chest ached with uneasiness.

Gavril may have wanted my flesh and my blood, but he was still the son of the queen. He was still willing to keep me here in a prison while he took what he wanted from me. He had told me so in his own words, and I wasn't foolish enough to forget that.

"Is that what you want, Starblessed?" His hand tightened in my hair, and I hated that name so damn much.

But I would not allow Gavril to know either of my truths. "Yes." I nodded and the tug of his hand in my hair brought out the smallest bite of pain. "Of course, that's what I want."

He let out a small, deep sigh against my skin, and his hand tightened even more. I could feel the tension radiating off his body as he held me in his hands, and I knew that if I didn't stop this, he was going to press his mouth against me once more.

He wanted to do more than that, and even though I had so willingly allowed his brother to touch me only a few days before, he was the only one to ever do so. The thought of Gavril doing the same made my stomach drop.

A loud knock on the door had Gavril's gaze flying up toward the sound, but he didn't release me from his hold as the door opened.

"Yes, brother?" Gavril gritted through his teeth, and my spine straightened as my gaze connected with Evren in the mirror.

He could clearly see everything that was happening in front of him. The way Gavril's body was pressed against mine, his hold in my hair, the curve of my neck that appeared so ready for his mouth.

It was on the tip of my tongue to tell him this wasn't what it looked like, but it was. Gavril was to be my husband, and the way he was holding me was the exact reminder I needed that I was his as I stared at his brother.

I was his, and the only options I had to change that also meant I would never be Evren's.

"Father is asking for you." Evren avoided meeting my gaze, and I let my own fall to the floor as he spoke.

I tried to remind myself of the cruel words he spoke as he left my room with traces of me still on his fingers, but it was no use. My body didn't care about what he had said. The moment he walked into the room, it sparked to life in a way Gavril could never do.

"What does he want?" His hand tightened again, and this time, I couldn't stop my wince as pain bit into my scalp.

Evren noticed. Of course, he had. His dark gaze finally met mine in the mirror, and he looked absolutely murderous.

"There are whispers of a new threat from the Blood Court. He has gathered his council to discuss our options."

"And are the whispers true?"

Evren looked back to his brother, and I couldn't place the look that glazed over his face. "They came from legitimate sources, but I am not at my post, so I don't know the validity of what has been told. But this isn't something we should be discussing in front of the Starblessed." He nodded toward me without truly looking at me again. "Let her finish picking out a dress for the ball while we meet with the king."

Gavril looked down at me as if he had almost forgotten that I was still pressed against his body in a hold he had yet to let me out of. His hand loosened in my hair, and he took a step back.

"Excuse me, Adara." He dipped into the slightest bow. "Duty calls, but we shall finish this conversation later."

He smiled softly, and I tried my hardest to return it. But I could feel Evren's eyes on me. I didn't look back up at him, but it didn't matter. I sensed his gaze deeper than any touch from Gavril.

The crowned prince walked past me, heading in the direction of his brother, and I gasped down a deep breath.

"I will head to the council room." He was no longer speaking to me but straightening his shirt as he spoke to Evren. "Please make sure that Adara makes it back to her room before you join us."

"Of course." Evren bowed his head to his younger brother, and the sight was unsettling. My chest ached as I watched him, and I knew that Evren wasn't born to bow to anyone.

I stepped away from the mirror and slowly lifted the jeweled chiffon from my shoulders and placed it on the table with the rest of the seamstress's belongings.

"I need a moment to change." I moved behind the small divider that was placed in the corner of the room and slowly pulled the fabric away from my skin. I was careful not to ruin any of the work the seamstress had done. There were pins and small marks of fabric chalk along the length of the dress where she intended to make it tighter.

"There's not much need for you to hide behind the screen." Evren's voice was calm and casual, and I hated the sound of it as he spoke. "It would appear that you don't have much left to hide from either of us."

I let the fabric fall to the floor in a pool and pressed my arm against my breasts as I tried to calm my heart. "Trust me, prince. I have plenty to hide from you both."

He scoffed, and I hurried to pull my dress over my hips and up my arms. The fabric fell against my upper arms and along my breasts, and accentuated parts of my body I wasn't accustomed to showing. I reached behind me, grasping for the ribbon that held the dress together, but it was out of my reach.

"Could you call for Eletta?" I grumbled even as I still tried to gain hold of the fabric.

"What could you possibly need your lady's maid for?" He chuckled without a trace of humor. "You really are getting used to the royal life, aren't you?"

I cursed under my breath and held the dress against my breasts. "If you must know, you ass. I cannot lace up my dress. It's impossible. I've tried."

He was quiet for a long moment before I heard his movement. I let out a low breath. I was thankful that he was going to get her. With Eletta here, that meant he would leave. He would leave, and I would try anything to distract myself from thoughts of him.

"Let me help you." Evren came into view around the screen, and I quickly took a step back.

"This is improper. You should call for Eletta."

He smirked, and that one small look made my stomach flip in a way that Gavril couldn't dream of. He gripped my upper arm in his hand and forced me to turn so that my back was to him. "I had my fingers buried inside you a few days ago. I think I can handle tying up your dress."

I gasped at his words, and I swore he moved closer to me.

"Unless you'd prefer that I help you out of it instead. The door is still open, but gods, could you imagine the rush of trying not to be caught while the bastard son of the king was buried deep inside you."

I jerked away from his touch and stared at him over my shoulder. "You cannot say things like that to me."

"Why not?" He ran his thumb over his bottom lip as he devoured my skin with his gaze. "Would you prefer that I call my brother back and let him whisper such words instead? Is that what he was doing when I entered? Was he promising you that he would do things to your body that would make you wish for the rest of the world to disappear?"

"Why do you care what your brother was whispering to me? I am his betrothed, and you would do well to remember that."

That only made him smile wider, and this time when he reached out for me, my mark buzzed with pleasure and my knees threatened to buckle. He wrapped his arm around my chest as he forced my back to press against him.

"Do you remember that, princess?" He grazed his nose over the back of my neck and my eyes fluttered closed. "I can scent how badly you want me. I don't think my dear brother could say the same. Poor crowned prince of Citlali destined to marry a woman who is getting wet at the thought of his brother's cock."

I attempted to jerk away from him and his harsh words, but he refused to let me go. His arm tightened around me, and his breath fell from his lips in a harsh rhythm against my neck.

"Why are you so cruel?"

"This isn't cruelty, princess." He chuckled softly, and the sound felt like a warning. "This is me doing everything in my power not to steal you away from this place so that I can keep you for myself."

"Do you want to keep me?" My words were desperate and full of longing, but I couldn't stop them.

"No," he growled, but his arm hauled me even closer against him, and I could feel how badly he wanted me against my backside. "I want to rid myself of this longing I have for you. I wish to fuck you out of my system so that I can kneel before you like the rest of the kingdom without dreaming of what you taste like between your thighs."

A shudder racked through my body, but I forced myself out of his hold. I shouldn't have been aroused by the words he spoke. He wanted to use my body then hand me back to his brother like he had never wanted me at all.

That thought was so simple for him, so true, but even though my chest ached at the thought, I still had to press my thighs together to stop the deep ache that had formed there.

"I told you to get Eletta." I took a small step away from him.

"And yet, I don't take orders from you." He adjusted his pants, and my gaze flew to the movement. "You're not the queen of this kingdom yet."

"And when I am?" I arched my eyebrow, and his dark eyes felt like they were holding back a thousand years' worth of words unsaid.

"What, princess?"

"Are you to take orders from me then?" I didn't know why I was asking him this. I wanted him to leave. To allow me to get back to my room and submerge myself in the bath while I tried to recreate the feeling he had caused in me with my own fingers.

"I doubt it."

"Isn't that treason?" I adjusted my dress against my chest and his gaze fell to my breast. He reached forward, one knuckle trailing along the exposed skin at the seam of my dress, and I didn't dare move.

"Turn around, princess." His voice was low and lacked the normal control that he usually possessed.

I did as he said, and I gasped when his fingers grazed my mark. He pulled the ribbons tightly behind me, tightening the dress against my body, and I dropped my hands from my chest as I felt him tying the strings into a knot.

"You didn't answer my question."

"I'm not sure how to answer." His fingers fell away from the ribbon and they skimmed down the sides of my back until they settled on my hips. "Every thought I have of you is treasonous, the way my hands ache to touch you, deceitful. Even my dreams make me a traitor of my own kingdom."

"Then stop," I whispered as I straightened my shoulders. The way he spoke of me as if I was a poison that was infecting every inch of him.

"That's the thing, princess," he whispered before his lips pressed against my bare shoulder. "I don't want to."

TEN

When I arrived at my door with Evren at my back, I could see the trepidation in Eletta's eyes. She didn't trust him, and I couldn't blame her.

I didn't trust him either.

She had stayed by my side for the rest of the night. Drawing my bath and pouring oils into the water to help me relax. She combed the tangles from my hair as I stared into the small mirror and thought of how Evren's touch had felt against my skin.

When she asked me if I was all right, I lied to the girl so easily.

But the way she watched my every move told me she didn't believe a single word.

Part of me wondered if she could see the way I longed for him when she looked at me. She watched me so carefully, and I knew that Eletta wasn't dumb. She saw more than most, and it was only a matter of time until she realized how deeply my want for the wrong prince went.

As soon as she left my room, I slipped my trousers on under the silk nightgown she had helped me into. I had to search for my boots, but finally found them tucked under the bed as if Eletta never wished to see them again.

I slipped my feet inside and wiggled my toes against the worn leather that felt so familiar and comfortable. I didn't change from my gown until the fire in my room was low and there wasn't a hint of sound coming from the hall.

I couldn't do this. I couldn't lie here in this gilded palace betrothed to a prince who was bad for me while I secretly lusted for another who was worse.

I had made my decision while I sank under the water of the bath, and I had stayed there until my lungs burned with need. I was going to run.

I wasn't sure how far I would make it, but I knew that I would never forgive myself if I didn't try. Sitting here and accepting what they wanted from me made me as bad as my mother.

And I refused to be like her. My father died trying to protect me, and my mother so willingly handed me over to the people who murdered him. I refused to do the same.

I refused to waste his sacrifice with blind obedience.

I quickly changed into one of my shirts and tucked it into my trousers before pulling my dagger from beneath my pillow and sliding it into my boot. The feel of it against my leg brought me comfort, and I took a deep breath before opening the door slowly and peeking into the hall.

I didn't see anyone. Not a single guard or servant. The halls were hollow and silent, and I gently closed the door behind me, careful to not disturb the palace's slumber.

I didn't bother grabbing any more of my things. Everything I took was just one more thing to slow me down, and I couldn't afford it. I was already so fearful of what they would do if they caught me, but I had to try.

I moved down the long hall toward the library, and I searched for the doorway I knew hid along the stone wall beyond the lamplight. I had seen it days ago, and I knew that it would be my easiest exit.

The door opened effortlessly, and the cool night air kissed my skin in a welcomed embrace. I looked back into the hall one last time before I stepped out of the palace. I should have been looking for anyone that could possibly see me, but deep down I knew that I was only looking for him.

I was looking for him, and it hit me in my gut how badly I needed to leave.

I slid outside, barely opening the door so no one would notice, and my heart felt like it was ready to beat out of my chest as the door closed softly behind me. The back of the palace was dark, but I knew that there would still be royal guards protecting all sides of the castle. I just had to sneak past them and manage to hide long enough until I could figure out how to get through the stone wall.

Nothing was impenetrable. I would climb over it if I had to, but that wasn't ideal. I needed to cause as little commotion as possible.

I moved down the wall and peeked around the corner. There were two guards standing there, and one was laughing at something the other had said. Neither one of them noticed me. Two royal guards and neither sensed my presence.

I quickly made my way through the small courtyard, watching my back at every turn, and once I made it to the thin cropping of trees, I let out a small breath.

I moved through the trees until I pressed my hand against the cool stone of the wall. It was imposing and suffocating, and I knew that if there were no openings in the stone, then I was going to have to use the trees to help me climb the thing that held me trapped inside.

I moved slowly, careful of every step as I trailed down the wall looking for any changes in the structure.

I heard the snap of a twig, and I crouched down against the

wall as I scanned the trees. There wasn't an ounce of movement, but it was far too dark out to truly be sure. I stayed like that for a long moment, praying that what I heard was nothing more than an animal or my fear.

My fingers trembled as I ran them over my dagger. I was just about to pull it from its sheath when I heard more movement to my right. A man I didn't recognize charged for me, and I couldn't even manage a scream before his sweaty hand clamped down against my mouth and forced my head against the rocky earth.

Pain shot through me, and my vision blurred as I tried to kick his body from mine. But he was far too heavy and too strong.

"Hold fucking still, you star witch," he spat at me while reaching for his pants, and my entire body froze with fear. I had no idea who this man was or what he wanted, but I knew that he wanted to hurt me one way or another.

He kept his hand over my mouth and his body pressed against mine as I struggled beneath him, and the scream I let out was muffled beneath his fingers as I watched him lift a small dagger. His hand fumbled with the weapon as he lifted it toward my chest, and I kicked my legs wildly to try to get him off me.

He wasn't expecting the movement, and I managed to budge my chest from under his. I screamed at the top of my lungs as his fingers lost their grip on my mouth.

"Fuck," he cursed and his hand came down hard on my upper thigh. I didn't realize what had happened until the burning pain tore through my leg.

He dropped the dagger quickly as he stared down at the cut he had just made in my flesh, and I knew then what he wanted. He was watching my blood escape from my skin as if it was a gift from the gods. He pressed his fingers against the cut as I hissed in pain, and when he lifted his bloodied hand into the moonlight, I knew that was my only chance.

I lifted my other leg and kicked him in the chest with every bit of power I had. He groaned deep and loud as he fell to his side, and I quickly crawled back from him and grasped for anything I could to help aid in my escape.

"You bitch!" His stare was murderous as he brought his fingers to his mouth and licked my blood from his skin. "You are going to pay for that."

I climbed to my knees before he could lunge for me again, but the sound of movement coming from the castle caught my attention. It caught his too.

He was to his feet before I could yell out again, and he disappeared through the trees as quickly as he came. Pain radiated from my leg as I tried to climb to my feet, and I heard one of the guards curse once they saw me.

"Get the prince," one of them ordered before coming to stand before me. "Are you all right, Starblessed?"

I watched over his shoulder as two other guards took off in the direction that my assailant had just left.

"I think she might be in shock."

"I'm okay," I grumbled, and pressed my hand against a tree to take some of the pressure off my leg. "I just need to get to my room."

The guards looked back and forth between one another. "You're bleeding."

"I'm well aware." My hand tightened on my thigh, and I pushed off the tree to force myself back into the palace. I didn't know what I was thinking. Here I was ready to run, ready to try to survive the world completely on my own, and I was attacked before I could even escape the wall.

I had a blaring reminder of who I was on my face and back, and no matter where I went, people would know. They would know what I was, and they would want and take from me as they pleased.

One of the guards reached out for my arm as I tried to pass him, and even though I wanted to refuse his help, I couldn't. My leg hurt worse with every step I took, and my head began throbbing in pain. I knew it would only get worse until I got back to my room and assessed the damage.

Damage caused by someone who was currently on the castle grounds. I hadn't recognized the man who attacked me, but I knew that he was nobility of some sort. He wasn't wearing a uniform of the guard, and the fabrics he wore were far too fine to be a servant's.

Which meant he was a trusted member of Gavril's court.

"We're almost there," the guard spoke softly, and I knew that he could see the pain in my face. "I could carry you."

"No." I shook my head and powered on toward the door I had left from.

I tried not to think about what Gavril was going to do or say once he saw me. I had no way to explain why I was outside the palace after dark. He would know the truth without a single word of confession from my lips.

I knew that he would be furious with his future bride, and I feared what that fury would bring.

The guard opened the door and helped me through, and my chest tightened as we made it back into the hall. The lack of air I felt hit me immediately, and I tried to calm my rising panic.

Instead of leading me toward my room, the guard turned past the library and pressed his hand against the stone wall. I sucked in a shocked breath as the wall groaned and the stone moved as if the strength in his hand alone made it so.

He tried to tug me forward, but I dug my heels into the ground.

"This way, Starblessed."

"Where are you taking me?" My voice didn't sound like my own. The panic was evident, and I watched as pity flashed in the guard's eyes.

"To the prince. Please don't make me drag you there."

I took a step forward, following him through the wall, and I blinked as the wall closed back behind us and the tight tunnel we stood inside came into view. It was dark inside the walls, but I could at least see in front of me as he led us down the small corridor and toward my consequences.

I could feel the blood coating my fingers with every step we took, and when he finally stopped and touched the wall again, I was desperate just to face the crowned prince and get this over with.

The wall opened to reveal the throne room, and I tightened my hold on the guard as I made my way into the light. But it wasn't the crowned prince who waited on the other side.

It was worse.

"What the fuck happened to you?" Evren growled as he marched toward me, but the pain in my leg was almost too much for me to care.

"Nothing." I shook my head and pressed my hand against my thigh. Blood had seeped through my fingers, and I clamped them together so he couldn't see the damage.

"Like hell." He reached for me, and I backed away until my heels hit the edge of the dais we were now standing in front of. "Let me see, princess."

"No." I stepped backward again, this time onto the dais that normally held his family higher than everyone else. The guard let me go, and I hated that he so quickly walked away and left me in the hands of the prince. "I want to go back to my room."

"A room you were trying to escape from?" His anger seeped through his words as he moved toward me still.

He was staring at me with so much fury, and when I looked down at his dark-stained fingers, I remembered that this man was capable of so much more than I knew. My fear hammered in my chest, but I still winced when the back of my legs hit the throne behind me.

"Please, Evren. Just let me go back to my room."

"Sit," he said the word like a command, and I obeyed him instantly.

The air around him crackled as he knelt before me and pushed my knees apart with more force than necessary. His gaze darkened as he stared ahead at my bloodied hand, but I didn't dare move it away from the wound.

"You are lucky," he hissed the words between his teeth, and I winced at the venom they held.

"To be attacked?"

"To still be alive." He lifted my trembling fingers away from my leg before letting out a curse. He pressed his own hand to my wound before reaching behind him with his other and pulling his dark shirt over his head. "You are lucky that my guards are loyal to their captain and came to me instead of the queen."

He was kneeled before me with his chest bare, and even as his hand caused pain against the cut on my leg, I couldn't stop myself from looking at him.

His body was sculpted in a way that could only be accomplished by years of work that wasn't done inside this castle.

"What are you doing?" I tensed as he pulled his shirt down his arms and reached out for my hand to replace his.

He ripped at the fabric of his shirt, tearing a strip off entirely. His abs bunched and tensed as he worked methodically on the task at hand, and I straightened in the throne as I stared at his muscles.

He had a long scar across his chest, and I wondered if he had gotten it defending the throne at which I now sat.

"I need to get this on to stop the bleeding. Then I'll take you back to my room, and we'll clean the wound." He slid the fabric under my leg and back around until he tied it in a tight knot.

"That's not happening."

His shoulders stiffened, and when he looked up at me, fear and lust mixed together and rushed through every part of me.

"Would you prefer that I take you to Gavril? To the queen?

Would you like to explain to them how you were stupid enough to try to run from a palace filled with fae and managed to get yourself hurt by someone who craves the power in your blood more than they do the favor of the crown?"

"It doesn't matter." I squared my shoulders.

"The fuck it doesn't matter, Adara." He stood before reaching out for me and pulling me to my feet. He was angry, but he was still careful not to hurt my leg. "They wouldn't be tending to your leg if they were the ones that found you. They would already have you locked up, and Gavril would be lapping at the blood seeping from your wound."

"But you're not going to?" I asked, and I could see the frustration eating at him.

"Does it look like I'm going to do either of those things? You may be a traitor to the crown, but I know what it's like to feel trapped. I don't blame you for trying."

I looked away from him as my chest ached. I didn't know what he wanted me to say. He could call me a traitor all he wanted, but being right here with him felt like the most traitorous act of all.

"Don't fucking do it again." He shook his head. "I'm already forced to watch you belong to my brother. I don't want to watch them torture you as well."

He bent down and gently slid his arm beneath my knees. He lifted me against his chest easily, and I quickly wrapped my arms around his neck before he dropped me. He started down the dais, and I tightened my hold on him.

"I can walk."

"It's easier and faster if I carry you," he grumbled without stopping, and I winced as my leg jostled against his chest.

"I can still walk."

"Fuck, Adara," he hissed my name. "Can't you just let me take care of you?"

I studied his face, and I knew it was foolish to think I could see his worry hiding behind his anger. Worry that caused my own heart to race.

"Who was that man who attacked me?"

He bit down on his bottom lip before he finally spoke. "I don't know." He moved down the hall quickly, in the opposite direction of my room, and I realized that I had no idea where Evren's rooms were. "He escaped my guards before they discovered who had done this, but I promise you, princess. I will find him."

Every part of me believed him. He was infuriated that someone had done this to me, and I didn't know if it was for my sake or the crown's. But I knew that he wouldn't stop until he had his dark fingers wrapped around the neck of whoever tried to hurt me.

We walked down a long hall at the opposite end of the palace, and I watched as black smoke dripped from Evren's fingers and into the intricate lock that held his door. I had never seen anything like his magic.

I had never felt anything like him.

My mark sparked to life under his touch and near his magic, and I clung harder to him as his door clicked open. He pushed through his doorway without any hesitation, and I searched his room as he kicked the door closed behind us.

It was set up similarly to mine, although it was far larger, and it hit me how little belongings he had throughout the room. A dark shirt was slung over the single chair that sat in the corner, and his dark bedding was tousled as if he forbade the servants to come in and make it for him.

He sat me down on the edge of his bed, careful with how he laid my leg against the soft fabrics, and he stared down at me for a long moment before he pushed away from me and stalked into his washroom.

I gripped the bedding in my hands as I stared down at his dark shirt wrapped around my thigh. Pain still thrummed through me, but I felt so on edge being alone in Evren's room that it distracted me from the discomfort.

He walked back toward me carrying a copper bowl that was steaming from the water inside and a stack of white fabrics. It felt like he barely noticed that I was currently sitting on his bed or the fact that my breath hitched in my throat, not from the pain but from the memory of his hands on my body as he kneeled in front of me.

He set the small basin at my feet before slowly untying his shirt from my leg. He didn't say a word to me as he worked, but I didn't need his words to know how angry he was. His normally controlled fingers shook with fury as he pulled the soiled fabric away from my skin.

He reached into my boot, surprising me when he quickly pulled my dagger from its home, and I didn't stand a chance as he moved it out of my reach.

"That's mine." I winced as I tried to move for the only thing that still felt like home to me.

"Calm down, princess." He pressed his hand against my chest and forced me back onto his bed before unsheathing my dagger and bringing it toward my leg.

I held my breath as he dipped his fingers into the tear in my trousers and pulled them away from my skin. Then my dagger followed. The metal grazed my skin just below my cut, and I didn't look away from it as Evren used my father's dagger to cut away my trousers from my leg.

"What you did tonight was reckless, Adara."

"I know," I hissed as the dagger tore through the fabric at my hip until my trousers were no longer held together on my left leg with a single thread.

Evren shook his head before setting my dagger next to me on the bed and sliding my boots from my feet. "Stand." His voice was demanding and crass, and for a moment, I wanted to defy him. I wanted to make him finally look up at me like I was more than some sacred blood that had tried to run from his brother.

Instead, I stood on shaking legs in front of him. He stared straight ahead at the apex of my thighs, and even though I shouldn't have noticed that look on his face when my leg was still aching in pain, it was impossible not to.

"Hold on to my shoulders." He gripped the back of my thighs, and I did as he said. He slowly pulled what was left of my shredded trousers down my legs before helping me step out of them.

I sat back down on the bed in front of him once he threw my trousers behind him, and I watched as he silently dipped his dark fingers into the steaming water. He wrung out a cloth before looking up at me, and this time, I could see the pity that was hiding behind all his anger.

I swallowed hard as I looked away from him. His anger I could handle. "Fuck," I cursed as he pressed the hot cloth against my cut. My hips jolted off the bed as my leg screamed in pain, but Evren pushed me back down as if I weighed nothing.

"I have to get it clean," he growled at me before pulling away the dirty cloth and grabbing another from the water.

"I can do it myself. I want to go back to my room."

Evren laughed before wringing out the cloth. "Are you going to stitch it yourself too? What are you going to say to Eletta when she sees it tomorrow or the queen when she accompanies you to your next fitting?"

"I'll say I slipped," I said the first thing that came to mind, and Evren's gaze darkened.

"The queen isn't a fool, princess. If she thought for a moment that you tried to run, she would do far worse to you than she ever did to…"

"My father?" I finished before he could.

He looked up at me again with that same pity in his eyes. "Your father or anyone else who dared betray her. You are everything she has been working toward, and she will not allow you to slip through her fingers."

He pressed the next cloth against my cut, and this time, I bit down on my bottom lip to stop myself from crying out.

"I don't want to be here." I curled my hands into fists and pressed them into his mattress at my sides even as they itched to reach out for him.

"You don't have a choice, princess." Evren didn't meet my eyes. Instead he was staring at my wound as he wiped the cloth against it and cleaned my tarnished skin. "I'm going to have to use magic to heal this."

"What?" My voice shook, and I knew that he could hear the fear that dripped from it.

"My magic can heal this quickly." He ran a finger along my inner thigh just below the cut, and I trembled. "Or I can use a needle and thread, but you'll risk…"

"Just do it." I clamped my eyes closed as his fingers pushed my legs farther apart.

"It won't hurt, Adara." His voice was soft and comforting, but I didn't dare open my eyes as my mark began to thrum in a steady pulse. My eyes were closed, but I could still sense darkness around me, darkness that was unusual yet breathtaking.

The shadows wrapped around me like a caress, and I couldn't differentiate what was Evren and what was his magic. But I knew that I didn't want it to end.

The pain seeped from my leg as if he was taking it into himself, and I sighed as the last of it left my body.

His magic fell away from me slowly, as if it was as resistant to leave me as I felt about losing its touch. But as the last embrace fell away from my skin, I blinked my eyes open and watched as the black smoke that healed me seeped back into Evren's fingers with a grimace on his face.

"Are you okay?" I unclenched my hands at my sides and pressed them into the soft fabric of his bedding.

"Don't worry about me, princess." He nodded toward my thigh. "Has that ever happened before?"

"No." I shook my head. "No one has ever used magic on me before."

"That's not what I mean." He lifted his hand and trailed it over where the cut had just been, and that was when I saw it. "Have you ever scarred like this before?"

I stared down at the starlight that shot across my thigh as if it were trying to hide my flawed skin. "No." I swallowed hard as my fingers met his against my thigh. "Never."

The starlight that marked my skin had been there since birth. Never before had a new mark shown up on my skin, even after all the injuries that had marred it.

And never had my star marks been shrouded in darkness like ink had been spilled on my thigh.

"You need to lie." Evren's fingers roamed over mine as he traced my new mark, and I felt it come alive under his touch as if it had been a part of me all along. "If Gavril or the queen sees this, you need to lie."

"What do I say?" I searched his face, and I could see the hint of panic on his face.

"Whatever it takes." His fingers contracted against my leg, and he lifted higher on his knees until his body was pressed fully between my thighs.

It fully hit me then that I was sitting on his bed in front of him in nothing but my undergarments and a shirt, and when his fingers tightened on my skin once more, I couldn't bring myself to be worried about the queen or the crowned prince.

"They must never know that I used my magic on you."

"What will they do if they find out?"

"I fear that neither one of us truly want to know the answer to that." His fingers skated up my sides until they settled along my hips.

I widened my legs for him without thinking, and Evren took

the opportunity to tug me closer to the edge of the bed and against him.

"And what if they find out about the way I've allowed you to touch me?"

My question brought a grin to Evren's face, and he slowly lifted his hand and moved my hair over my shoulder before letting his fingers fall against my neck. "Are you going to let me touch you again?"

"No," I said the word without any authority, and Evren knew it.

He grinned harder as his hand pressed against my neck and his fingers dug into the soft flesh of my hip.

"You say one thing, but your body says another." He leaned forward and pressed his mouth against my jawline. It wasn't quite a kiss, but like his lips were trying to discover who I was simply by the curve of my jaw. "You don't need to be ashamed of wanting me."

I swallowed hard as I took in his words. "A moment ago, you were ready to kill me."

"I'm still ready to kill you, princess. You put yourself in real fucking danger tonight, and you could have been killed." His hands tightened further as if he was trying to control himself. "But my anger with you does nothing to extinguish my want. If anything, I somehow want you even more now. I want to mark your beautiful skin with proof of my touch so everyone knows that you belong to me."

"I don't belong to—" My words were cut off as his teeth grazed over the sensitive skin of my neck. I inhaled deeply as I reached out and grasped onto his forearms for support. My chest heaved against his, and I could feel his heart racing.

"Don't say shit like that to me tonight," he growled. "It already took everything I had not to bend you over that throne and fuck you until no one was confused about the fact that you were mine. Not whoever tried to harm you, not the queen, and definitely not my fucking brother."

It was on the tip of my tongue to remind him that his brother was exactly who I belonged to, but when I looked at how possessively he was looking at me, all I could do was attempt to press my thighs together as moisture gathered there.

"And now?" I asked hesitantly.

"And now I'm kneeling between your thighs that are marked with a mix of your magic and my own, and I am still desperate to mark you with my fingers just as harshly. But you already have enough to hide, princess." His fingers tightened once more before he slowly stood before me.

I looked up, searching his face for what he would do next.

"You need to sleep."

I looked down at my bare thighs before us. "Am I to head back to my room like this or are you going to allow me to borrow some of your royal trousers?"

He chuckled low and soft before reaching down and wrapping his arm around my middle. He pressed his knee into the bed between my thighs before his grip tightened, and he quickly lifted me and dragged me to the top of his bed along with him.

My head hit his pillow, and the scent of him overwhelmed me as if I was smelling it for the first time. Evren laid at my side with his head propped onto his hand, and he stared down at me for a long moment before pulling his bedding up over our bodies.

"Tonight, you sleep here. My guards will bring you clothes to change into, and we'll get you back to your room before sunup." He dropped down beside me, and I could feel his breath against my cheek.

"I should go back to my room tonight."

"No." He shook his head against me before lifting his fingers, and the light slowly drained from the room. "Tonight you stay with me."

Evren wrapped his arm around my middle and tugged me

into him until my back was pressed against his chest. The warmth of his bare chest seeped into me, and even though I knew I shouldn't, I let a deep breath fall from my chest as I settled against him.

He pushed his knee forward between my thighs and ran his nose along the back of my neck as if he was breathing me in.

"Sleep, princess. Everything else can wait until morning."

His request felt impossible, but as his warmth surrounded me, my eyes fluttered closed and I slept more deeply than I had since I had arrived in this kingdom.

ELEVEN

"You've barely touched your pastry," Gavril said from my side before slowly pushing my braid over my shoulder. "Is this not what you want?"

Of course, this wasn't what I wanted. I wanted to be back in Evren's room, wrapped in his arms, before the guards had knocked on his door and broken the illusion I had fallen into. He had somehow made me forget where I was. He obliterated any thoughts of duty.

The only sense of responsibility I felt was that of my own wants. I felt no obligation to the prince who sat at my side. Instead, I longed for the one who had dropped me back at my room as if he were in pain to do so.

"It's fine." I smiled up at Gavril before lifting the cup of warm tea to my lips. "I'm just not very hungry."

"That's all right." His fingers trailed over my shoulder before slipping around my back. Gavril tugged my chair closer to his, and I feared that he would be able to smell the traces of his brother on my skin. "You smell divine."

"Thank you." I looked away from him just as two women around my age walked into the room. Both of them were eyeing

Gavril as if I wasn't there, and I didn't blame them. He was as handsome as he was powerful, and I should have wanted him.

"Adara, have you met Quinn and Lydia Etkin?" Gavril nodded toward them, and both women quickly dropped into perfect curtsies.

"I have not had the pleasure." I smiled even though I had no interest in meeting these women.

The one with long brown hair sat at my side and smiled at me. "It's an honor to meet you, Starblessed. We have heard so much about you."

"Yes." The one with hair of honey sat near Gavril, but now her eyes were only on me. "We have heard many tales of what you offer to our kingdom and our soon-to-be king."

"Quinn." Gavril said her name with exasperation, and his hand tightened around my shoulders. "Quinn and Lydia are both daughters of Nobleman Etkin. We have all grown up together in the palace."

Quinn nodded her head with a smile before studying me. "We know the crowned prince better than most, so if there is anything you have questions about, please feel free to use me to help you with your betrothal."

I was startled by her words, but Gavril didn't seem bothered by them in the least. His fingers were still trailing over my shoulder as if the woman in front of me wasn't letting me know that she had already had my soon-to-be husband.

"I will keep that in mind." I balled my hands into fists in my lap. It didn't upset me that she had been with him before me, but it infuriated me that she had the gall to say it to me without a trace of unease.

"And Evren?" she asked casually.

"What of him?"

Her gaze slammed back into mine at my question. "I was just asking the prince if he has seen him. I would love to be able to spend some time with him before he leaves once more."

I gritted my teeth as my heart began to race and my head ached. This woman had not only had her hands on the crowned prince, but now I was imagining her touching my prince. And the second thought infuriated me far more than the first.

"So you know both of the princes well?"

"I do." She nodded as her smile widened. "If it wasn't for you, I would be in line to be betrothed to Gavril."

I could practically taste the venom in her words. "I bet you hate me then."

Gavril laughed at my side, and Quinn's face fell. Perhaps she hadn't expected me to have a backbone.

"I don't think there are too many in our kingdom who do like you, Starblessed."

"Quinn." Gavril sat up straight as he chided her for her words, but I wanted to hear them.

"No. It's fine. I'd actually like to hear what she has to say." I leaned forward and pressed my elbows into the table. "I'd love to know why I'm giving up my entire life for a kingdom that doesn't want me."

Everyone was silent as my words rang through the room, and Gavril's hand stilled on my shoulder.

"Please, Quinn." I motioned my hand in her direction. "Don't hold your tongue now."

She simply stared at me without saying a word. She thought that she could intimidate me with her intimate knowledge of a man I was supposed to fall for, but all she did was fuel my hate.

"Am I interrupting?" Everyone looked toward the doorway where I knew Evren now stood, but I kept my gaze on Quinn and watched the way she adjusted her hair as she looked at him.

"Prince Evren." She and her sister quickly stood and dropped into a bow that didn't dip nearly as far as they had with Gavril, but they were showing him honor just the same. "I was hoping to see you before you left."

"I'm not heading out until after the ball." Evren moved

toward the table, and I finally looked up at him when he stopped directly across from me and lifted a strawberry to his mouth before nodding in my direction. "Starblessed."

"Evren." I watched as he bit into the berry, and I couldn't look away as he traced the juice from his lips with his tongue.

How could that one move turn me on far more than his brother caressing my skin with his fingers?

"Prince Evren, are you attending the ball alone, or are you bringing someone?"

I tensed against Gavril as I heard the question. I hadn't even thought of Evren bringing someone else to the ball. I hadn't thought about what it would be like to watch him with someone else the way he was forced to watch me.

"It will just be me and my sword." Evren smiled at her and my chest ached with jealousy. "I am a member of the guard, remember."

"And a member of the court." Quinn smiled up at him playfully. "I can remember several things that you've done that had nothing to do with your duty to the guard."

"Hear, hear." Gavril chuckled as he lifted his glass of wine, and I turned to him to avoid seeing the way Evren was now looking at her.

Gavril looked back at me, a smile playing on his lips, and he ran his fingers back over my braid as his gaze ran over me. "Duty and pleasure."

"Is that what you and the Starblessed are calling it?" Evren asked with a laugh that felt like a curse. "The two of you look awfully intimate over there."

"We make a beautiful couple, do we not?" Gavril looked back to his brother, but I refused.

"That you do. Adara will make the loveliest queen we've ever seen. Don't you agree, Quinn?"

I looked back at him then, and I watched as Quinn looked back and forth between the two of us quickly.

"She will. Absolutely lovely."

Gavril's hand slipped from my hair and fell against the small of my back. He pressed his hand there, drawing my attention back to him as the feel of him thrummed through my mark, and he lifted his other hand to trace along my jaw.

"And she's all mine." He smiled up at me, but I could see his possessiveness staring back at me. Gavril was being kind to me, but everything about him felt like a game.

"Well, and the kingdom's." Evren chuckled as he took a seat at the table. "She is here to save us, after all."

"True." Gavril nodded but didn't pull his gaze away from me. "But everyone else can simply look upon her. They can dream of what her mark will feel like under their fingers and running through their veins. None of them will ever be able to truly experience that besides me."

I glanced up at Evren just in time to watch his jaw tense. This was exactly what Gavril wanted. Brothers or not, Gavril was making it clear where things stood.

"Can you imagine the envy in their eyes?" Gavril chuckled before slowly running his hand down my arm.

Chill bumps broke out across my skin, but it wasn't because I was liking what he was doing.

I wanted him to quit touching me.

Especially in front of Evren.

But he did no such thing. His hand tightened along my forearm, and he lifted my arm. His fingers tangled with mine before he gently turned it over and exposed my wrist to him. He looked back up at his brother then, just as he was lowering his mouth to my skin.

"I would be wild with jealousy if I wasn't able to taste her."

I went rigid against him, but he didn't notice. He was too busy watching his brother for a reaction.

A reaction that Evren refused to give him.

"It's a good look for you, brother. Although, I can't imagine you tied down to just one woman. That's going to be a change of pace for you, isn't it?"

Gavril laughed although it held no trace of humor. "I'm more than willing to pass them all down to you. Give you your fair share of the spotlight."

Quinn and Lydia both snickered, and I wanted to demand that they stop. Instead, I stood, pushing my chair back with my knees, and Gavril finally looked back at me.

"I'm going to the library." I wasn't asking his permission or waiting around for his approval. I may have been his betrothed, but I refused to sit here and listen to this. Especially when I was dying inside to look to his brother and never look away.

"Are you all right?" he asked as if he couldn't possibly see why I'd want to leave.

"Of course." I nodded. "I'm just tired and would like to read for a bit."

"Okay." He stood and placed a soft kiss on my forehead. My gaze met Evren's as soon as Gavril's lips were pressed against my skin, and he looked as if he was ready to come across the table. "Join me for dinner tonight?"

I nodded because I didn't trust my voice. Not when Evren was looking at me like that.

Gavril held my fingers in his until I walked away and forced him to drop them. I didn't look back as I pushed out of the room. I didn't say a single one of the million things that was running through my head.

And I didn't let the whispers of Quinn's voice as I left the room run through my head over and over. I didn't like that girl. It wasn't because of the way she acted in there or the fact that she made it clear that she had been with my betrothed, but I couldn't stop imagining the ways she could've possibly touched Evren as I sat down in the library and grabbed a book.

I slammed my book closed in frustration and walked back to

the shelf to grab another. I didn't know what I was looking for as my hand trailed over the leather spines.

I just needed something, anything, to take my mind off of him.

My hand stalled next to a solid black book with no writing on the spine. I pulled it from the bookshelf, and the front looked the same. Not a title or marking anywhere in the leather.

I walked back to my seat with the book in hand and searched the doorway before I sat. My fingers traced over the black leather, feeling the supple fabric that had to be much older than me before I slowly opened the cover.

I was greeted by yellowing pages with black handwritten ink. This wasn't just some book; this was a journal. I flipped through the pages as I scanned over the writing. There were notes of the palace and a hand-sketched map of the grounds.

I flipped past those quickly, and only stopped again when I noted the words *curse of the stars* staring back at me. The words looked like they had been scribbled so quickly that I could hardly read them, but below them was a sketch of a woman with dots spread out across her chest and running down the center.

An arrow pointed toward the markings and the words *star mark* were written alongside it.

My gaze ran over the page looking for more information, but it was basic things. Things I already knew. I flipped to the next page quickly, devouring the information and searching for more.

It wasn't until I got to the final page of the book that I found what I was looking for.

Starblessed are a blessing and curse on our world. Their power can be extraordinary yet wicked. A mated Starblessed equals a threat.

I read the words over and over, but I was confused. I had never heard of a mated Starblessed before. Only fae mated, and even that was rare. It was another thing that I had only heard of in stories passed down to me by the mouths of those in my village.

But no one had ever spoken of a mated Starblessed.

"Have you gotten your fill of reading yet?"

I slammed the book shut in my lap and snapped my head up to look at Evren. He was standing in the exact same spot he had been the first time he found me in the library, but something seemed different about him.

Dangerous almost.

"Is there something I can help you with?"

"I don't know, princess. Is there?" He ran his hand along his jaw as he watched me, and I felt like he was eating me alive with his gaze alone.

"I don't know." I pressed the book to my chest as I stared at him, watching every move he made. "You seem upset."

He pushed away from the wall and took two small steps in my direction. "Frustrated."

"By what?"

His gaze ran over every inch of me, and he didn't hide a moment of it. "That my brother can touch you, can talk about you like you're his."

"I am his, Evren. We'll be married soon enough."

His gaze darkened as he stepped closer, and I could see the barely tamed fury that hid there. "You will never be his, princess. I don't give a damn if your hand holds his ring or if your head holds his crown. You still won't belong to him."

I swallowed hard as I stared up at him and watched him approach. I wished with everything inside of me that his words were true, but I knew they were nothing more than a fantasy. I couldn't be married to one man but belong to another.

My heart wouldn't allow it.

And Gavril would kill me for it. He didn't need me to love him to be his betrothed, but I knew the future king would never allow the woman that was meant to be his to fall into the arms of another. Especially not another that shared his blood.

"This book." I held it up just as he stood directly in front of me. "It says that Starblessed can be mated. Is that true?"

His brow scrunched in confusion, and I had my answer before he even spoke. "I've never witnessed it, but that doesn't mean it isn't true. What else does it say?"

I was hesitant to show him, but I still flipped to the back pages of the book before handing it over.

"Extraordinary yet wicked." He chuckled softly as he read the words aloud. "That sounds just like you."

A blush crept up my cheeks as I thought about the ways in which he had made me wicked.

Him and no one else.

"I'm not wicked."

"Aren't you?" He cocked his head to the side as he watched me. His fingers tightened around the book as he pressed it closed. "You're the most wicked little thing I've ever met."

I shook my head even as my chest tightened.

"Only someone wicked could make me want to fall to my knees before her and pledge my loyalty to her with my tongue. My family be damned."

"I haven't asked for your loyalty, Evren."

"No?" He stepped even closer to me and ran his knuckles along my hand. "You've simply demanded it of me with every breath you take. You may not have asked, princess, but gods, you have it regardless."

"And what if I don't want it?" I raised my chin and my stomach flipped. Gods, I wanted it. I wanted anything he was willing to give me.

"We both know that's a lie." He lifted the book in his hand and ran the supple spine against my wrist before slowly moving it up my arm. Everywhere it touched, chill bumps followed behind, and it felt impossible that he was capable of making me squirm while not even touching me with his skin. "We both know you are dying for things you shouldn't want."

He pressed the book edge against my collarbone before slowly dragging it along that sensitive skin to meet my neck. He didn't stop there. His gaze led the trail before the book slowly followed down my chest, between my breasts and over my belly button. My stomach tensed beneath his touch, and he slowed.

He was barely moving as his gaze dipped between my thighs. "I think that you want it right now. I think that you would give almost anything for it."

He moved the book at a painful pace as it dropped lower and lower, and even though I knew I shouldn't have, I spread my legs almost unnoticeably.

But of course, he noticed.

A smile graced his lips, but he didn't pull his gaze away from my thighs. "That's a good girl, princess." He pressed the spine against my lower stomach, and I gasped for breath. "Open for me."

"Evren," I whispered his name, and his gaze flew up to meet mine.

"Yes, princess?"

"We can't do this." I shook my head, but my legs still inched wider. My mind and my body disagreeing with one another.

"Why not?" The book dropped lower and lower until I felt nothing but the pressure of him and that spine pressed against the spot where I needed him most.

"You heard what your brother said before."

"What was it that he said?" He cocked his head to the side as he watched my lips open in a sigh. "That no one else can touch you." He pressed the book harder against me, and my back straightened against the chair. "Technically, I'm not laying a single finger on you, princess."

He moved the corner of the spine in small circles against my sex as if he was trying to prove his point. A moan slipped past my lips, desperate for more of what he was giving me.

But he simply kept up his teasing pace as he watched me. Not an inch of his skin touched mine, but I could feel him all over me.

"He couldn't be threatened by a book, could he?" Evren licked his lips as he watched the work he was doing with the book against me. I wrapped my fingers around the arms of the chair, and my knuckles turned white as I tried to keep myself from calling out for him. "I told you, princess. You're a wicked little thing."

Moisture pooled between my thighs, and I pushed my hips forward, chasing the feeling he was giving me.

"That's it," he encouraged me, and I bit down on my bottom lip as I began moving my hips in the smallest circles. "Take from me what you know he'll never be able to give you."

I reached out for him, but he pulled back slightly out of my touch before shaking his head. "No touching, princess. That'd be breaking the rules."

"I think we've already broken them, don't you?" I answered him breathlessly before closing my eyes and pressing my head back against the chair. My stomach tightened as my pleasure built inside of me. Warmth rushed through me and my marks were aflame. He wasn't even touching me, and still, my mark knew him.

My body would know him without a single word or sight. There was a feel of him that was vastly different from everyone else.

"Eyes on me, princess," he commanded, and my gaze snapped open to meet his. "I want to watch you while you fall apart beneath me. Let go. Let me see all of you."

I fell apart as soon as he spoke the words. He pressed the book harder against me as I clamped my thighs closed around it. I moaned his name softly, desperate to taste it across my tongue.

"Good girl. Come apart for me right here in the library where anyone could catch us."

"Please, Evren." I slammed my head back against the chair as wave after wave of pleasure shot through me.

Evren's hand finally touched me then, his thumb stroking roughly against my bottom lip, and when I opened my eyes again, he was staring back at me with so much lust I could choke on it.

"Open." He pressed his thumb against my lips, and I did as he said. He slid his thumb into my mouth, tracing my tongue with the tip of his finger as he slowed the movement with the book. "Suck it for me, princess. I want to imagine you with your mouth open and my cock sliding along your perfect lips when I take care of myself later."

I closed my lips around him and hollowed out my cheeks as I sucked his thumb. I rolled my tongue along the bottom, and he groaned before slowly pulling it back out and shoving it back in. He did that over and over, fucking my mouth with his thumb, and I reached forward because I was desperate for it to be something else.

I wanted to see him, to touch him, to taste every part of him that he would allow.

My hands connected with his thighs, and he growled low and deep but never took his eyes off my mouth. "You're so fucking perfect."

He pulled his thumb away with a pop and saliva fell against my lip.

"I want to touch you." My hands dug into his trousers, and he ran his hand along my jaw.

His hand was rough and frantic against my face, and I knew that the prince was so close to losing every bit of control he still managed to possess.

"Not tonight." He shook his head gently as he stared down at me, but I didn't want to listen to him. He had brought me pleasure twice now, and I had yet to touch his skin beneath my fingers.

"Please, Evren," I begged. I actually begged this man in front of me who I should have been walking away from.

"You've given me more of yourself tonight than I should have ever asked for, princess. Let me escort you back to your room."

He reached his hand out for me, but instead of taking it, I dropped to my knees before him.

"Fuck." He ran his hand over his mouth as he watched me before quickly looking back toward the library door.

I wasn't prepared for his power or the effect it had on me, and I gripped onto his thigh as a swarm of black magic fell from his fingers and filled the room around us. It encapsulated every inch of the library except exactly where we were.

My spine straightened as his magic met my skin, and I felt that shock of him all the way to my core. I raised my trembling fingers to the top of his trousers, and although I had no idea what I was doing, I was still desperate to try.

I wanted to bring him pleasure like he had given me. I wanted to erase anyone who had come before me out of his mind.

"Can I?" My hands hesitated at the buttons on his trousers, and when I looked up, Evren was staring at me with so much want that it made me press my thighs together with need.

"You can do anything you want with me, princess. I'm yours." He ran his hand over my hair almost lovingly, and I concentrated my attention on getting his buttons undone with my fumbling fingers.

Evren didn't rush me. He stood above me wordlessly as I finally lowered his trousers enough to see him. I swallowed hard at the first sight of his length. I slipped his trousers lower until his cock was released, then I brought those same trembling fingers to meet his skin.

He was soft, so much softer than I had imagined. I hadn't known what to expect, but I felt desperate to figure out every part of him. I wrapped my hand around the width of him, squeezing tightly as I tried to press one finger to my thumb, and he hissed.

I pushed my fist up and down his length, testing the feel of him in my hand, and his hand tightened in my hair.

"Can I taste you?" I asked as I looked up at him, and Evren clamped his eyes closed before quickly opening them back up to look down at me.

"Gods please, princess." He buried his fingers against my scalp. "I've been dreaming about what that mouth of yours can do."

I looked back at his cock, and I was so intimidated by the size of him. I had no idea what I was doing, but I knew that I wanted to feel him in my mouth in the same way I had just felt his thumb. I wanted to create that same reaction in him as well.

I licked my lips and moved closer to him, and I glanced up at him just as I ran my tongue over his tip.

"Fuck," he growled and his hand tightened even further in my hair. There was a bite of pain there, but it felt like it was directly connected to between my thighs.

I ran my tongue along the underside of his cock, tasting the entire length of him, and his thigh shook beneath my hand.

"Am I doing this right?"

Evren chuckled as he let out a harsh breath. "There is nothing you can do that would be wrong, princess. However you want to touch me is more than I could ever beg of the gods."

I took his words as encouragement and wrapped my lips around the tip of him. My mouth felt so full as I slowly slid him inside me, pressing my tongue flat against the underside of him. I did exactly as I had with his thumb, and I hollowed out my cheeks as I took him in farther and farther.

I took him until he hit the back of my throat, and I gagged around the tip of him.

"Fucking hell." Evren pulled my head back by his grip on my hair before he slowly slid back inside. He did that over and over again until his handle on his control seemed to slip away.

He really began to move then, his cock slamming into the back of my throat before almost pulling completely out of my mouth. I stared up at him as he did so, and I had never been so turned on in all my life.

Evren was always beautiful, but unhinged was a stunning sight.

I let my hand fall away from his cock and held on to his thigh as he slammed into my mouth over and over. My body shook with pleasure as I stared up at him and saw the way he was watching me.

It almost felt lewd to watch him as he came apart as if this was the most vulnerable Evren ever allowed another to see him, but I couldn't look away. Even as I lifted the skirt of my dress and slid my fingers beneath, I still watched him.

My fingers met the exact spot where he had been working the book against me only moments before, and my legs trembled instantly. I was so close to falling over the edge already, the feeling of Evren in my mouth was more than I could handle.

I dipped my fingers inside myself, gathering the moisture that pooled there before lifting it back to my cluster of nerves and rubbing small circles. I tried to keep up with the pace that Evren was setting, but once he saw what my hand was doing, it became almost brutal.

His other hand pressed against my jaw, his thumb caressing my skin as I continued to take him, and I knew he was close to falling over the edge as his thrusts became merciless.

"I'm going to come, princess," he warned me, and I moaned around him as I felt myself chasing that high that only he had been able to give me.

I sucked him harder into my mouth as his magic seemed to surge and swirl around us. My marks were aflame against my skin. I felt it touching every inch of me, and even the hand that was buried between my thighs didn't feel like my own.

I felt the first release of his pleasure hit the back of my throat, and I moaned around him as my fingers could hardly keep up the pace. I was falling apart, harder than I had earlier, and I was drinking down his pleasure as eagerly as I chased my own.

He roared in pleasure, and I watched him as he bared his teeth and the sharp points of his canines seemed more predominant than earlier. I should have been fearful, but pleasure still coursed through my body.

Evren slowed his movements, and his hands loosened their hold against me. He pulled out of my mouth before he gently ran his thumb along my swollen lips. "Are you okay, princess?"

I nodded because I wasn't sure I was capable of words. Evren's magic still swirled around us, and I didn't know if it was by choice or if he simply had lost control of it.

But I welcomed it either way as he pressed his hands beneath my arms and lifted me on shaking legs.

"Like I said. A wicked little thing." He leaned forward and pressed his lips against mine, and I never wanted to leave the cloak of him or his magic.

TWELVE

There was a firm, loud knock at my door, and I took a deep breath before moving toward it. My dress swirled around me like glitter as I walked, and I knew that this was exactly what the queen wanted.

Attention.

And she was sure to have it.

I opened the door and was surprised to see Evren standing on the other side instead of one of the guards.

The smile on his face fell as his gaze roamed over every inch of tight fabric that showed off my body that the dress was meant to cover, and I watched his hand ball into a fist as he noticed the long slit that crawled up my thigh.

"Princess." He cleared his throat roughly before bringing his gaze back up to meet mine. "I've come to escort you to your first ball."

"Shouldn't Gavril be doing that?" I asked even though I was more than happy that it was Evren instead of his brother.

"The crowned prince is already in attendance at the ball. His grace was presented with the king and queen."

"But not you?"

"Not me." He smiled again, this time the move looked genuine as he stared down at me with his dark eyes.

He was wearing his signature black attire, but his dark trousers were finely pressed and perfectly tucked into leather boots and his shirt was molded to his skin like it was made for no other. And for the first time since I first met the prince, he wore a pin of his father's royal crest along his chest.

"You look…" He hesitated for a moment and his gaze fell to my bodice which was barely covered in white satin and the sheer jeweled fabric that fell along my shoulders. "Unbelievable." He shook his head.

I could feel heat rising in my chest as I looked away from him. All I could think about was the way I had been on my knees before him only the night before. "You look handsome as well."

"I do not compare, princess." He ran his hand over the front of his trousers. "Whatever I am, it does not measure to you."

I tried not to let him see how much his words affected me, but it was impossible. I was completely and irrevocably altered by his words.

"Thank you, Evren."

He held out his hand for mine, and I placed it there without hesitation. My star marks sparked to life with the first touch of his skin to mine, and it was odd to feel him against my thigh along with my back and cheeks.

I had hardly noticed the night before because I had felt him everywhere.

He tucked my hand into the crook of his arm as he slowly closed my door behind us and led us down the hallway toward the ball. A ball that was being held in my honor although I had zero interest in attending.

"I don't want to do this." I dug my fingers into Evren's bicep, and he stopped in his tracks.

The hallway was quiet and empty, and even though I knew

the palace was filled with others waiting to see me, when I looked up at him, I felt like we were alone.

"I'll be there the whole time, princess. No one is going to hurt you." His dark eyes looked over every inch of me. "You have been hurt under my watch once, and I refused to allow it to happen again."

But being physically hurt wasn't what I feared the most. I didn't want to be paraded around their ballroom like a prized cattle who was nothing but a trophy before she was to be slaughtered. I didn't want to feel their eyes or their hands on me.

I felt desperate to hide away. To run.

But as Evren stared down at me, I knew that wasn't a choice. He swore no one would hurt me, but it would be by his family's hand that I would suffer the most.

He lifted his hand before tracing his thumb over my jaw and my bottom lip faintly. I could smell traces of leather on his skin, and even though I knew I shouldn't, I pressed my tongue against the tip of his thumb before he could pull it away.

His gaze darkened and his thumb pressed harder against me as his fist tilted my chin to look up at him. "You're playing a dangerous game, princess."

"And what game is that?" I baited him. I wanted an argument, anything that would take me away from the fate that was set in front of me.

"The game where I take you back to your room and fuck you instead of going to this absurd ball." He pressed closer to me, and I didn't dare back away. I was desperate to feel how badly he wanted me. "Instead of this perfect fucking version of the Starblessed they've created, you'll arrive to them depraved and sated." He leaned forward and his mouth pressed against his thumb and my lips. "My brother will look at you, and every bit of doubt he's had about your desires will knock the breath from his lungs. He'll have no choice but to see how badly you need me, how easily I taught you things I've been dreaming about since I first laid eyes on you."

My stomach tightened and moisture pooled between my legs. "And what if that's not what I want?"

He laughed soft and low. "We both know that it is, princess. I can smell how badly you want me right now. I can't get the thought of you on your knees before me out of my head. I can still remember exactly what you tasted like off my fingers. I'm dying to see if it's any different when my head is buried between your thighs and you're pledging your loyalty with a scream of pleasure."

"Evren," I whispered his name in warning, but it sounded like I was begging him to do exactly as he promised.

He moved a hand around me, and he pressed his rough fingers into my exposed back. "Gods, Adara." He ran his nose along my jaw, and my chest rose and fell quickly against his. "You undo me every time my name is uttered from your lips."

My back arched as his power thrummed through me, and a deep ache started between my thighs. An ache I hadn't been able to get rid of since I met him.

"We're supposed to be at the ball."

"We are." He nodded against my neck, breathing me in deeply. "Lots of people are expecting to see the future queen of Citlali."

He spoke the words, but he didn't move away from me. If anything, he pulled me tighter against him until I knew that my dress would be wrinkled from his touch.

"But gods, I must taste you before they have their fill." Evren walked backward, pulling me with him, and I almost tripped over the skirts of my dress as he fumbled for the stone wall and ran his hands along the smooth stone.

For a moment, I wondered what he was doing, but then the stone moved, just as it had for the guard, and Evren pulled me inside the dark corridor that was lit tonight by a few lanterns that hung from the wall. The stone had hardly closed before he wrapped his hand around my neck and tugged me toward him.

"What is this place?" It was small enough that the two of us standing together were forced to be close, but the corridor stretched on for as far as I could see.

"It's the guards' passage." He forced me back against the wall and ran his lips along my neck. "We use it to get where we need to be in the palace quickly."

"And does the queen know of it?"

His teeth grazed over my collarbone, and my eyes fluttered closed at the sensation.

"There is very little that the queen doesn't know, princess. But she is far too busy tonight to wonder what's going on in the halls of her castle." He brought his mouth up to meet mine then, and he kissed me roughly, as if it was taking every bit of his control not to consume me.

And I kissed him back just as carelessly.

He groaned when my tongue met his, and I could taste the hint of ale on his tongue.

"Put your hands on the wall, princess." He pushed me forward until I was forced to comply with his words, and I pressed my hands into the stone just above my head as Evren held on to my hips. "Fuck, you're beautiful." He ran his hand from the top of my shoulders down my spine, and I inhaled a sharp breath when I felt him drop to his knees behind me.

He pulled my skirt to the side, the slit at my thigh allowing him access, and his fingers grazed over my undergarments in a whisper of a touch. I jolted when he pressed more firmly against my sex, and I heard his soft laugh behind me.

"So ready for me. Aren't you?" He slid the fabric to the side and dipped his fingers beneath until they met my flesh. "So damn wet."

I clamped my eyes closed as he gathered my moisture with his fingers before slowly sinking them inside me. I widened my legs to give him better access to my body, and he pressed a gentle kiss to the back of my thigh.

"Do you want my mouth on you, princess? Do you want me to taste what lays between your perfect fucking thighs?"

I nodded my head before looking behind me to where he kneeled. He was watching me so intently, and I knew that I would never experience this again. No matter what happened in my life, I would never experience a lover as possessive as Evren.

"Has anyone tasted you before, or does that honor belong to me?" He nipped at my thigh and my knees threatened to buckle.

"Only you," I whispered and reached behind me to touch him. I ran my fingers along the back of his neck and felt the way his hair fell through them.

He lifted my skirt then and his tongue caressed the bottom curve of my backside. My hips surged back, searching for his mouth, desperate for his tongue to be exactly where I needed him.

Evren's hand slipped away from my sex and roughly grabbed my hips before he ripped away the delicate lace of my undergarments.

"Fuck, you taste even sweeter than I imagined."

"Oh gods." I pressed my forehead against my arm just as he jerked my hips backward and forced my bottom to arch almost uncomfortably so.

I wasn't prepared for what he was doing, and when the first swipe of his tongue met my sex, I cried out against my arm.

"That's it, princess," Evren spoke against my skin. "Let me hear exactly what I'm doing to you."

He sucked my flesh into his mouth before he gently lapped at it with his tongue, and I was far too aroused to even consider being embarrassed by the fact that the prince was eating my flesh like a man starved.

His tongue worked me softly before moving faster, a constant change of pace that was driving me crazy, and just when I was about to scream in frustration, Evren spun me around to face him and slammed my back against the stone.

He lifted my thigh in his hands, the one that now held a mark that was somehow equal parts me and him, and his tongue ran over the starlight and shadows just as he hooked my thigh over his shoulder.

The move felt like a direct line to my sex, and I quickly brought my hand down to chase that feeling while he teased me along my magic.

"That's not happening, princess." Evren quickly pulled my fingers away from my core before dipping them into his mouth and licking away the evidence of what I had just done. "Your pleasure is mine and mine alone."

There was no more teasing after that. He widened my legs and sucked my sensitive nub into his mouth in one move, and I quickly gripped my fingers in his hair to keep myself from falling over. The pleasure was explosive and obscene, and I cried out his name as it began coursing through my body.

Everything inside me felt like it was pulled taut, and I knew I was going to snap before I could stop it. "Evren, please."

He slid two fingers inside me unexpectedly, and he curled them toward himself as he sucked harder on my nub.

"You're mine, Adara. Regardless of who you dance with tonight or who you're presented as. You belong to me. Anyone who has you after this will have you with traces of the bastard prince left on your skin."

His fingers on my hip tightened, and I fell apart with a cry as I rode his face until every drop of pleasure coursed through my body.

"That's it, princess. Scream my name while they eagerly await you. You are their savior but my demise. You are to ruin every part of me."

He pressed a gentle kiss between my thighs, then another along the new mark on my leg, before he slowly lowered it and made sure I was steady on my feet. He was still on his knees before me, and as I looked upon him, I could still see my moisture coating his lips.

He lowered my skirt, straightening it back to where it belonged, before he stood in front of me. I was still bracing my back against the wall as I stared at him, and he grinned as if he knew.

"Would you like to know, princess?"

"Know what?"

"What it is you taste like off my lips? It seems unfair that I've tasted myself from yours, but you haven't had the pleasure to know how sweet you are against my mouth." He leaned forward before I could answer and pressed his mouth to mine. He forced his tongue inside before I could object, and he groaned as I chased the taste of us mixed together with my own.

"I don't want to take you to this fucking ball," he growled before taking a step back away from me.

"But?"

He pressed his hand to the wall again, and this time it opened far easier than the last. "But, I must, princess."

He reached out for me, and I let him take my hand. He pulled me back into the hallway where this all started, and I pressed my legs together as the fact that I was no longer wearing undergarments hit me full force.

"Unfortunately, everyone will notice if you don't show."

He placed my hand back in the crook of his arm before he ran his other hand through his hair, then he started forward as if he hadn't just completely unarmed me. If I was unprepared to face everyone at the ball before, I was wholly defenseless now.

The closer we got to the ballroom, the louder and louder the music became, until the loud crescendo felt like it was teasing the racing of my heart in my chest.

"I'll be here the whole time," Evren whispered before he placed an inconspicuous kiss on the top of my head.

We rounded the corner to the ballroom, and a few of Evren's guards stood watch just outside the doors. All three of them bowed as we approached, and I fidgeted with my dress to make sure there wasn't an inch out of place.

Would the guests be able to see where Evren's hands had bunched the fabric and moved it out of his way as he dove into my flesh, or would they see me exactly like the queen hoped?

"Starblessed. Captain." One of the older guards moved toward us. "The queen is waiting for you."

Evren nodded once in his direction before leading me toward the door, and I took a deep breath and closed my eyes before I had to face the reality of the night ahead of me.

"Breathe." Evren's voice was a plea, and when I opened my eyes again, we were stepping into the ballroom surrounded by hundreds of faces of people I didn't know.

Every one of them stopped what they were doing to watch me as we made our way through them. I could hear their hushed whispers and gasps of surprise as I passed. My mark. Every one of them turned their heads to stare at my mark on my back.

I had almost forgotten about it when I was with Evren. It was almost as if my mark didn't matter when I was with him. But that was absurd.

My mark mattered more than my own life. It was everything that I was and everything that this kingdom wanted from me. And tonight, I was here to show it off.

The crowd moved as we walked, clearing a path for the Starblessed escorted by the bastard prince, and I knew that was how they all saw us. Neither one of us was more than what they had labeled us, and as Gavril came into view, his gaze searched me out and he didn't even notice his brother at my side.

It was a mistake on his part.

Because his brother was all I could see.

He started toward us with a grin on his face, and he bowed deeply once he stood in front of me. "Adara," he sighed my name before reaching his hand out for me. "You look breathtaking."

"Thank you." My hand clenched against Evren before I mustered the courage to drop my hold on him and allow his brother to pull me away.

Gavril pulled me into his side without acknowledging his brother, and he led me toward the dais where the king and queen waited. "Gods, you're beautiful." Gavril ran his fingers down my spine, and chill bumps were left in his wake.

I was still so raw from his brother, so on edge.

The urge to bow before the queen was overwhelming, but I somehow managed to keep my head held high like I hadn't just let the other prince of their kingdom eat from my flesh.

"You look different, Starblessed." Those were the first words she spoke, and my breath rushed out of me as fear consumed me.

"What?" There was no way for her to know. No possible way that she could see the way Evren had marked my soul with his touch.

"Your thigh." She nodded toward the slit in my dress. "That star mark hasn't always been there." She narrowed her eyes as she studied it. "It's different than the others."

"Oh." I pressed my fingers to the new mark Evren had given me and looked down at the scar as my heart raced. "No, Your Majesty. It's new."

She smiled, although the motion held no trace of pleasure, and looked back and forth between her son and me. "It would appear that this betrothal will bring out the best in both of you." She paused for a long moment as her gaze fell back to my thigh. "Please dance. Let our guests gaze upon the magic that mars your skin."

I watched as her hard gaze fell on Evren before she looked back at me slowly, and my stomach sank at her assessment. Her eyes narrowed on me before they fell back to my thigh, and my hands trembled at my sides. Whatever she was seeing was wrong. I had to make sure she believed that.

I turned toward Gavril and smiled at him with as much joy as I could muster. "Then let's dance."

He pulled me toward the middle of the floor where others were already dancing, and for the first time since I walked into the room, I noticed how handsome he looked. His brown hair was pushed back out of his face perfectly, and his clothes hung close to his body in a way that drew you in.

"I didn't think you were ever going to get here." He laughed as he lifted my hands and placed them along his shoulders. He ran his fingers slowly down my arms, and I tried not to tense under his touch.

"This dress took a long time to get into."

He laughed softly, and his gaze fell to my chest. "I bet it did. Did I tell you how beautiful you look in it?"

"You did." I smiled and looked away from him, and I was reminded of how on display we were.

Everyone in the room was watching us, assessing their future king and me, and I could see them waiting for me to make a mistake.

"There will be a few noblemen who will ask for your hand in a dance tonight."

My gaze flew back up to meet Gavril's.

"The queen has requested that you accept."

"Requested or demanded?" My heart raced at the thought of having to dance with anyone else. Of having their hands on me.

Gavril gave me a tight smile. "I guess they are one and the same."

I nodded because I knew exactly what that meant. I didn't have a choice.

"But trust me, Adara. The thought drives me mad." His hands tightened around my waist as he whirled us around the dance floor. "I don't wish to see any other man have his hands on what's mine."

His words stiffened my spine because I feared what he would do if he was to ever find out about the way his brother had touched me. The way he has taken what was his right under his nose.

"I'll do what I need to."

I looked toward the queen where she was talking to a few men, but her eyes were directly on me. Watching my every move.

I would do whatever it took to make her not suspicious of the son that wasn't of her blood and me. I searched for him throughout the sea of people and finally found him standing near the door with a few of his guards. They were speaking to one another, all three with grimaces on their faces, but Evren's eyes were tracking me.

The music slowed before the final notes floated through the room, and Gavril held me firmer against him as our footsteps stopped along with the sound.

"Come on." He smiled down at me playfully, and my chest tightened. "Let's get you some wine before you're forced to dance with some men who aren't nearly as good of a dancer as I am."

"You think you're a good dancer?" I teased, and I hated how heavy it felt in my chest. Gavril was being kind to me, and I was doing nothing but betraying him anytime he simply looked away.

"I have been told that a time or two." He chuckled and wrapped his hand around mine. "Do you think I need more training?"

"Maybe." I laughed as he pouted. "But I'm certain that the two of us will get more than our fair share of training tonight."

"That we will." He dropped my hand long enough to grab a goblet of wine from a long table that was filled with alcohol and food, and he handed it to me before grabbing his own. "And this should help."

I took a long sip of the wine and tried to allow it to calm my nerves. I would need far more than a single glass, but I was thankful for the small reprieve.

I finished the glass quickly, and Gavril didn't say a word as he took the empty glass from my hand and gave me another. He simply smiled as if he knew how much tonight was going to take from me. He smiled at me like he wasn't the prince who was forcing my hand in marriage because he wanted me for my mark and not for me.

And for a moment, it hit me that Evren probably wanted the same. There was no doubt in my mind that the bastard prince wanted me in a way that was indescribable. He wanted my flesh, and I wanted him just as badly, but would he crave me the way he did if I hadn't been the girl who was destined?

I sought him out again, my gaze knowing exactly where to find him, and he was watching us both so intently as if I was standing with the enemy and not his blood.

"Excuse me, Your Grace." I was caught off guard as an older man bent into a low bow in front of Gavril, drawing my attention back to him. "May I ask for the Starblessed's hand in a dance?"

He stood back to his full height, and I felt like I couldn't breathe. There was something familiar about this man, something I couldn't quite put my finger on, but I knew that I knew him.

"Of course." Gavril patted his shoulder before turning to me with a smile. "Adara, this is Nobleman Etkin."

"It's a pleasure to meet you, Starblessed." He smiled at me kindly, but my back was straight and the muscles in my legs tight and ready to flee.

"Likewise." It was the only word I could manage.

He held his hand out to me that was worn from age, and I looked to Gavril as I hesitated. But he was smiling up at the man like he couldn't imagine there being anyone else better for me to dance with.

He wasn't going to stop this no matter how badly I was begging him with my eyes.

I slipped my hand into the nobleman's and allowed him to pull me away from Gavril and back to the dance floor.

He held one of my hands in his own, and I lifted my other to rest on his shoulder. I looked anywhere but at him as he started leading me around the floor, but my back was turned to Evren. I just needed to look at him once.

"How are you enjoying the kingdom of Citlali thus far, Starblessed?"

I was forced to look up at him then, and I quickly studied his eyes as I answered. "It's been lovely."

"Good." He nodded once, his gray hair barely moving out of place. "And everyone has been kind to you?"

My stomach dropped as I listened to his words. I knew this man. I knew him, but I didn't know from where. I didn't recall meeting him throughout the castle, but I had to be wrong.

"Have we met before?" I studied his eyes and watched as a flicker of fear entered them at my question.

"No, Starblessed. I just arrived in the capital a few short days ago."

It hit me then who he was, and my entire body stiffened as he tried to turn me along the floor.

"Are you all right, Starblessed?"

I nodded even as my heart raced, and I looked over his shoulder, praying that Evren was still where he had been when I last sought him out.

His eyes met mine instantly, and I sighed in relief. Here I was dancing in the arms of the man who had attacked me only a few nights ago, and all I needed was to see Evren. He shifted as soon as he saw the look on my face. One simple look, and he was marching toward us with determination.

"My daughters told me that they had the pleasure of meeting you yesterday. Both were honored to spend time with the Star-blessed."

His words quickly drew my attention back to him. "Quinn and Lydia are your daughters?"

"They are." He smiled like a proud father and not the man who had shoved a knife into my leg with no remorse. "They grew up in this palace with Gavril. It feels like home to them."

"Excuse me, Nobleman Etkin." Evren stopped at my side, close enough that we had no choice but to stop our dance. "I would love to have a dance with the Starblessed if I can interrupt. She did promise to save me one."

"Of course," he said quickly, although his face contorted in annoyance. "We shall talk again later." He nodded toward me, and I quickly returned the movement.

Evren didn't hesitate as he took my hand from the man and pulled my body into his. He held me closer than even Gavril had, and I tried to put some space between us but he refused. He spun us around the floor effortlessly, getting us lost in the mix of the others, and only then did he open his mouth.

"What's wrong?" He searched my face quickly, scanning every inch of me.

"I don't..." I shook my head because I didn't know how to put into words what I believed to be the truth.

"What is wrong, princess?" He said the words through his teeth, annunciating each one.

"Who was that man?" I nodded to where I had just been dancing.

"Did he say something to you?" His gaze turned murderous, and I quickly shook my head.

"No. Who is he to you?"

"He is Quinn's father." He nodded toward where the girl was dancing with someone else. "He has been a part of my father's court for as long as I can remember."

"But he doesn't live in the palace?"

"Not anymore." His hands tightened against the small of my back. "Why are you asking?"

I shook my head because I didn't want to tell him. What if I was wrong? What if he wasn't the man I had seen that night?

"Fucking tell me, princess." He growled at me, and my heart raced even harder.

"It's just..." I looked back for the man, but he was nowhere to be found. "I think he was the man who attacked me."

Evren's body went rigid under my hands, and I knew that I shouldn't have said anything.

"I'm sorry. I must be mistaken. I shouldn't have said that."

He looked down at me, and I could see the anger burning in his gaze. My hands loosened against him, and for the first time since I met Evren, I truly feared the man standing in front of me.

"I'm sorry."

"Do not apologize." He shook his head before looking over my shoulder with the same ferocity that he had just been directing at me. "Don't you dare fucking apologize for that coward."

"But what if I'm wrong?" I shook my head and tried to pull away from him, but he held me tighter against him. "He's a part of your father's court."

"I don't give a damn if it was my father himself, princess. No one will hurt you and not see the end of my blade."

I was shocked by his words, but when I looked up at him, he was staring down at me with nothing but truth in his gaze. I wanted Evren desperately, but he was still my enemy. The blood that ran through his veins was the very blood that was trapping me here, but he was also something more.

He would destroy anyone who hurt me, but would he do the same when it came to his brother?

"You should never be afraid of telling me the truth of what is bothering you." He lifted his hand and pushed a stray strand of my hair out of my face, and the urge to lean forward and kiss him was overwhelming. He had just had his head buried between my legs, but it wasn't enough.

If anything, it only made me crave him more.

"Evren," I whispered his name as I turned my face into his hand, and that was when I remembered where we were. Faces I didn't know were staring back at me, but I easily recognized the look they were giving me as they looked back and forth between their bastard prince and me.

They could see everything I had been trying to hide.

"The queen is watching us." Evren pulled his hand away from my face before putting the slightest distance between us. To everyone else, it would appear as nothing, but to me, it felt like he was a thousand miles away. "I will find you after."

He slowly bent into a bow as the last notes of the song rang out through the room, and I couldn't look away from him as he rose before walking away from me. He left me standing alone in the middle of the dance floor, but everyone was still watching me.

When I turned back to face the queen, Evren was right. She stared at me with a cold, shrewd stare, and I could barely look away from her. Not as Gavril came back into my view with a charming smile on his face or when he wrapped his arms around my waist and pulled me back into a dance.

The queen watched me through it all, and I knew that she was dissecting the way I held on to Gavril versus Evren. But even knowing, I wouldn't be able to convince her.

"I'd like to show you something."

I looked away from the queen long enough to look up at my betrothed, and his smile was tight as he watched me.

"Okay." I nodded even though I didn't want to go anywhere but back to my room. I wanted to find Evren and disappear in his darkness for just a few more moments.

But that wasn't going to happen.

Gavril took my hand in his, and he laid a gentle kiss against my knuckles before he pulled me toward him. I followed behind him as we left the ballroom, and every eye was on us. This was what I needed them to see. I needed them to feel how in love I was with their crowned prince.

I needed them to believe something that would never be the truth.

Gavril pulled me into the hall, and I finally took a deep breath as I walked to keep up with him. He took me down the hall where I knew Evren's room was, and he kept going even after we passed his door.

He didn't say a word as we walked, he just pulled me along after him, and the farther we got from the ballroom, the harder my heart raced in my chest.

"Where are we going, Gavril?" I could hear the fear in my voice, and so could he. His hand tightened its hold on me as if he feared I was going to run.

"To my rooms." He glanced back at me for only a moment, but he didn't stop even as fear crawled up my chest and threatened to bubble over into a scream.

There was nothing for me in Gavril's room. Nothing that I didn't fear.

He stopped in front of a large set of double doors, and I glanced at the two guards that stood outside them. I pleaded with them with my eyes to do something, anything, but neither of them held my gaze for long.

They simply nodded toward their future king as he pushed through the doorway and pulled me behind him.

His room was massive and lit up with dozens of candles and lanterns throughout the space. A fire roared in the far corner and a bead of sweat dripped down the long expanse of my exposed back within seconds of entering the room.

Two more guards stood in the room near Gavril's bed, and when I noticed them, I stalled and jerked my hand from Gavril's.

"What are we doing?" I backed up until my back hit the doors with a loud thump, and Gavril turned to me with so much mistrust in his eyes.

"How did you get that new mark, Adara?" His gaze slid down to my leg, and I quickly tried to cover it with the sides of my dress.

"I don't know. I told your mother—"

"The queen doesn't trust you," he cut me off before I could finish. "She doesn't believe a word that slips past your lips."

"And you?"

He shook his head, and I knew that Gavril didn't have the opportunity to form his own thoughts. Whatever he believed of me was fueled by his mother.

"I believe that this union is going to save our kingdom. You and I are going to be the very thing our people have begged and prayed for. It doesn't matter where you got that new mark as long as it fuels us to be the strongest king and queen that this court has ever seen."

It was on the tip of my tongue to ask him if he cared about what his brother had been doing to me. Did he care that I was betrothed to him but desperate for someone who should have been the most loyal in his court?

"What are we doing here, Gavril?"

The door pushed open behind me, and I quickly moved out of the way so it could open fully. I wanted to run before any of them could stop me, but I wasn't able to do a thing as the queen walked into the room and the door closed silently behind her.

"Good. You haven't begun yet."

"Begun what?" I took another step backward toward the fire I felt desperate to get away from and looked between them. But I already knew the answer. I knew the moment I walked into this palace what they wanted from me, but I wasn't ready for them to take it.

They couldn't just take from me.

"Gavril, take her to the bed." The queen nodded toward his massive bed that was centered in the room, and I jumped when Gavril reached out for me.

"Please don't do this. I'm not ready for you to do this."

There was no sympathy on his face as he grabbed my wrist in his hand and tugged me toward him. I tried to pull away, to fight against his hold, but it was no use.

He pulled me into his chest and wrapped an arm around my back. He lifted me against him as if I weighed nothing, my feet dangling above the floor, and a tear slid down my cheek as he moved us toward the bed.

"Please, Gavril."

"Hush, Adara," he commanded me. "This will be pleasurable for the both of us."

I pushed against his chest as he led me to the bed, and when my gaze connected with the queen's over his shoulder, I began kicking in an attempt to get away. Someone grabbed my arm, and I cried out as I looked behind me and found one of the guards now trying to hold me still.

"Put her in the chair," Gavril commanded him, and he pushed me into the arms of the guard as he moved toward his bed.

I slammed my head back, connecting with the guard's face, and he let out a curse before the other guard joined him in his hold on me. Their hands dug into my skin, the bite of pain fueling my fear, and even though I barely budged an inch, I didn't stop fighting them as they forced me down into the chair and held me against it.

I watched as Gavril lifted a dagger into his hand and unsheathed it before him. He was going to use that dagger on me. He was going to pierce my skin against my will and take from me.

And I couldn't just sit here and allow it to happen.

"You said that this wouldn't happen until we were married." I looked up at the queen as I kicked and tried my hardest to pull out of the guard's hold. "You promised me."

"I underestimated you, Starblessed." The queen stepped closer to me, and I stilled with every inch she closed in on me. "That mark on your leg didn't just appear. That is the result of magic. I'm not a fool."

I clamped my mouth closed as I stared at her. There was no way that I would tell her the truth of what happened. I would never tell her that Evren was the cause of that beautiful scar on my skin.

"If you won't tell us where that mark came from, then Gavril will taste it within your blood. We shall see how powerful you make my son before he is forever attached to a girl with nothing but lies on her tongue."

Gavril came back into my view with the dagger held in front of him and determination in his gaze. Nothing I said was going to stop him.

"Gavril, please," I begged a man who I knew didn't really care about me, but he refused to meet my eyes.

"This will only hurt for a moment, Adara." He dropped to his knees in front of me, and when I kicked out toward him, he pinned my knees in front of him, pressing his torso against my legs. "Hold her still."

Both guards had a hold of my arms, pinning them down to the chair, and I didn't stand a chance of getting away from them. I whimpered when I tried to struggle free again and didn't budge an inch. I hated that I was showing so much weakness in front of Gavril and the queen, but I couldn't stop the panic that was crawling over my skin. Even my mark burned against me as if in warning of what was to come. It knew this wasn't right. This wasn't what we wanted, but I had no choice. My blood was going to be drained from me despite my desires.

Gavril lifted his dagger, never once meeting my gaze, but I

didn't look away from him as he pressed the metal into my inner wrist, and pain sliced through my skin.

My blood pulled there, seeping through the cut on my arm and dripping down the side of my wrist and onto my pristine dress.

"I'm sorry, Starblessed." Gavril dropped the dagger at his side before leaning forward and hovering his mouth over my wrist. I didn't know what to expect, but I felt so violated as he stared down my blood with more admiration than he had ever given me.

"Please, Gavril," I begged him again with fear coating my words. "Please don't do this. Not tonight."

But he still wasn't listening to me. He leaned forward, closing the space between his mouth and my blood, and when his tongue swiped out of his mouth and lapped at the blood on my skin, I screamed.

I closed my eyes as I cried out, praying that anyone would hear me, that anyone would dare go against the queen to save me, and I hated that there was only one name on my lips. One name that I shouldn't have dared whispered.

Evren.

I screamed for him as Gavril sealed his mouth over the cut and began sucking the blood from my veins. My scream cut off as the sensation overpowered me, and I opened my eyes to watch my betrothed as warmth raked through my body and my mark burned against my skin.

My mark had only felt so real when Evren had touched me, but that was different. This was, it felt… a soft moan slipped past my lips.

I watched as he fed from me, and even though I wanted to pull my arm away, I was frozen exactly where he wanted me. A rush of pleasure shot through me as he sucked deeper, and my eyes rolled back as I tried to make sense of what was happening.

I didn't want this, but my body buzzed with desire.

"Please." The word slipped past my lips coated in longing, and even I didn't know what I was asking for. My stomach tightened with a need I didn't understand, but even through the pleasure, I could feel myself losing part of me to him.

It seeped out of me slowly, lazily moving through my veins and into Gavril's waiting mouth.

"That's enough for tonight," the queen barked, but I could barely hear her words. They felt muffled and so far out of reach.

I could barely feel the hold of the guards on me either. Everything felt so centered around Gavril and what he was taking from me.

"Gavril!"

He lifted his head then, his tongue brushing over his lips as he looked up at me, and I blinked my eyes open and closed to try to force myself out of the spell I felt trapped in.

"How do you feel?"

I glanced toward the queen when I heard the question leave her lips, but she wasn't talking to me. Her gaze was directly on her son as he climbed to his feet before me.

But I couldn't focus on either one of them.

Instead, my distorted gaze slammed into Evren. He stood in the room with his back against the door and hostility filled his gaze. I tried to lift my hand to reach out for him, but I felt so sluggish and my arm fell back against the chair.

I glanced back down at the cut on my arm, bright red blood coated my wrist and dripped from the cut. The cut where Gavril had just taken from me against my will. I looked back toward Evren and saw him staring at the exact same spot.

Had he watched him? Did he know what his brother had planned for tonight when he was whisking me around the dance floor and making declarations about others hurting me?

Of course he had. Evren didn't belong to me. He belonged to this court. They were his family, the court that he served, and his loyalty lay with them and them alone.

I had just let him do things to me in that hallway I had never let anyone else do before, and all the while, he knew what his brother had planned for me at the end of the night.

He had me begging for him to feed from between my thighs moments before I would beg his brother not to feed from my blood. Did he think about that when he was bringing me pleasure? Did he know that I would hate him by the end of the night?

Because when he looked back at me, that was the only thing I could think. I had trusted him, and I hated that I had allowed myself to do so. He was the enemy, and I had put far too much hope into who I thought he was.

But he was no different than the rest of them. He was the captain of their guard, the son of the king, and I was a fool.

"Gods, I can feel her running through my veins."

I looked back at Gavril as he spoke and watched as he clamped his hands into fists before slowly letting them relax.

"It's never felt like this before."

Before. When he had fed from other Starblessed. Had he done so against their will also, or had they been more than willing to serve their future king?

Gavril glanced back at me as the queen came to his side, and I could feel the fog from what he had done slowly lifting. My blood still coated his lips, but his eyes shone bright as he stared down at me.

"Are you all right, Adara?"

I didn't answer him, and when he stepped closer as if he was going to touch me again, I flinched back into the chair.

"I think she's had enough for tonight," Evren growled at his brother, but I didn't dare look back to him.

Gavril did, though. His gaze slammed into his brother, and I tensed as I saw the venom in his eyes. "I am not going to feed from her again tonight." Gavril lifted my wrist in his hand, and I winced at the pain.

He reached out behind me, and one of the guards handed him

a roll of cloth. I wanted to pull my hand away from Gavril, but I didn't have the strength left in my body. Even though my mind felt like it was clearing, my body felt as if I had spent hours working in the sun.

Gavril slowly wrapped the gauze around my wrist, over and under, meticulously wrapping it over my cut, before he tied it off.

"But Adara is my betrothed, Evren." He squeezed my wrist gently in his hand before looking back toward me. "I will feed from her as I see fit."

I stared up at him, and I hoped that he could see the fear and hatred in my eyes. I had softened to the prince in the last few days, but that feeling was long gone now. When I looked up at him with the knowledge that he was the man I was to marry, to spend the rest of my life with, I felt sick.

Gavril lifted my wrist to his mouth, and I once again struggled in his hold. But he pressed his lips gently against the gauze and his eyes softened. "I'm sorry, Adara," he whispered before dropping my wrist, and I pulled it against my chest.

"I'm taking her back to her room." Evren made his way toward me but stopped suddenly as if he had been hit in the chest. But no one was within reach of him.

"Mind your place, brother." Gavril seethed as he said the words, and his hand lifted forward as pain crossed Evren's handsome face. "I am perfectly capable of taking my promised back to her room for the night."

He dropped his hand, and Evren jolted forward. "More than capable." Gavril looked down at his hand and turned it back and forth as he marveled at what he had just done.

"I am Captain of the Guard, brother, and as such, it is my duty to protect the Starblessed."

"From me?" Gavril laughed, but Evren was already making his way toward me once again.

"From anyone." He looked back and forth between Gavril

and the queen. "I serve our father, and he demands that she be protected."

His words felt like a slap in the face, and I couldn't stop the way my heart was racing in my chest. The words he spoke to his brother and the words he whispered to me earlier were so vastly different.

"Come, Starblessed." He reached his hand out for me, but I refused to take it. Instead, I gripped the arms of the chair where I had just been held down and stood on shaky legs.

I could see how displeased Evren was, but he didn't open his mouth for a second to argue with me. What was there for him to say?

"I wish to go back to my room." My voice was as weak as I felt. "I would like to be alone."

No one answered me, though. There was a loud knock against Gavril's double doors before a guard I didn't recognize pushed through. His gaze bounced around the people in the room, frantically looking back and forth between them.

Everyone seemed on edge as we waited for the guard to speak.

"Captain." He nodded toward Evren, and I stiffened where I stood. "I need to have a word with you."

"What's happening?" Gavril questioned before Evren could take a step in his direction.

The guard looked back to Evren, seeking permission, and Gavril huffed in frustration.

"I am your future king. Tell me what's going on."

The queen stepped toward the guard, but Evren simply nodded his head. One simple move and the guard opened his mouth.

"There are whisperings, Your Highness."

"Whisperings of what?" the queen demanded.

"Vampyres in the capital."

My stomach flipped as his words rolled through the room,

and I could feel magic stirring around us. I didn't know where it came from, but from the feel of it against my mark, my gaze slammed into Evren.

"That's impossible." The queen shook her head and grabbed the bottom of her dress in her hand as she moved even closer to the guard. "We haven't been under attack in centuries."

The guard looked back and forth between Evren and the queen, and I could see him battling with what to say to her.

"What numbers are we talking about?" Evren asked, ignoring the queen completely.

"Inside the capital, our intel is guessing close to fifty. We're not certain what waits for us outside the capital's borders."

The queen turned toward Evren, and for the first time since I met her, I could see the panic on her face. "I thought you said our borders were protected."

"They were when I left them." Evren stared at the queen without an ounce of fear. "But I haven't been at the border in quite some time. I don't know what's happened since I've been in the capital."

"What do we do?" Gavril asked, and it hit me how unprepared he was to be king. He may have been who the queen wanted, but Evren was far better suited to rule.

Evren looked back and forth between the queen and his brother, and I knew he was probably thinking the same thing as I was. "We protect the capital. Send any guards we can spare from the palace to protect our people."

"No," the queen replied quickly. "We must protect the palace and the Starblessed."

"If the vampyres reach the palace, the Starblessed will be no concern of yours. They will wipe out every one of us with a vengeance you cannot grasp."

"Take her away." Gavril moved toward his brother without even looking in my direction. "We need the Starblessed, and she must be protected. Now that I've fed from her, take her away. Take her to Nabál until we know the threat is over."

Evren shook his head as he looked at his brother. "That's a bad idea. They know she's here, and they are going to be looking for her. Do you know what the Blood Court could do with such a powerful Starblessed in their hands? We don't have guards capable enough to keep her protected."

"You go." Gavril nodded toward him. "And take your best men. I'm not sure what I'm capable of now that her blood runs through me, but I can take care of the palace."

"And our people?" Evren growled.

"Are the least of our concerns. We must protect Adara and our home."

Pain sliced through my chest as Gavril showed me who he was again and again.

"These people trust us." Evren pointed to the wall where the city lay just outside the stone. "You cannot leave them defenseless against the Blood Court. It will be a massacre."

"It is not your decision to make, Captain." Gavril stared at Evren, and the feel of magic flared in the room. "You have your orders, and you will obey them."

"Of course." Evren dipped into a small bow, but his jaw tensed as he did so. "We will leave in the early morning hours when everyone least expects it."

Evren finally looked toward me, and I could see the hesitation in his gaze. He didn't like this plan any more than I did. I had no interest in staying in the palace, but I also didn't want to be taken somewhere else where I would remain their prized prisoner.

And I didn't want to be taken there by him after what he had just allowed his brother to do.

"Come, Adara. I'll take you to your rooms until we are ready to depart." He outstretched his hand, but I passed by it without taking it. I didn't want anyone in this room to touch me. They had all done enough already.

I moved toward the door and pulled it open, and I took a deep breath as I stepped outside of Gavril's chambers. I was leaving this palace tonight, and I had no intentions of returning.

THIRTEEN

I didn't speak to Evren as I pressed my hand against the stone hallway and slowly made my way back to my room. It didn't matter that he reached out to help me or that he tried over and over to speak to me.

I didn't want to hear a word that he had to say.

And by the time I made it back to my room, I could feel the strength Gavril drained from me slowly seeping back inside me. I slammed the door in Evren's face, to Eletta's shock, and I quickly began gathering the things I brought from home from my small trunk.

Eletta was stunned with fear when I told her what I had just found out, but she quickly got herself together and helped me bathe and dress in the clothes I had brought with me.

It was the most comfortable I had felt since I arrived in the Citlali, and I laid down in my bed fully dressed along with my boots and dagger. I knew that I should try to get some rest, but my mind wouldn't allow it.

I stared up at the ceiling as I ran my fingers over the dressing on my wrist that Eletta had redone. She hadn't said a word when she saw the deep cut along my wrist, but we both knew where it came from. She was loyal to the people who had just taken from me, and she didn't dare say a word against them.

I jumped to my feet when my door opened, quickly grasping my dagger from its home, but it was only Eletta returning with a warm cloak and a small satchel full of food and water. I thanked her before lying back down with my heart racing. I didn't think it would ever calm, but eventually, my eyes became heavy and the pull of sleep too hard for me to withstand.

I didn't know how long I slept, but by the time I was awoken with a soft hand gently shaking my shoulder, the fear of the threat had slipped away in my dreams.

"Evren," I whispered his name into the dark as I saw him standing over me, but when I saw the grim look on his face, the reality of tonight came back to me quickly.

"We must leave, princess." Evren looked back toward my door. "The threat is larger than I feared."

He reached for me, but I pushed his hand away as I stood and checked to make sure my dagger was still in place. I wasted no time adding the cloak around my shoulders and slipping the satchel over my head. Evren watched me wordlessly before moving to the door and holding it open for me.

I followed him through the halls, in the direction that I had tried to escape, and the cool night air hit me the moment we stepped outside.

Jorah was mounted on a gray mare dressed in all black, and two other guards I had seen around the palace were mounted at his side. One black horse stood next to him, with his reins in Jorah's hand.

Evren mounted the beast quickly before reaching down for me to join him.

"Where is my horse?" I took a step back, and Evren's face formed into a grim smile even though he attempted to hide it.

"You're riding with me, princess. We can't risk you on your own."

"I am more than capable of riding my own horse."

"I didn't say you weren't, but if we are attacked, I need to have you with me. We can't escape them if you are not with me."

I looked between him and the horse, and even though I knew he was trying to protect me, I didn't trust him.

"I want to ride with Jorah."

There was a scoff from one of the guards, but I didn't dare look away from Evren.

"That's not fucking happening, princess. Now mount the horse before I have to come down there and get you. We need to leave."

I growled in frustration because I knew he spoke the truth.

I reached up for the pommel of the saddle and tried to pull myself up, but Evren reached down for me and placed his hands under my arms before pulling me up. He settled me in front of him, my back pressed against his chest, and I stiffened in the saddle against him.

"Let's go." He kicked his heels into the horse, and the animal took off quickly through the dark night.

We trampled through the palace grounds as we made our way to the gate which was already open as we arrived. I looked back over my shoulder one last time to the dark palace behind us, and the horse only seemed to run faster away from it as I did so.

It was only as we passed through the gate that I noticed what hung on spikes just outside the palace walls. Three heads, each detached from their bodies with a sure blade. We passed by them quickly, but not before I recognized the faces of all three men that now hung lifeless.

The two guards whose names I didn't know hung side by side. The two guards who had held me down while Gavril had fed from me. Their hands had been touching me only hours ago, but here they hung with blood still dripping from what was left of them.

The third was harder for me to recognize, but once I saw the cold, calloused grimace that still marred his face, I knew the man to be of the royal court.

Nobleman Etkin was staring ahead at me as we passed, and I looked away as quickly as I could.

Three men hung from those spikes. Three men who all had a hand in hurting me, and I knew deep in my gut that the man responsible was the one who rode behind me. But he didn't say a word as we passed.

He kicked into the horse's side, pushing him harder as we left them and the palace behind, but I knew it was him just the same.

My stomach tightened as I thought about what he had done, of what he had risked, but I refused to let my guard down around him.

Jorah led us quickly through the capital streets, taking sharp turns I would have never been able to manage on my own, and before I knew it, we were outside of the capital and sprinting at full speed through the land that surrounded it.

My thighs gripped the sides of the horse to keep me as far away from Evren as I possibly could manage, but they had already started to ache even though we had only just begun our trip.

We rode hard and fast for a long while until we finally came to the edge of the Onyx Forest. We slowed as if the horses were as spooked as the riders as we approached the dark trees.

"Are we going in there?"

"We are." Evren nodded behind me. "We have no choice unless we go through the human lands."

"Then let's do that." I looked around the woods and noticed how perfectly still everything seemed.

"It will add days on to our trip, and we can't afford that. We need to get you safe as quickly as possible."

"Do you really think the vampyres will try to capture me?"

Evren groaned behind me and his chest pressed harder against my back. It took everything inside of me not to sag against him and let his body take the weight of mine. "You are the Starblessed to the future king. You are the future queen of Citlali. To the Blood Court, you are everything."

My heart raced as I let his words take hold of me. I was nothing more than a chess piece to be used how they saw fit.

"The Onyx Forest is dangerous, but it's dangerous for them as well. We will all face things in these trees that we'd rather not, and we hope to use that to our advantage. My guards and I have traveled through this forest more times than we can count."

I wasn't sure that made me feel any safer, but despite everything that had happened in the palace, I still trusted Evren more than any of the others. If there was anyone I believed could get me through the Onyx Forest alive, it was him.

But I didn't say as much. Instead, I kept my mouth clamped shut as we pushed through the forest edge and a magic like I had never felt before washed over me. My marks buzzed in a dull throb, but the new cut on my wrist burned like fire. I pressed my hand against the bandage, and Evren looked down at the movement.

"Are you okay?"

"I'm fine." I pulled my cloak tighter around me as the chill blew through the air. It felt colder somehow, even though we had just moved beneath the blanket of darkness the trees provided.

We continued on through the forest wordlessly. I was on high alert, my gaze snapping to every possible movement I thought I saw in the trees, but after some time, the movement of the horse had my eyelids feeling the weight of the lack of sleep I had.

They would flutter closed before I would snap them back open, and I looked ahead of us at Jorah. He pushed ahead as if there was no threat around us, and my eyes fluttered closed once more.

When they finally opened again, it was because our horse had slowed almost to a stop, and my head gently rolled to the side. I let them flutter closed again, disoriented from sleep, and I breathed in the scent of Evren as my nose pressed against his neck.

I moaned softly as his hand pressed against my stomach, holding me against him, and I pushed back against him. His body was molded against mine, holding me up on the horse, and I didn't want to move away from the warmth of him.

"Princess."

"Hmm?" I breathed him in again. How did he always smell so good?

"Princess, I need you to wake up. We're going to set up camp." He pressed his hand harder against my stomach, and my thighs tightened around the horse.

I moaned softly against his neck. I needed his hand to drop just a few inches and take care of the ache that throbbed between my thighs.

"Princess, I swear to the gods." Evren turned his head into me and spoke softly against my ear. "I will rip you off this horse and fuck you right here in front of my men if you don't stop making those damn noises."

I blinked my eyes open then and lifted my head away from his shoulder. Evren was right. His men were tying their horses to trees, but all three of them kept glancing in our direction. I shot away from Evren, putting as much distance between us as I could, and he laughed behind me before gently running his hand from my stomach to the small of my back.

Evren dismounted then, climbing off the horse as if it was nothing before he reached his hands up for me. I wanted to deny him, to do it on my own, but my thighs ached with more than my need for him. I was sore from riding, and as I lifted my right leg to swing it around, I couldn't do it.

"Here." Evren placed his hands on my sides before lifting me off of the saddle and against his body. He slowly lowered me until my feet touched the ground before him, and I could feel him through his trousers. He wanted me as badly as I wanted him.

And I wished that I didn't.

Everything would have been so much easier if I hadn't wanted him at all. But as I stood there looking up at him, I could barely force myself to step away.

"We need to set up camp and get some rest before we continue riding."

I looked up at the sun that was trying to peek through the trees. "But it's daylight."

"It's the only time one should sleep in the Onyx Forest. We need to be completely alert by nightfall."

"Okay." I nodded, and Evren reached out and moved some hair out of my face.

"You camp with me."

His words pissed me off. After everything, here he was still bossing me around like nothing had changed.

"Did you kill those men?"

"What?" He searched my face, but there wasn't an ounce of shock on his at my question.

"The men outside the gates. The men that held me down and Nobleman Etkin. Did you kill them?" I needed to know. Even if deep in my gut I already knew the truth, I had to hear him say it.

"I told you that no one will hurt you and not see the end of my blade."

"Except your brother?" I held up my bandaged wrist in between us and forced him to look at it. I forced him to face what he had allowed. "Is he the only one allowed to harm me?"

Evren's jaw tensed as he gently gripped my wrist in his hands. I tried to pull it away from him, but he forced it to his mouth and pressed his lips gently against the bandage. He held his mouth there as he stared at me, and his jaw clenched with unspoken words. Words he wouldn't allow himself to say to me.

"I can heal this."

"No." I shook my head and pulled my hand against my chest. This time, he let me go. "I don't want to lose the reminder of what they did to me. Of what you allowed."

His gaze darkened, and he stepped impossibly closer to me. "I didn't allow that."

"You did." I took a step back and almost ran into our horse. "You're just as bad as your brother."

I didn't wait for his response. I dropped my gaze from his and moved toward where the guards stood, providing hay for their horses.

"Jorah, is there somewhere that I can have a bit of privacy?"

He looked up at me, and I knew that he hadn't expected me to come to him.

"You can go just behind these trees, but we will have to stand guard, Starblessed. It's too dangerous."

"Fine," I huffed and headed in that direction. "But I'd like you to be the one to do so."

He looked back toward Evren before turning back to me. "Okay."

I stepped past him into the trees, and I could feel his footsteps directly behind me. "Also, Jorah. Please stop calling me Starblessed. My name is Adara."

"I'm sorry, Adara."

I stopped beside a tree that was far enough away from the rest of them before twirling my finger in the air. Jorah grinned before turning his back to me.

Neither one of us spoke as I relieved myself and Jorah was stiff as a statue until I came back to his side.

"I'm sorry you ended up on this job." I straightened out my cloak, and Jorah finally looked down at me.

"Don't be." He shook his head. "I will always be at Evren's side."

"Why is that?" I looked ahead of us as Evren fed our horse before pulling things out of the saddlebags. "Why are you so loyal to him?"

Jorah looked at me for a long moment before he finally spoke. "Evren has earned my loyalty over and over. I am loyal to him and him alone."

"But not to the crown?"

"Only if that's where Evren wants my loyalty."

I was shocked by his answer, and I turned to look at him fully. Jorah was so handsome even if his face was typically severe in a scowl. "Were you born in Citlali?"

His back straightened, and for a long moment, I didn't think he was going to answer me. "No. I was not."

"Where were you born?"

"Jorah," Evren called out to him, and I looked back to see him watching me. "I need you for a moment."

Jorah left my side without hesitation and made his way to his captain. They spoke close to one another in hushed tones, and I wondered what they were discussing. None of the other guards seemed to mind them as they laid out bedrolls against the hard ground.

I sat down next to them, and all three looked in my direction.

"No fire?"

"No." The one with light blond hair shook his head. "It draws too much attention."

A chill ran down my spine, and I couldn't stop myself from looking over my shoulder. I didn't see anything lurking in the trees, but I knew that didn't mean anything. Things that lurked in the darkness knew how to not be found.

I wrapped my cloak tighter around me as I looked back at them. The air seemed to get cooler and cooler the farther we made it into the forest, but I would make do just like the rest of them.

"What are your names?"

They looked up at me curiously as if they hadn't expected me to talk to them at all.

"That's Landry." Evren dropped a bedroll beside me as he pointed to the guard who had just spoken to me. "That's Achar." He pointed toward the handsome guard who had his shoulder-length hair pulled back with a leather string. "And that heartthrob over there is Caelum." He pointed to the last man of the group whose beard was so large that it took up most of his face. He smiled, large and genuine, and I decided right then that I liked him.

"It's nice to meet you all." I nodded in their direction. "I'm Adara."

Evren chuckled before dropping another bedroll beside the one he had just put down. "They know who you are, princess."

"Don't call me that."

Evren didn't reply. He just sat down on the bedroll before looking to his guards. "Get some sleep. Jorah's taking the first watch."

All three of them obeyed him immediately, but I didn't blame them. I knew they had to be exhausted from riding all morning. Jorah probably was too.

"I can take first watch so Jorah can sleep."

"That's not happening, princess." Evren patted the bedroll next to him. "You need to get some rest. We've got a long night ahead of us."

"I'm not sleeping beside you."

"You are." He laid down and rested his head against his arm. "You can either sleep next to me willingly or I can tie you to a tree and sleep next to you there. It's your choice."

"Such great choices," I huffed and looked up to see Jorah watching us.

"Just fucking get on your bedroll, princess. I'm not going to be able to get any rest unless you're beside me."

I wanted to argue, to tell him exactly how little I cared about him getting any rest, but the truth was he was the one responsible for getting me safely to where we were going. If I wanted to make it through the Onyx Forest alive, then I needed him. I needed all of them.

I untied my cloak from my shoulders before standing and moving to the bedroll Evren had provided for me. He watched my every move as I laid down with my back facing him and covered myself with my cloak.

"How long until we arrive in Nabál?"

"A few days at best." Evren spoke softly before I could hear him rolling over behind me.

He wasn't touching me, not a single inch of skin next to mine, but I could still feel him over every part of my body. He was so close to me. If I scooted back even an inch, my body would have met his.

And I felt desperate to do so.

"And at worst?"

"I don't know." He sighed behind me. "I don't want to think about it at worst."

"And what happens when the threat is over?" I whispered my biggest fear. I was scared to death of the Blood Court and what they could mean for our world, but I was more fearful of going back to that palace.

I didn't want to be Gavril's betrothed. I didn't want him to feed from me while his brother watched.

"I don't know, Adara." His fingers trailed over my back, and I jolted forward at the contact. "I have no idea what's going to become of us."

He meant us as in his kingdom, his family, but the word hit my gut as if he was speaking about the two of us alone.

"I'm not going back," I whispered only loud enough for me to hear, but Evren's hand stilled on my back.

"Get some rest, princess."

I allowed my eyes to flutter closed as he pulled my cloak over my shoulder, and with my enemy at my back, I fell into a restful sleep.

FOURTEEN

I awoke to the sound of men talking and groaned. I hadn't had enough sleep. I snuggled harder into my bedroll and relished in the warmth. My body ached from sleeping on the ground, but as I buried my face into the heat, I sighed.

"Good evening, princess." Evren's rough voice rumbled beneath my head, and I jerked back. But Evren tightened his arm around me and forced me back down against him. "Not yet."

"Let me go," I grumbled even though my body desperately wanted to burrow into him and let him hold me until I forgot about our reality.

"You're the one who snuggled into me, princess, and I'm going to enjoy it for a few more moments."

"I said let me go."

Evren chuckled before his arm dropped to my side. I pushed myself up and looked around the camp before looking back down at him.

"Everyone else is already packed up and ready."

"I know." He nodded before leaning up on his elbow. "But you needed rest after everything that happened last night."

The memories slammed into me quickly, and I tried to force them from my mind even as my wrist burned as a reminder.

"You should have woken me."

I stood from the bedroll before reaching down for my cloak. Evren handed it out to me with a soft smile on his face, and I hated it. I hated how easily he could pretend like things were normal between us.

But as he climbed to his feet and loaded our things back into the saddlebags, it felt more normal than anything I had done since I had arrived in the fae realm. Running away with Evren felt like a dream I had wished a hundred times over.

"You ready?" Evren climbed onto his horse and settled in the saddle before reaching his hand out to me. I hesitated for only a moment, but he noticed. His gaze darkened and the soft smile fell from his face. "Princess?"

"Yeah." I nodded and put my hand into his. He pulled me up, and the moment I wrapped my leg around the horse, he pressed his chest into my back.

"We'll be there soon," he murmured against the back of my neck, mistaking my indecision over him for hesitancy for the rough travel.

"I'm fine, Evren." I stiffened against him even as he pressed his hand to my stomach and forced me farther back in the saddle.

We rode like that for a long time before either of us spoke again. The sky had darkened above us and the moons were the only light with which we rode by.

Jorah had ridden ahead of us several moments ago, and I searched the trees as we waited for his return.

"He'll be fine, princess. Jorah is the deftest soldier I know."

"I'm not worried." I looked away from the tree line I had been searching, and Evren's thighs tightened around mine.

"You could have fooled me." He ran his nose along the back of my neck, and I stiffened. "You seem awfully worried about the things you claim to hate."

I clenched my jaw as I rolled his words over in my head. "I have never claimed to hate you."

"Haven't you?" he murmured against my skin. "You've barely been able to look at me since we left the palace without hate in your eyes."

He was right. I was so confused about how I could feel so much animosity and want at the same time, but they battled inside me like the enemies who were now at our doorstep.

Jorah came through the trees, and I was thankful for the distraction as he rode toward us.

"It's clear."

"Okay." Evren nodded his head and pulled the reins. "We'll rest here for a few hours."

"What? Why? We haven't been riding that long."

Evren pulled us to a stop, and my legs ached at the movement.

"You need your rest, and so do my men."

Jorah dismounted, and I could see the tiredness in his eyes.

"Jorah needs the rest." Evren spoke only loud enough for me to hear.

I dismounted without questioning him further and wrapped my arms around myself once my feet hit the ground. I didn't wait for Evren. I simply stepped away from him and looked around the forest. For something that was rumored to be so ominous, it felt peaceful.

I ran my fingers along the dark bark of one of the trees, and comfort settled into my bones. It felt like it was calling me, begging me to venture farther.

I dropped my hand from the tree and moved to the next. The bark scratched against my fingertips, but the feeling was the same. It was as if they were welcoming me.

I looked back over my shoulder, and neither Evren nor Jorah were paying me any attention. Both men were tying off their horses as they spoke quietly, and the three other guards were still dismounting from their horses.

I took another step into the woods.

Evren hadn't believed me when I said that I wasn't returning back to his brother's palace, or maybe he had. Maybe he cared as little about what I wanted as his brother did.

But I hadn't been looking for his permission.

I felt that I owed it to him to tell him the truth, but regardless of how he felt, I couldn't go back.

And his loyalty to his father's crown would force me to.

Another step into the dark forest, and the trees began shadowing my steps. There was a slight breeze in the air, beckoning me forward, and I allowed it to do so.

My steps were silent even through the brush, and I let out a rushed breath when I slid behind a larger tree and out of Evren's sight.

"Princess!" his voice called out to me immediately, and my marks sparked to life. They begged me to turn back to him, to stop listening to the trees, and turn to the man I knew I couldn't trust.

But I refused.

I took another step forward, my boot sinking into the soft earth as they carried me away from him, and I heard him call for me again.

But despite how badly I didn't want to run from Evren, everything inside me knew I should run from his brother. I should run and never look back, and I didn't know if I would ever have another opportunity.

"Adara, where the fuck are you?" Evren's voice echoed through the trees, and my heart hammered in my chest.

I moved faster and faster, careful to keep my footsteps light, and the trees seemed to pull me further as if they knew I needed the protection. I dared a glance behind me, but all I could see was the darkness that surrounded me.

Panic poured through my veins, but I pushed it down. I couldn't handle the fear when I needed my strength. Both had to coexist, but the choice was mine to make. And I couldn't be scared of a forest when I was running from my enemy.

"I swear to the gods, princess." I could barely make out Evren's voice now, but he was following me. He was searching for me, and my bones ached with the truth that he wouldn't stop.

But the more distance I put between myself and the palace, the better. Gavril had a plan for me, and I needed to derail it.

I came across a small creek, and even the water that flowed through it looked as dark as the night sky. I squatted down as I stared into the black depths, but all that stared back at me was my reflection.

The starlight on my cheeks was the only glow of light to be seen.

I lowered my hand to press my fingers into the water, but something in my gut warned me against it. I clenched my hand into a fist before standing back to my feet, and I leaped over the water and onto a large rock that jutted out in the center. One more jump and I was across.

I didn't look back again as I took off. My feet carried me swiftly through the forest, and it didn't matter that I had no idea where I was going. Nothing mattered at that moment except for the way everything inside me begged me to turn back to Evren and the will I found not to do so.

He was my enemy whether I wanted him to be or not, and those were the words I repeated over and over in my head as I forced my feet to carry me farther away from him.

FIFTEEN

I t had been hours since I ran. Hours that my feet had carried me forward and the ache that had set in reminded me of that fact over and over.

Daylight should have shown its face by now. It should have peeked through the trees and greeted me like an old friend, but darkness was the only thing that remained.

I stopped and turned in a small circle. Every tree I passed looked eerily similar to the one I had just left, and I couldn't make sense of where I was going. Evren's voice had faded out quickly as the trees welcomed me into them, and the sound of the leaves rustling was the only thing I could hear.

Fear trickled up my spine, and even though I had feared Evren would catch me, the panic of the idea that he wouldn't gripped at my chest. Because I was completely and utterly lost.

I leaned against one of the dark trees as I tried to tamp down my rising panic. My marks burned against my skin, a warning that I should have heeded.

A cautioning that hardened my stomach and made me jump at every possible noise.

I looked behind me and contemplated turning back in the

direction I came from, but I felt so disoriented. There were no tracks from where I had just walked; the forest had consumed them as if I had never been there at all.

That fact could have been my savior but also my foe. The forest had helped me get away, but now, I didn't know what I was thinking.

My hand clamped down against the bandage on my wrist, and I took a deep breath to harden my resolve. The forest was frightening, but nothing scared me more than being back in Gavril's control.

Keep walking forward, I repeated over and over in my head as I pushed away from the tree. My body was tired, but I couldn't afford to rest. Evren was fearful of what lay in this forest, which meant I was to be too.

I couldn't let my guard down even as my body begged me to lie down just for a moment.

I had made it three steps when I heard a whisper of sound in front of me. My legs trembled as I searched the woods and prayed to the gods that I was alone. I reached for my dagger just as a deep, harsh voice echoed through the trees.

"You won't need that here, sorceress." The voice coiled around me as if it was carried on a phantom wind.

I still didn't see anyone, and I slowly turned as I adjusted my grip on my knife. "Who are you?"

"Osiris. Although no one has called me by my name in a long time." His voice made my spine straighten and my marks blistered against my skin in warning.

I couldn't even see this Osiris, but he was a threat.

"Why can't I see you?"

Laughter fell around me like a song before I caught movement near one of the large trees. Then there they were, stepping out from behind the shadows, and I gasped as my feet faltered and I almost fell to the damp ground.

She looked like she belonged to the trees, or maybe they

belonged to her. Moss and bark grew along her torso as if it were a part of her skin, and a long gauzy skirt fell against her legs and trailed along the ground.

But none of that was what drew in my attention. It was her solid black eyes that trapped my breath in my lungs and forced me to stay where I was.

"I could heal your wound." Her head cocked to the side and those strange eyes studied the bandage on my wrist.

I pulled it against me and tucked it beneath my cloak. She smiled slow and sinister before her gaze slid back to meet mine.

"You are the Starblessed destined, but for what?"

Fear crawled up my spine as she studied me with such an unnatural stillness.

"You are destined for far more than they realize."

"I don't understand." I shook my head and took a step closer to her. "What am I destined for?"

"Your soul." She spoke slowly as she studied me. "It is irrevocably attached to another." Her gaze slid back to my wrist, and I shook under her stare even as my heart pleaded for her words to be false.

"What if I don't want it to be?" Gods, I refused to be bound to Gavril for eternity. Was it because he had fed from me?

"You don't have a choice, sorceress." She said it so undoubtedly, but I refused to believe her.

"Stop calling me that." My voice shook with a boldness I found faltering. "I'm not a witch."

"Aren't you?" Her eyes narrowed and my marks flared harder. "I can feel your magic from here, but I can feel his as well."

Coldness dripped along my skin as if I was standing in a pouring rain. Everything about this woman warned me away, but I needed to know, I needed to hear what she knew.

"And what they say about me saving the kingdom?"

She studied me for a long moment before she spoke again. "Which kingdom is it that you'd like to save?"

She was speaking in riddles, and my anger started to overtake my fear. "I don't understand."

"Blood and magic have been woven together throughout our land for centuries, but you are the blade with which they will sever it."

"You're not making any sense." I stepped toward her again, and her smile widened.

"Your stars burn brighter in the shadows, witch. But it is you who must decide which darkness you cling to." She stepped back, and part of her body was shrouded by the trees.

I didn't want her to leave. I thrust forward, desperate for her to stay, and her eyes tracked my every movement.

"You aren't telling me anything," I growled in frustration. "What darkness? What does that mean?"

She took another step backward, and my marks screamed in frustration against my skin as I tried to reach her. "Please," I roared, and power shot from my fingers as I outstretched my hand.

"Witch," she cursed the name as my magic fell upon her.

Terror and wrath like I had never known dug its claws into me. My hands shook as I stared down at them, at where the magic had just fallen from my fingertips. I didn't know whose power I possessed, mine or the prince's, but a familiarity I shouldn't have recognized wrapped around my hand and caressed my arms.

"I'm sorry. I…"

She was retreating, running from me when I should have been the one who was fearful of her.

"Princess!"

My magic drew into me, pushing me back, begging me to turn at the sound of Evren's voice.

"You choose your darkness." The woman looked at me once

more before her gaze slid over my shoulder to where I knew Evren was coming up behind me. "Choose wisely."

I didn't know if that was a warning against the prince who found me or the prince who stole from me, but regardless, my magic still called to him. It coaxed me back, step after step, until I turned away from the woman and faced him fully.

His eyes were wide and filled with rage and terror, and even from where I stood, I could see sweat beading along his skin.

"What the fuck are you doing?" He reached for me, his hand grasping my arm before he jerked me toward him. He searched over my head, and I knew who he was seeing. Black smoke fell from his fingers, and it hit me how similar my magic had looked to his.

"Don't hurt her," I cried as he tugged me behind him.

"What?" He looked at me, and rage poured from every part of him.

"Please don't hurt her."

"I'm not going to hurt her, princess, but you're lucky that she didn't harm you." His fingers pressed into me, and they trembled with his barely controlled power. "You're blessed that I don't fucking punish you until you scream. You used my feelings for you against me, and I put my trust where it didn't belong."

I jerked out of his hold, but he refused to let me go. I knew that he wouldn't let me out of his hold ever again.

He had trusted me, and I demolished that trust when I ran.

"I won't let you punish me." My voice shook even as I stared at him with as much courage as I could muster. The woman's words echoed in my head as I stared at him.

You choose your darkness.

"You think that you'd have a choice, Adara." He pulled me into him until my chest slammed against his and his face lowered to mine. I stared up into his dark gaze as his jaw clenched. "If I decided to punish you, then there would be nothing you could do to stop me."

"You're cruel."

He laughed, and the sound ran along my skin like a kiss from a lover. "You have no clue how cruel I can be, princess. All you've tasted is the pleasure at which my body can bring. You wouldn't dare to learn my malice."

I tried to swallow down the harsh breath, but it wouldn't come. Panic. Pure unpolluted terror ran through my veins as I feared what Evren would do to me.

"Please, Evren."

His hand cemented against me, and his face softened as he searched mine. "I have never known fear like what you just evoked in me. I have searched these woods to find you, and I would have done so endlessly."

He lifted his hands and ran them through my hair as he pulled me toward him. "I'm angry with you because I shouldn't feel anything for you, princess. But I would have taken on the world to get you back."

"I can't go back to that palace, Evren." I shook my head even as my heart hammered from his words. "I won't let them take from me again."

"I know. I fucking know." He tilted my head back, and his gaze dropped to my lips. "But I can't protect you unless you let me. You have to fucking let me."

I was at war with myself as I searched his face. I wanted him to kiss me, to make everything disappear except the two of us, but there was another part of me that held on to the distrust I had for him.

"Captain?" Jorah's voice called through the trees, and Evren sighed against my lips before he looked in his direction.

"Here!" he yelled back. "I have her."

Jorah came into view, and his own anger with me shone in his eyes as he took me in. "Are you all right, Starblessed?"

"Yes." I nodded my head even though I wasn't sure that I was.

"I found her with a nymph," Evren answered, and I looked back to the trees where Osiris had just retreated. I saw no signs of her, but I could still feel her watching me. "We need to get out of these woods."

"Agreed." Jorah came to our side, and I finally noticed the other three guards behind him. All of them looked exhausted, and I knew I had been the cause. "We should ride at once."

SIXTEEN

W'e had been riding for hours, and my thighs ached with a desperation to get off the horse.

"Just a little bit farther," Evren spoke from behind me. "We'll stop for camp shortly."

I nodded even though I wasn't sure I could handle even a few more feet. My body was exhausted, and I could only blame myself.

"You've done so well so far."

I gritted my teeth at his compliment. He had found me, but still, I had no interest in his kind words. I just wanted off this damn horse.

"Captain."

I rubbed my thighs as Evren looked up toward Jorah.

"Evren!"

I heard his name just as an arrow whizzed past me.

"Fuck," Evren groaned before wrapping his arm around my middle and jerking me down from the horse.

We landed against the ground hard, and my head slammed down against Evren's chest.

"Stay down, princess." Evren moved out from beneath me,

and I watched in horror as he reached for the arrow that was embedded in his left shoulder and snapped it just before his flesh.

"Evren," I called out for him as he pulled a black dagger from his hip, but he was already on the move.

I scurried back from the direction he was going as rocks and sticks tore at my hands. My back hit the base of a tree just as our horse spooked and kicked up on his hind legs. Another arrow was shot in my direction, and I quickly pushed to my feet and reached for my own dagger.

I could hear shouting before I ever saw the five men that surrounded us. One was pulling his sword from Caelum's neck, and I gasped as I watched the guard I had just met a few days ago drop to the ground.

Evren launched his dagger at the man who was dressed in a uniform of all black, and he hit his target perfectly. The soldier's eyes bulged as his hand met the dagger that was launched into his neck, and I watched as he searched for his killer before his gaze landed on Evren.

Evren stormed toward the man, unaffected by the others fighting around him, and he jerked his dagger from the soldier's flesh before kicking his boot into his chest and knocking him to the ground.

Evren moved on to the next, launching his dagger into the back of the soldier who was currently facing off with Jorah. The man fell to his knees instantly as blood leaked out onto his dark uniform, and Jorah raised his sword and finished him before he could truly know what was happening.

Another soldier surged forward, his sword held high over his head as he aimed for Evren. The prince didn't have his dagger back yet, but he charged the soldier before he could bring his sword down and knocked the both of them to the ground.

"No!" I gasped, but I couldn't clearly see what was happening.

Landry lay on the ground behind Jorah, but I couldn't see his chest well enough to see if he was still breathing. He had to be breathing. This couldn't be happening.

I was trying to find Evren as the two of them fought on the ground, but my head was jerked backward with a cruel jerk of my hair. I screamed as pain shot through me and raised my hand to stop the man.

But it was no use. He pulled me backward, making me lose my footing, and he dragged me against the forest floor as I tried to fight against his hold.

I slammed my other hand behind me, trying to blindly hit the man with my dagger, but the way he held me made it impossible.

"Come on, star whore." He lifted me to my feet, holding nothing but my hair, and I whimpered. "I want to see what all the fuss is about."

I fought against him, kicking and swinging my arms, but his blade was swift, and he cut my cloak away from my body within seconds.

"Please don't." I searched for Evren, but the man behind me had pulled me farther into the forest and all I could hear was the grunts of men fighting and the sound of metal clanking against one another.

"Hold still." He jerked me back harder before I felt his blade against the back of my neck. The cold metal induced a fear in me like I had never felt before, and I screamed out Evren's name as his blade tore through my shirt and sliced it open all the way to my trousers.

Chill bumps broke out across my skin as the cold forest air kissed my skin and my mark, and the man's hand tightened in my hair. I tried to force power from my hands like I did before, but nothing came from my trembling fingers.

"Holy gods," he murmured, and I clenched my shaking hand around my father's dagger. "The Blood queen has no idea..."

I didn't let him finish his sentence. I slammed my dagger

backward and connected it with his thigh. He roared in pain, but he was caught off guard enough that his grip slipped from my hair. I fell to my knees in front of him before quickly pushing up on my hands and trying to scurry away as quickly as I could.

The man reached for me, jerking one of my ankles until I slammed back to the ground on my stomach. I groaned at the pain, but dug my fingernails into the forest floor.

"Drop your hands from her now." I looked up as Evren pushed through the trees and headed in my direction. The look on his face was murderous, but blood trailed down his temple and along his cheek.

The man didn't loosen his hold on me. Instead, he said, "My prince." Two words were all he was allowed before Evren's smoke soared through the air and launched into the soldier's chest.

His hand gripped my ankle roughly as a gurgled groan left his throat. I looked behind me just as he leaned forward, his other hand going to his chest, and he ripped at his shirt as if he could fight against Evren's power.

I cried out as the weight of him slammed into me, pressing me harder against the ground, and I tried to scurry out beneath him. My fingers screamed in pain as I dug my nails into the earth as tears streamed down my cheeks, but then Evren was there.

He groaned hard and raw as he pushed the man off me, and I quickly climbed to my knees and slammed into his chest as I wrapped my arms around his shoulders.

"Shh." He ran his hand over my hair, and I winced in pain but didn't stop him. "It's over."

"The others?" I barely recognized my voice as I clung to him harder.

"Dead."

"What?" I pulled away from Evren quickly, and he winced at the movement.

"The Blood Court soldiers are dead."

"And ours?" I asked even though I didn't want to know the truth. I wasn't sure I could handle it.

"Jorah is the only one still alive."

I reached forward, touching my fingers to Evren's temple, and he recoiled. The injury looked relatively mild, but blood poured from the wound and down his handsome face.

"You need care."

"I'm fine, princess." He lifted his hands and ran them over my face. He touched every inch of my skin, his fingers trailing delicately. "Are you hurt?"

"No." I shook my head. "Not really." But I was lying. I could feel the areas where my hair was ripped from my scalp already drying with my blood, and my body ached with every move I made.

"Princess, I…" His gaze searched my face as he searched for the words to say. "I've never been more frightened in all my life. I thought he would kill you."

He swallowed hard, and I tried to catch my breath as his words slammed into me. "But you saved me."

"I allowed them to hurt you." He shook his head as guilt filled his eyes.

"Evren."

"Let's find Jorah." He pressed his hands under my arms and helped me stand before climbing slowly to his own feet without meeting my eyes. He was just a step behind me when I heard his deep groan, and he collapsed to his knees.

"Evren!" I reached for him as he hunched forward and pressed his hand to his abdomen. Blood coated his fingers instantly, and I didn't know how I hadn't noticed it before. "Jorah!" I screamed for him as Evren fell to his side and took a deep breath.

"I told you I was fine, princess." He grimaced, and I slowly lifted his hand and pulled it away from his wound.

"You are far from fine." I quickly unbuttoned his black shirt before pulling it away from his skin, and I gasped as I saw the size of his wound. There was a clean slice against his stomach, longer than my entire dagger, and blood poured from the wound rapidly.

"Fuck." Jorah fell to his knees at my side, and I could see the fear in the normally stoic guard's eyes. "Fuck, fuck, fuck."

"What do we do?" I lifted my trembling fingers over Evren's wound, but I had no idea how to help him.

Part of an arrow still protruded from his shoulder, but I couldn't focus on that when I was looking at his stomach.

"Take her." Evren shifted before groaning. "Get her the fuck out of here, Jorah."

Jorah nodded once toward his captain, but they were out of their minds.

"I'm not leaving you."

Evren didn't look at me. Instead, he spoke directly to Jorah. "Tie her to the damn horse if you have to, but get her out of here. Don't stop until you've reached our destination."

"I am not leaving," I growled, and finally he looked up at me. "I will fight Jorah every step of the way. We are not leaving you."

"I can't ride like this, princess." Evren motioned toward his stomach.

"You have magic. Use your magic." I ran my hands over my trousers. "Please."

"It doesn't work like that." He shook his head gently, and it took far too much of his strength for just that small movement. "I could possibly stop the bleeding, but I can't… I can't heal this. It's too much."

I shook my head as I stared at his wounds. I knew he was telling the truth, but I didn't want to believe him. I couldn't just leave him here to die.

"Feed from me." I jerked up the sleeve of my shirt and

exposed the wrist where Gavril had fed from me just days ago. "Take my blood."

"What?"

"Take my blood, Evren." My voice broke as I pushed closer to him.

"I thought you said you'd never let another feed from you again?" He looked up at me and looked so relaxed. "I am not my brother, princess. I won't take something from you that you don't want to give."

"I want to," I cried as I tried to get him to see reason. "I want to save you."

"I'll be fine, Adara, but you need to get out of here." He looked back to Jorah. "Those men didn't recognize it was me, not until the end, but they knew her. Don't let them catch sight of her again."

"Stop," I cried again and lifted my dagger. I was about to press it to my own wrist before Evren placed his hand over my scar.

"Don't, princess."

"Then feed from me," I begged him. "I'm begging you to feed from me."

Evren looked at me for a long time, and I knew that he was contemplating what he should do. But the decision was simple. Evren wouldn't survive these woods without my blood, and I worried I wasn't going to survive without him.

His fingers wrapped around my wrist gently, and I wasn't sure if he was simply trying to be careful with me or if that was all the strength he could muster. "I don't want to hurt you."

"I don't care." I shook my head before forcing my wrist closer to me and my dagger. "I won't let you die."

"She's right, Evren," Jorah spoke to his friend and captain, but Evren was still staring up at me.

"I don't need your dagger." He pulled my wrist toward him,

and I helped him close the distance between me and his mouth. "I told you what I am."

Evren opened his mouth, and I held my breath as he gently ran his teeth along my sensitive skin before sinking them in deeper. I gasped as pain shot through my arm, pain like I had never felt before, and Evren's hand tightened around me as if he feared I would pull away.

His teeth sank deeper and deeper until I feared he would hit my bone.

His eyes fluttered closed as I felt a part of me draining out of my veins and into him. But it was different. Even as the pain still radiated through my arm, I knew that what was happening with Evren was so much different than with Gavril.

My marks came alive against my skin as Evren's lips sealed over my wrist, and they felt like they were burning in an exquisite kind of pain. It was as if they hadn't truly been a part of me until that moment, but now, right then, they were branding into my skin.

The urge to scream was overwhelming, but I wouldn't allow myself that weakness. Evren would stop if he knew what was coursing through my veins. Pleasure and pain mixed until I couldn't tell one from another.

He would stop, but I refused to let him.

My wrist trembled against his mouth as he fed, and I worried about what would be left of me when he was done. I had been told a hundred times over that Gavril was my destiny, but what if they all had it wrong? What if I was Evren's destiny instead?

What if I was a Starblessed not meant to save a kingdom, but instead, meant to save a bastard prince?

The pain flared inside me, peaking to a new height until I didn't think I could handle another moment of it, then it changed. Warmth rushed through me, coating every inch of me until my eyes felt heavy.

The feeling didn't stop. It created pressure everywhere it

went, and my stomach tightened as that insistent rush centered between my thighs. I gasped, desperate for a breath I couldn't seem to catch, but it did nothing to ease the need that grew inside of me.

With every drop of blood that Evren pulled from my body, he gave something back. Something that I couldn't grasp on to no matter how desperately I chased the feeling through my body.

He took, and he took, but gods, it made me feel frenzied with my own hunger.

"Evren," I said his name gently, but the sound was a little more than a moan. I wanted him. More than I had ever wanted anything before in my life. I wanted Evren more than I could bring myself to want my own freedom.

And it wasn't just physical. Every fiber of who I was, was screaming for him as he took from me. My marks burned so deeply, yearning for his touch.

I wanted to open my eyes to look at him, to see the man I felt so desperate for, but I couldn't. As every bit of what he gave me ran through me, I was capable of doing nothing else but endure what he gave.

And it was a sweet torture.

Evren shifted beside me, and I whimpered when he lazily pulled his mouth away from my wrist. He pressed his lips against the new wound that would no doubt cover the one before it, and I felt that small move all the way to my core.

"Please," I begged as I pressed my thighs together.

Something had snapped inside of me. Something I couldn't hold on to, but I knew that I would never be the same again after today. When Gavril had fed from me, he had made me feel like a shell of who I was before. But Evren? Evren made me feel more like myself than I ever had.

"It's over, princess," Evren whispered, but his words felt like they were crashing against my skin in waves. Everything was too much yet not enough all at once.

"Evren."

His hand wrapped around the back of my neck before he pressed his forehead to mine. "Open your eyes, Adara."

I did so as if he had commanded me to. I blinked my eyes open and stared at the man before me. His dark eyes were filled with heat and power, and I felt it thrumming from him as if it was tangible.

"I'm burning," I said, the only thing I could think. I wanted to touch him, to see that he was okay, but all I could focus on was the burning need that coursed through my veins.

"Fuck." Evren looked away to Jorah, I was sure, before looking back at me. "I hurt you?"

I shook my head quickly, but I didn't know how to explain to him what I was feeling. I couldn't put into words the heaviness in my chest or the way my body was begging me to reach out for him.

"I need you."

"Tell me what you need, princess."

Evren's hand pressed against my cheeks as if he was trying to figure out what was wrong with me. But everywhere his hands touched felt like fire. The need inside me igniting under his fingertips.

"I don't know." I shook my head as I tried to clear my thoughts, as I tried to make sense of what was happening inside of me. "I just need you."

His fingers tightened against my skin as I pressed my thighs together, and his dark gaze slammed into me, and his lips parted. I didn't need his words to tell me the truth of what he was feeling, I could feel it.

More than I had ever felt his magic before, his power, the essence of who he was. It ran through every fiber of me as if it was trying to get to know me.

Everything about him felt different.

It felt real.

I had no idea if Jorah was still there, but I couldn't bring myself to care. Not when every part of me felt like it was going to combust if he didn't touch me. I had never felt a thirst like this in all my life. It was as if something inside me was shifting, changing, begging to become his.

Black magic leaked from his fingers and felt like a soft graze against me. It wrapped around me slowly, binding me in his magic, and I moaned as it pressed along my back.

"I've got you, princess," Evren spoke, and his words reverberated in his magic. He lifted to his knees in front of me, and his fingers pushed my hair out of my face. "Whatever you need from me. It's yours."

"Touch me," I begged him as I reached forward and tried to close the space between us. "Please touch me."

"Princess." He sighed, and I could see it on the look on his face. He was going to deny me. He had every reason to. I was being irrational and absurd, but I couldn't explain it. I couldn't control the urge that raced through me.

"I feel like I'm going to die if you don't touch me."

His gaze slammed into mine. I had barely wanted to be around Evren only moments before all this happened, but now? Now, I wouldn't dare pull away from him.

His magic crept along my neck, and I let my head fall back as I felt the power of him against me. His hands moved down my sides, stopping along my breasts, and his knuckles skimmed the sides of my sensitive flesh. Even through my shirt, his touch was overwhelming.

"You are so damn perfect, princess." His hand pressed fully against my breast, and he ran his thumb over my sensitive nipple. "I will forever be in your debt for what you did."

"It was nothing." My breath rushed out of me, and I pushed my chest forward, silently begging him for more.

"It was more than anyone should ever ask of you." There was a slow caress down my spine, and I couldn't tell if it was his hand or his magic. "It was far more than anyone should ever take."

I didn't want to think about that. I didn't want to remember the way Gavril had taken from me or the way Evren had watched. Remembering that made me hate him, and right now, it was the last thing I wanted to do.

"I should kill my brother for what he did to you. I wanted to spike his head on that gate, just like all the others who had hurt you."

I blinked my eyes open just as his hand kneaded my breast harder, and a soft moan escaped me. "You are loyal to your brother."

"I am loyal to no one who hurts you, princess. My loyalty broke the moment I walked into that room and saw him wiping your blood from his deceitful mouth."

His words ricocheted through me, and I tried to turn them over in my mind, but all I could concentrate on was the way his hand slowly slid down my stomach until it met the top of my trousers.

"My loyalty to my brother broke the moment he hurt something that is mine." He shoved his fingers into my trousers, and I gasped as he met my wetness.

"Godsdamn, princess," he cursed and pressed his forehead into my neck. "I feel so damn crazy for you."

His fingers began working against me, moving the moisture and sliding it over my sensitive nub again and again. I could feel myself breaking apart before he had barely even touched me, and the feel of his magic continuously wrapping around me, getting to know every inch of my body, was more than I could handle.

His tongue lapped at my neck before his teeth grazed over the sensitive skin, and my hips surged forward in his hand.

"Please, Evren."

"Let go, princess." He kissed my neck over and over, making

his way up to my mouth. "Let my magic that flows through you give you exactly what you need."

I cried out as he spoke, my body thrumming with need and overwhelming pressure, and when he pinched my nub between his fingers, I fell apart with a scream.

Evren's magic caressed my lips, muffling the sound before it was quickly replaced with his mouth, and he slowly brought me down with his fingers and his lips against mine. My body felt heavy, impossibly so, and I pressed my weight into him as I tried to make sense of what had just happened.

Even now, even sated as I was, every part of me still longed for him.

"Come, princess." He pressed his mouth to my forehead. "The forest isn't safe."

SEVENTEEN

I t had been hours since we mounted our horses and left the bodies of the guards lying in the forest. It infuriated Evren to do so, but both he and Jorah had decided that we didn't have time to bury them if we wanted to make it out without another attack.

No one hardly spoke as we rode. Evren was still behind me, his hold on me so much harder than before, but I didn't fight it. I welcomed his touch, even as my gaze devoured every inch of the trees. I felt on high alert, and Evren's whispered words that we were okay did nothing to calm me.

Not until the line of trees thinned and I could spot the trails of sunlight just beyond the edge of the forest. We passed through that line, and a weight lifted off my chest as the sun beamed against my skin. I felt instantly warmer, but I still leaned back against Evren as I tried to make sense of what was to come.

"There's a small town just ahead," Evren spoke against my neck. "We'll stop there for the night and rest."

I nodded my head, although I wasn't sure stopping was the best idea. But real food and a real bed sounded lovely, and I wasn't foolish enough to pass it up. And even though Evren said that he was healed, I knew the prince needed to rest.

And I needed my space.

I stared down at my wrist as we made it to the edge of town. The scar that Gavril had caused was now covered in a new mark. The starlight and shadows stared back at me and reminded me of what we'd done. The difference between a mark due to what was taken and what was willingly given was stark.

I only noted two buildings in the town as we approached. A tavern with billowing smoke escaping from a small chimney and what I assumed was a blacksmith across the dirt road. There were no people out on the street even though I could make out small houses in the distant fields.

"This is Iladonia." Evren nodded toward the small village. "They've kept watch on the border of the forest for centuries."

"What are they watching for exactly?"

"Any threat to the kingdom."

Jorah led his horse directly in front of the tavern, and Evren followed suit. We stopped there, and Jorah dismounted before grabbing the reins from Evren.

"I'll find boarding for the mares."

Evren nodded. "We'll get us a room."

Evren dismounted before helping me down from the horse, and I shook out my stiff limbs. "Come on, princess. If nothing else, I know this place has some decent ale."

He clasped my hand in his, and my hand zapped with his power. He pulled me inside behind him, and the large fire that took up the majority of the back wall roared with heat.

I trembled against the heat, and I hadn't realized just how cold I was.

"Here." Evren led me to the back of the tavern that was only filled with a few other patrons. None of them paid us any notice as he pulled out my chair at the table closest to the fire. "I'll be right back."

I rubbed my hands together as he walked up the long bar that took up one entire side of the pub. There was a young girl working behind it, and she smiled softly at Evren as he approached. Jealousy bloomed in my chest, but I forced it down.

She nodded at whatever the prince was saying before opening the sole door behind her. She disappeared for a moment before she returned and began speaking to Evren as she grabbed three glasses and began filling them with ale.

A young boy pushed through the doorway she had just gone through, and he balanced three wooden bowls in his hands. He blinked up at me as he approached, and the smell of stew made my stomach growl.

I hadn't realized how hungry I was either.

"Ma'am." He dipped his head before sliding one of the bowls in front of me.

"Adara." I grabbed the spoon quickly and shoveled a bite of the hot stew into my mouth. The boy watched me as he set the other two bowls at my sides.

"I'm Ren."

"It's nice to meet you, Ren." I looked over the boy who was covered in dirt and soot. He was dirty, but he looked healthy. The muscles on his small frame telling of the life he lived.

"It's nice to meet you as well." He looked over his shoulder to where Evren was now taking a key from the woman. "Are you here with the captain?"

"I am." I nodded and took another bite. The flavor was divine and the meat tender. "This is delicious."

"Thank you." Ren blushed as he watched me eat. "I can get you another bowl. I made it myself."

"That's very kind of you, Ren, but I shouldn't." I took another large bite, and my eyes fell closed as the stew warmed my belly.

"Hi, Ren." Jorah's voice drew my attention, and I opened my

eyes just in time to see him sitting down beside me. "What's the special today?"

"Rabbit stew with root vegetables." Ren beamed proudly.

"It's amazing." I pointed my spoon to my almost empty bowl.

"It looks like it." Jorah laughed before grabbing his own spoon. "But it usually is."

"Where are you and the captain heading today?" Ren shifted on his feet just as Evren approached the table and set the large glasses in the center.

"I can't tell you all my secrets, Ren. What kind of captain would that make me?"

"I didn't think of that." Ren rubbed his chin as he stared up at Evren, and admiration shone in his eyes.

Evren mussed Ren's hair with his hand before pulling out the seat at my side. "Keep training. You're going to make a fine captain one day."

Evren flipped him a coin, and Ren caught it in his hand before smiling broadly. He ran back behind the bar and spoke to the woman who I assumed was his mother.

"That was kind."

"He's kind to us." Evren nodded toward Jorah before pushing an ale in his direction and the other in mine. "Why wouldn't I be so in return?"

"There are lots of men in this world who don't return kindness."

"Well, I'm not one of those men." He shrugged as if his answer was that simple, but it wasn't.

Evren said it so simply, but it mattered far more than he realized. He was a part of the royal family that I hated, but I had begun to trust him more than I had ever trusted anyone else in my life.

"Have some ale." He pushed it toward me before laying a key in front of Jorah. "Then we'll all get some sleep."

"Where's my key?" I held out my hand just as Jorah choked on his ale.

"Here." Evren held the key in his hand but pulled it away as I reached out for it. "Not happening, princess. We're sharing a room."

My stomach tightened at the thought, but I had to force away my want for him. I needed to think, to try to make sense of what I was doing, and I couldn't do that with him in the same room.

"I want my own room." I pressed my hands against my thighs as I spoke.

"There are only two available, and I took them."

"Then you room with Jorah." I nodded to the guard, who was quietly eating his soup.

"That's not happening." Evren shook his head and took his own bite.

"Why not?"

"Because, princess. We were just fucking attacked, and I'm not letting you out of my sight for even a moment. You can room with me, or all three of us can room together. Those are your two choices."

He stared me down, and I matched his gaze. I knew he was being reasonable, but I didn't want to be. I wanted to demand that he leave me alone while every part of me was screaming for him to stay.

I raised my ale to my mouth and took a long pull as he watched me. I wiped my lips with the back of my hand. "Can I at least go to the room while you two finish eating, or is that against the great captain's regulations as well?"

Jorah laughed before he quickly cleared it with a cough.

"Straight to the room." Evren dangled the key in front of me. "Remember, if you try to run, I will find you."

The urge to tell him that I couldn't run again if I wanted to was overwhelming, but I wouldn't give that much of myself away. Not when he already had more of me than I had ever intended to give.

"Noted." I snatched the key out of his hand before standing. He watched my every move as I pushed my seat back in and moved around the table.

"Up there." He nodded toward the stairs. "Second door on the right."

I nodded and quickly made my way up the old wooden staircase. It creaked under my weight, but held true until I finally made it to the top. There were four doors in the hall. Two on the right and two on the left. They all looked identical except for the varying stages of wear, and I shoved the brass key into the second door and pushed it open.

The room was small and most of the space was taken up by a tiny bed and copper tub. I stood at the tub and stared as every part of my body ached.

I kicked off my boots at the end of the bed and pulled my dagger from them before laying it against the cover. My clothes were soiled and ripped, and had traces of mine and Evren's blood.

I felt desperate to take them off and crawl into the bed wearing nothing, but that wasn't possible. Not unless I could somehow manage to barricade the doorway closed with the tub.

A soft knock sounded at the door, and I jumped. Pressing my hand to my chest, I cracked the door open and peeked outside to see the woman from downstairs standing behind it.

"I just thought you might like a change of clothes." She held up a white cotton dress in her hands along with a towel. "Evren thought you might like for me to run you a bath as well."

"That would be amazing." I opened the door wider, and she ducked her head as she stepped inside. "Thank you."

"Of course." She blushed before setting the fabrics on the bed. "If you lay your soiled clothing outside the door, I will have them cleaned and mended for you before you wake."

"You don't have to do that." I shook my head as she lifted her hand, and water streamed from the wall like a waterfall.

"It's no problem, miss. The captain pays us more than our share when he stays here. It's my honor to take care of his guest."

"Well, thank you." I tucked my arms against my chest. "I don't have money, but you do have my gratitude."

The woman stared at me for a moment as if she was trying to figure me out, then her face softened before she turned back to the tub. The water inside was steaming as she poured in an oil from the pocket on her apron. "That should help your muscles." She pushed the stopper back in the jar before pulling out another filled with what looked like herbs and flowers. "And that should help with the captain."

"Help how?" I laughed, and she smiled at me over her shoulder.

"However you want it to."

The smell drifted through the small room as the steam billowed about the space, and I took a deep, relaxing breath.

"I'm betrothed to the crowned prince of Citlali," I told her, and she cocked her head to the side.

"Yet, he's not the one who holds your heart."

It wasn't a question, but I still felt the need to answer her. "My heart belongs to me and me alone."

"You are a brave but foolish girl." She put her last vial back in her apron before she waved the flow of water away. It disappeared instantly as if it had never been there at all. "Love makes us foolish."

I didn't answer her because I didn't know what to say. Love? I wasn't in love with the man who sat downstairs drinking ale. I wanted him more than I had ever wanted anyone before, but that wasn't love.

"I'm not in love." I stepped out of her way as she moved to get by me.

She hesitated with her hand on the door before looking back at me. "Just place your clothes right outside the door. The soap is next to the tub." Then she opened the door and slid outside without another word.

I undressed slowly, careful to try to keep myself covered in case I had any more visitors, then I dipped a toe into the bath. It was blissfully hot, and I sighed as I sank down inside it and tossed my shirt into the pile on the floor.

Steam rose off the surface of the water, and I breathed in the heat before holding my breath and slowly sinking below the water. I closed my eyes as the water engulfed me, and I tried to clear my head. My lungs began to burn, and all I could think about was Evren and what he was doing down in that pub right now. What were he and Jorah talking about?

Were they strategizing? Were they discussing me?

Had Jorah watched as I begged Evren to touch me in the middle of the woods?

I surged up out of the water and gasped for breath. Running my hands over my face, I pushed the water out of my eyes and stared down at my body. There was bruising along my skin, and I didn't know how much of it had been there from my night with Gavril and how much of it was new from our attack.

I gently scrubbed the dirt away from my skin with my fingers before the mark on my wrist caught my eye, and I lifted it out of the water to get a better look. Seven dots of starlight danced along the dark skin there. I could no longer make out the scar from Gavril beneath, but it was still there, just hidden beneath Evren's mark.

I traced the starlight with my fingers, connecting them along my skin as if they were freckles. My mother had done that once upon a time to the marks on my face. The thought made me both angry and sad.

"What are you thinking about?"

Water splashed out of the tub as I screamed, and Evren chuckled as he raised his hands in surrender.

"Hell, I didn't mean to scare you." He was lying on the bed with his back against the wooden headboard, and he looked so damn at ease as he watched me.

"When did you get in here?" I covered my breasts with my arm causing him to grin. "Did you use your magic to do so?"

"No." He wiggled his black-stained fingers in the air. "I used these hands to open that door while you were apparently having a moment under the water. It's not my fault you didn't check your surroundings."

"Get out."

"I'd much rather watch." He smirked and lifted one of his arms behind his head. "The view is perfect from here."

I shifted in the tub, giving him my back, and heard his deep inhale.

"Gods." He stood from the bed, and I watched as he made his way to me.

"What are you doing?" I tightened my arm on my breasts and pressed my thighs together. He was still wearing his black trousers, but his boots had been removed along with the top buttons of his shirt.

"Your back." He touched my shoulder, and I tensed. "It looks awful."

"Thank you."

"That's not what I mean." He dropped to his knees beside the tub before his fingers skimmed along my shoulder. "You are breathtaking, but you're bruised. If I could go back and kill him again, I would."

"You mean my mark is breathtaking?" I asked as I scooped some water in my hands and let it trail over my knees.

"No, princess. I mean you. With or without those marks, you are the most exquisite thing I have ever seen."

I turned to look at him, and he was staring at me like he meant every word that had just passed through his lips.

"Please let me take care of you." He didn't wait for my answer. He unbuttoned his shirt sleeves before slowly pushing them up his arms. Then he grabbed the soap and poured it out into his hands. "I need to take care of you after I let this happen."

He dipped his hands into the water, gathering moisture, before rubbing his hands together.

"You didn't let this happen."

"I did." He stared up at me just as his hands met my shoulder. "I am more responsible for these bruises on your body than you know."

He wasn't to blame, but if he needed this to help clear his conscience, then I would give it to him.

I lifted my hair off my back as his hands roamed over me and gently washed my skin. It felt divine as he touched me with so much care and precision. He poured more soap into his hands before he raised them to my hair and scrubbed the soap throughout.

I bit down on my lip as he met the spot where my hair had been pulled from my scalp, but I tried my hardest not to let him see the pain.

"Have you washed many women before?" I chuckled softly as he moved to the ends of my strands and worked the soap through.

"No. You'd be my first." He smiled. "I have never wanted to care for someone like this before you."

My chest ached, and I tried not to read into what he was saying.

"You take your duty seriously, Captain."

He met my gaze as he let my hair fall against my back, and the urge to lean backward and kiss him was overwhelming. "I do." He nodded, and his hand slid behind my neck and back into my hair.

He dipped me backward into the water, and I blinked up at him as he cupped water in his hand and let it cascade through my hair. "But what I feel for you has nothing to do with my duty, princess."

I swallowed hard and looked away from him as he finished his job. I hated every word he was saying to me. I couldn't want that between us. I couldn't have it.

And I knew it would do nothing but hurt us both in the end.

Because regardless of what he said, I was nothing more than the Starblessed and he was the captain of the royal guard. No matter how you looked at it, our fates would never align.

He lifted my head before resting my neck against the back of the tub, and his gaze was questioning as he poured more soap into his hands. I dropped my hands timidly, and he ran his soapy hands over my shoulders and down my arms.

"How is your wrist?" He lifted it into his hands before gently rubbing soap over the new scar.

"It's better." I looked at the markings he left there just as his fingers pressed against them and made them thrum with life. "It's so much better than it was before."

"The starlight suits you." He cupped some water and rinsed away the suds he had just created. "I have never met another Starblessed more befitting to wear these marks."

"It feels weird to have new ones." I lifted my hand and ran it over the markings on my wrist. "They feel different than the others."

"How so?" He took my hand in his and quickly worked the soap up my other arm as he listened to me.

"The markings on my back and face, they feel like me. They are no different than my skin or my hair. They are just a part of me despite how people want to use them, but these new marks, they're me but not. They also feel like you."

His hands stalled on my arm for a long moment. "What do you mean, they feel like me?"

I bit down on my lip as I thought of how to explain it. "I have always been able to feel you along the markings on my face and back." I raised my hand to touch my face, and Evren moved his hands to my neck and chest. "Whenever you touch me or use your magic, I can feel you along my markings more than anywhere else. But with these new marks, they feel aflame around you. It's like they recognize you before I even get the chance."

Evren stared into the water for a long moment with his hands motionless against my upper chest. "Does this happen with anyone else?"

"I can feel others. Others with magic." I shook my head gently. "But it's not the same."

"And with my brother?"

"I can feel him, but it doesn't compare. Everyone else feels dull compared to you."

A tremor ran down Evren's spine as he stared into the water. "You can't say things like that to me, princess."

"It's the truth."

"It doesn't matter." He shook his head just as his hand dipped below the water, and he cupped my bare breast in his hand. "Hearing you say that makes me want to cover you with my marks. I want the whole damn world to know that your skin is adorned by me and me alone."

I gasped as he pinched my nipple between his fingers.

"I want no one to look at you and be confused about whose you are."

"But I'm not yours, Evren." I pushed my head back against the tub as he kneaded my breast in his hand while he watched through the water.

"The fuck you aren't." His hand pushed through the water before he cupped my sex in his palm. "Every part of you belongs to me. Everyone else be damned, princess." His finger slid between my folds, and I whimpered as he barely grazed over my nub. "Even your body knows it. It calls to me like a fucking prayer."

I lifted my hips in the water, chasing his hand, and he growled. He wrapped his hand around my thigh, the edge of pain turning me on more, and I wasn't prepared when his grip tightened further and he hauled me from the tub.

Water dripped from every inch of me as he fell back on the floor against the foot of the bed and hauled me against him. I had no choice but to straddle his lap as he forced my chest to his, and I could feel just how desperately he wanted me beneath my thighs.

"Gods, princess. You drive me fucking crazy." He shoved his hand into my dripping wet hair before he pulled my face down to meet his. He kissed me, hard and thoroughly, and I kissed him back with just as much need. We were lips and tongue and teeth, and it became impossible to tell where one of us began and the other ended.

I pushed my hips down against his as he kissed me, the wetness between my thighs having nothing to do with my bath, and Evren groaned.

He pulled my hair back in his hand, and I whimpered as my neck was fully exposed to him. He ran his nose along the length of my neck, breathing me in before his lips began tasting me. His other hand pressed against my bottom, and he encouraged the way I had started grinding my hips against him. His teeth bit down so hard I was worried he'd break skin.

"You have no idea, Adara." He spoke against my neck as I sped up my movement. "I could feed from you right now and put us both out of this misery. I could bring you more pleasure than you could possibly imagine."

"What?" My voice trembled as I tried to make sense of what he was saying.

"That need you felt in the forest? Just think about how fucking good that would feel while I am fucking you. Think about my magic running through your blood while my cock is buried deep inside of you."

I trembled against him as I continued to chase that high.

I wanted everything he spoke of. I feared it, but gods, I wanted it.

"I want you," I whispered, and his hands tightened in my hair.

"You have me, princess. For whatever you want." He kissed me again, and I raised my trembling fingers to his shirt. I fumbled with the buttons, nervous yet eager to get it off of him, and Evren didn't rush me. He pushed my hair out of my face as I worked the buttons down his abdomen and pulled his shirt from his trousers.

I pushed it from his shoulders, revealing his torso, and I slowly ran my fingers over him.

"What are these scars from?" I ran my fingers over the scarred skin, and he let out a harsh breath.

"Too many battles," he said it so easily. "Each one leaves a scar."

I looked up into his eyes, and I knew that he meant more than just what it left on his skin. What had he been through? What had they used him for that now haunted his soul?

"I hate the queen." I leaned forward and pressed my mouth to the largest scar.

"As do I."

"And your brother." I spoke the truth that both of us already knew.

Evren groaned, and his hands tightened against me. His eyes pleaded with me, but his mouth was held in a harsh line as he stared at me.

"I know that he's your family and I'm meant to be betrothed to him, but I hate him."

"I know." He nodded, but he didn't return my sentiment. "I fucking know."

"But I don't want to think about them." I pushed my hands up his chest and wrapped them around the back of his neck. "I want you to make me forget that they exist."

Evren kissed me again, this time more rushed than before, and he wrapped his arms around my back. I tightened my hands on his shoulders as he shifted, and I held on to him as he lifted us off the ground and stood.

He carried me easily to the bed and pressed my back against the mattress. He kissed my shoulder before slowly making his way down my torso, and I gasped as he pressed his mouth against my hard nipple.

"You're mine, princess." His mouth grazed over my ribs before he gently bit down against them, causing me to squirm. "Every single part of you belongs to me."

I nodded my head even though we both knew it wasn't true. This moment didn't have any room for reality. This was about us, and everything we wished could be true.

His mouth pressed against my stomach before he dropped even lower and ran his tongue along my hipbone.

"Evren," I called out his name as I squirmed against him.

He lifted his head, looking up at me before he blew a slow breath against my sex. "Yes, princess?"

"I need you."

"Then tell me you're mine." Another slow, agonizing breath. "Tell me you're mine, and I'll give you anything you want."

"I'm yours." I ran my fingers through his hair and tried to pull him where I needed him most. "I will always be yours."

Evren growled, low and frightening, before he lifted my legs in his hands and spread them impossibly far. My knees hit the bed on either side of me, fully exposing me to him, and he didn't hesitate as he ran his tongue against me.

"Oh gods." My hips shot off the bed, but Evren kept me in place with his hands on my knees.

He sucked my nub into his mouth as he stared up at me, and I had never seen anything more erotic in all my life. This man wasn't mine. He wasn't meant to be anything more than my guard, but seeing him feast from me was more than anything I could have ever wanted.

My marks buzzed against me, the same feeling that was building in my stomach flowing through them, and everything was so overwhelming.

Evren lifted his hand, sliding it up my body before it tightened around my throat gently. "Suck," he commanded, releasing my neck to bring those fingers to my mouth. He slid two inside, and I did as he instructed. I ran my tongue along his fingers before I sucked them deep into my mouth, and Evren groaned against my sex.

He pulled his fingers from my mouth, and I watched as he brought them back down to my sex and slid them inside me. There was no hesitation, no gentleness left in him, and I pressed my head back against the bed as he slid them in and out of me over and over.

I didn't think I could handle much more, everything he was doing made me feel flooded with pleasure. Then he curled his fingers inside of me as he bit down against my nub, and I screamed.

Loud enough that anyone in the pub below could hear me, but I couldn't bring myself to care. The pleasure he drew from my body was too much.

"Fuck." Evren bit down on my thigh before pressing a kiss to my star mark, and another wave of pleasure shot through me. "I need to be inside you, Adara."

"Please."

Evren stood and made quick work of his trousers. He slid them down his legs before kicking them off behind him. Then his hands were back on my legs, and he gripped behind my knees and jerked me closer to the edge of the bed.

I stared at his cock and how hard he was in his own hand, just as he bent my knee and pressed it against his chest. He rubbed his cock through the wetness that still coated my sex, and I squirmed every time the head of him hit my nub.

"Are you sure, princess?" He looked up at me, and I could tell he was barely holding on to the bit of control he had left as his throat worked.

I nodded my head as I pressed my hand to my mouth.

"That's not good enough." He pressed his cock harder against me. "I need your words. I need you to tell me you want this as badly as I want you. I won't do it otherwise."

"I want you, Evren." I reached out for him, and he locked his fingers with mine. "You're the only thing I want."

Evren's gaze darkened, and he lifted my hand and pressed a kiss to my knuckles before pressing another at the bottom of my stomach. He stood back to his full height and ran his cock through me one more time before he hesitated at my entrance.

He sat there for a second, but it felt like so much longer. I could see indecision running through his gaze, or maybe it was guilt, but his want for me won over. He slowly slid inside of me, and I panted as I tried to adjust to his size.

He stretched me inch by inch, and he was so damn gentle as he did so. "Are you okay?"

I nodded because there was no chance of me forming a single word. Pain sliced through me with every inch that he moved, but he replaced that pain with pleasure with every swipe of his fingers against my skin.

"I'm almost there." He groaned as he pushed the smallest amount farther. "Gods, you're so tight."

He pressed his forehead to my neck when he was fully inside of me, and both of our rushed breaths mingled together. Pleasure and pain. It mixed together so perfectly, and even though I still felt so sore around him, I was desperate for him to move.

I rolled my hips against him, and I whimpered when I felt him so deep inside of me.

"Fuck, princess." Evren's breath rushed out as he kissed my neck. "You can't fucking do that, or I'm not going to be able to be gentle with you."

"I don't want you to." I pulled on the ends of his hair and forced him to look up at me. "Please don't treat me like I'm fragile. I'm not the Starblessed. I'm yours."

Evren growled before he slid out of me almost to the tip and slammed back inside. My eyes rolled back in my head as pleasure and pain surged through me.

Evren gripped my head, tilting me toward him, and he kissed me roughly as he slammed inside me again. "Is this okay?"

"Yes," I moaned before biting down on his bottom lip.

Evren groaned, then pressed a kiss over the star mark on my cheek. They practically purred beneath his touch, and a chill ran through my body.

"I've never seen anything more beautiful." He rose until he was standing at the edge of the bed, and he pulled me tighter against him. He held my knee in his hand as he stared down at where we connected. "More perfect." He slammed into me as his fingers pressed against my nub, and I lifted my hands and kneaded my breasts as I watched him.

"You may be blessed by the stars, princess, but you were fucking made for me. Fate be damned."

Evren pulled out of me completely and then used my knee in his hand to flip me over onto my belly. I pressed my hands against the bed as I tried to figure out what he was doing, but Evren's hands gripped my hips and lifted me until I was on my knees.

My hands slid out from under me and my face pressed against the bed.

"Evren." I knew he could hear the slight panic in my voice by the way his hands softly caressed my back.

"I've got you, princess." His words were muffled as he swiped his tongue through my sex, and my knees threatened to buckle beneath me. "You taste like sin."

His mouth moved away from me, and I searched for him over my shoulder just as he stood back to his full height and ran his fingers over my bottom. He was caressing and spreading, and I closed my eyes just as I felt his cock press inside me once more.

He slammed inside of me, and I moaned as my pleasure rose to meet him. His hand slid down my spine, touching every inch of my star mark, and something inside me stirred. It was stronger than I had ever felt before, and I bit down on my lip as I tried to focus on what he was doing.

"Gods, I can feel you." His hips rolled and another surge of pleasure rose inside of me. "It's like your body knows me."

He was right. Since the moment I met him, it was as if my marks knew him better than I ever did.

"Evren, I'm so close." I gripped the bedding in my hands as he slammed into me, and another cry passed through my lips.

"I know." His thumb pressed roughly against my spine and my knees trembled beneath me. "Let go with me, princess. Let me feel you fall apart around my cock."

I did as he commanded, and I screamed into the bedding as he slammed into me again and again. I could feel his seed filling me as I clamped down around him. Evren roared from behind, and his hands became as rough as his hips.

Every touch pushed me further. Every moan dragged the pleasure from my body.

My knees buckled beneath me, and Evren pressed his forehead to my back as he tried to catch his breath.

"Are you okay?" He kissed my spine, and another chill ran through me.

"I'm more than okay." I nodded.

"Me too, princess."

He dropped beside me on the bed and pulled up the bedding to cover me. He ran his fingers over my face as he searched my eyes, and I wanted to live in this moment forever. I didn't want to think about what was to come after we left this room.

"Me too."

EIGHTEEN

I awoke to a soft knock on the door and the sound of muffled voices. I lifted the blanket higher against me, and the fabric felt blissful against my skin. My very bare skin.

I blinked my eyes open just as Evren was closing the door. He was wearing nothing but his trousers only halfway buttoned, and his hair was mussed from sleep. But he held a tray of food in his hands and my clothing in his arms.

"Morning," he mumbled when he noticed me looking up at him.

"Morning," I groaned as I pushed up in the bed until I was sitting. There was a slight ache between my thighs that reminded me of what we had done the night before, but I didn't need the reminder.

Every part of my body still hummed with the memories of the way he had touched me.

"Gadira brought your clothes back." He tossed them on the bed beside me before pushing the tray filled with pastries and meat in my direction. "And breakfast."

I lifted a piece of fried meat to my mouth and moaned as the flavor hit my tongue. I was starving. "Do we continue our travel today?"

"Yes." Evren nodded before sitting down on the edge of the bed and pulling on his boots. "It'll take another two days' time for us to arrive in Nabál. Jorah sent word back to the palace this morning."

"Back to Gavril?"

Evren's back stiffened as I spoke his name, and it took him a long moment before he was able to answer me. "Yes, princess. Back to Gavril."

My chest ached, and my stomach turned at the thought. Of course he had sent word back to his brother. He was the captain of his guard, and I was his job. So, I didn't know why it felt like a betrayal.

"And have you gotten word about the attack on the capital? Of the happenings there?"

"No." He shook his head before running his fingers through his hair. "No one in the village has heard any talks of an attack. There is no news."

"That's good then, isn't it?"

"Or it's very bad." He stood and buttoned his trousers without looking back in my direction. "Either way, I have no way of knowing unless word gets passed to us. Right now, we're blind."

"Do you want to go back?" I pulled the covers higher on my chest to shield myself from his answer.

"What?" He finally turned to look at me. "We left to protect you. I can't take you back."

"I didn't mean for me to go back. You." I nodded in his direction. "Jorah can take me the rest of the way. I can see that not being there bothers you."

Evren stared at me for a long moment, and I squirmed under his scrutiny. "You think I'd rather be back there than be here with you."

"I think that you are the captain of the royal guard."

His jaw tightened, and he narrowed his eyes. "I am much more than that, princess."

"I know that."

"Do you?" He cocked his head before he leaned forward on the bed and pulled the breakfast tray away from me. "It would appear that you need a reminder." He reached under the blanket, and his hand wrapped around my ankle before he jerked me toward him.

I squealed as I attempted to keep myself covered, but it was no use. Evren pulled the blanket from me, exposing my naked body to him, and his tongue ran over his lips as he stared down at me.

"Where exactly do you need the reminder, princess?" He dipped his fingers into a small pot of honey that was accompanying the pastries, and I gasped as he raised them above me and let the sticky substance drip onto my breasts. "Here?"

"What are you doing?" I tried to cover my breasts, but he caught my hand in his and pushed it down against the bed at my side.

"Reminding you of the things I told you last night. They seemed to have slipped your mind." More honey dripped from his fingers down my sternum and into my belly button. "I want to make sure you have a clear fucking understanding before we leave this inn."

"I do understand," I grumbled, but Evren wasn't listening to me.

"No, princess. You don't." He lowered his hand still, and honey dripped from them and over my sex. "Or you wouldn't think for a moment that I could possibly leave you."

More honey dripped down my thighs and slowly rolled across my skin and to my bottom. "And I'm more than fucking happy to make sure we've got things clear." He dipped his honey-coated fingers into his mouth and sucked away the evidence of what he had just done as he stared down at me.

Then ever so slowly, he dropped to his knees before me and slid each of his arms beneath my thighs.

"Evren, we need to get ready." My voice shook with the anticipation of what he was about to do.

"What I need." He pressed a soft kiss against my inner thigh as he used his arms to lift my hips into the air. My shoulders pressed firmly into the mattress, and I couldn't look away from him as he spoke. "Is to find out if this honey tastes even sweeter off your sex."

He ran his tongue along my bottom, catching the honey that was still falling there, and I clamped my eyes closed as embarrassment flooded me. "Eyes on me, princess," he growled, and I opened them immediately. "I need you to watch while I fuck every inch of you with my mouth. I don't want there to be a trace of confusion left."

He licked away every bit of honey from my skin, his mouth touching every part of me except where I needed him most. He ran his teeth along the top of my sex, careful not to touch my aching nub, and I groaned in frustration as his mouth moved up to my stomach.

"What's wrong, princess?" He chuckled against my skin, but I refused to give him what he wanted. I wasn't going to beg him for the pleasure he was denying me.

I pressed my head back into the mattress as his tongue dipped into my belly button. "Gods, you're so sweet," he rumbled against my skin, and my legs shook in his hands. He brought his head lower, just over my sex, and my stomach tightened in anticipation.

"Ask for what you want, princess. Tell me what it is you need."

"You," I moaned as I looked up at him. "I need you."

He dove into my flesh hard and fast, feasting on me like a

man starved, and I cried out as every bit of my frustration throbbed between my thighs. I rolled my hips against his mouth, far too desperate for him to sit still, and he groaned against me.

"That's a good girl. Fuck my face like you were always meant to be mine."

"Oh gods." I gripped the bedding as his words and his mouth consumed me. Pleasure rushed through me, fast and all-consuming, and I knew that I was so damn close to falling over that edge. "Evren."

"That's right, princess." His words vibrated against me before he sucked me into his mouth. "Let the whole fucking kingdom know who you belong to."

I pressed my thighs against his head as my pleasure shot through me, but he didn't stop. I covered my mouth with my hand, trying to bury the sounds of my cries as he continued to draw out my pleasure. He took, and he took, until my legs trembled and I could hardly catch my breath, and only then did he rise to his feet and run his thumb along his lips before he pushed my moisture that was coated there into his mouth.

"You're a sticky fucking mess, princess." He took that same thumb and rubbed it along the star mark on my thigh, causing me to quiver. "Let me run you a bath."

He lifted his hand and black smoke shot from his fingers in a whirl and bounced around the room as water began pouring from the wall. Evren looked down at his hand almost as if he was confused by his magic before he reined it back in.

The tips of his fingers were still stained black, and I wasn't sure why I loved the look of it so much. He had called it a mark of his dark magic, but it just felt like him.

"You rarely use your magic," I noted out loud, and Evren looked to me.

"I use it when I need to."

"Did you use it on those men? The ones hanging at the gate."

"No." He shook his head and reached his hand out for me. I

placed my hand in his without hesitation, and he helped me from the bed. "What I did to those men was with my bare hands."

A shiver ran down my spine, but he barely seemed to notice as he led me to the bath and held my hand as I stepped into the tub.

"Does the queen know what you did to those men?" I sank into the water as I stared up at him, and he leaned down until his face was so close to mine.

"I think the queen would be far more concerned with what I've done to you, princess." He pressed his mouth to mine and kissed me softly before pulling away. "But I don't give a fuck what the queen thinks."

NINETEEN

W'e waved goodbye to Ren as we rode away from the village, but that felt like hours ago. Every moment took me farther away from the kingdom, but somehow felt like it was taking me closer to my doom.

Evren had sent word to Gavril, and I had no idea what he had told him. Would Gavril meet us at Nabál? Would he come once the threat was over?

Evren's hand tightened around me as if he could sense the thoughts running through my mind. "Do we need to stop?"

"No." I shook my head quickly and tightened my hands on the pommel of the saddle to keep myself from leaning back into him. I didn't want to get too comfortable, too used to this thing that was happening between us.

"Are you sure? Your back went rigid. Are you sore?"

I was. Increasingly so with every mile that we traveled, but that wasn't what was bothering me. "I'm fine, Evren. I'm just ready to arrive."

He was silent for a long moment behind me, and I thought that he was going to drop it as I looked over at Jorah. He was watching the tree line dutifully as we traveled, and he took the last attack as personally as Evren had.

"Are you angry about what happened at the inn?" Evren cleared his throat, and a chill ran down my spine. "I didn't mean to hurt you. I shouldn't have..."

"You didn't hurt me." I shook my head and turned to look at him over my shoulder. "I told you I wanted what happened back there."

"Then what's wrong?"

The urge to tell him that I wished we could just ride away from this place and never return was on the tip of my tongue, because I would. If Evren asked it of me, I would follow him wherever he was willing to take me.

Away from both of our duties and fates.

"What role will I have as Gavril's queen?"

He went stiff behind me at my question. "What do you mean?"

"Gavril is meant to rule over both the fae and human realms, is he not?" I looked forward again and thought about the home I had left.

"He is."

"And what about me? Will I have that same rule?"

"Princess?" My nickname was a whisper from his lips.

"I refuse to sit in that castle with servants and feasts while people around us starve. Have you ever seen someone who is truly starving, Evren? Have you witnessed what that's like?"

More hesitation and I worried I had crossed a line. I was about to tell him to forget what I had said just as he spoke. "I've witnessed more of it than I dare speak of. It isn't just your human lands that are starving, princess."

I hadn't thought of that. I hadn't considered that fae who possessed magic could ever get to that point.

"Ren was little more than skin and bones the first time Jorah and I stopped in Iladonia." His voice was gruff and laced with anger. "We make a point to stop there every time we travel now. Without my coin, they would barely survive."

My stomach ached as I thought of Ren's smiling face. I couldn't imagine him any other way. I couldn't see him the way Evren described.

"And your father? Why doesn't he do anything about it?"

"Kings are rarely concerned with things that don't fill their coffers, princess. A man could be starving in front of my father, and I'm not sure he would extend him a piece of bread."

"Doesn't that bother you?" I shook my head. "That you serve a man who could be so cruel?"

"He is my father."

"And he killed mine. Just because someone is your blood doesn't mean they deserve your loyalty."

Evren sighed, and I knew there was more he wanted to say. There was so much more he wasn't willing to tell me.

"Princess, I..."

"Yes?" *Please talk to me.*

"I wish that the world was different. I dream of a place where these burdens don't exist."

"And what of your mother?"

"What do you mean?" His hand tightened against me, and I knew he didn't want to talk about her.

"What is the world like where she lives?"

"I... I don't know."

My mark burned against my skin as he spoke of her.

"But I can't imagine that it could be the same as Citlali."

There was so much power in his voice, and my marks burned in warning. Was he lying?

"Do you miss her?"

"Do you miss yours?" he countered quickly.

"Sometimes." I shrugged. "When I'm with Gavril or the queen. When I'm longing for a home I barely knew."

"And when you're with me?"

"I don't think of her at all."

His breath rushed out against the back of my neck, and I feared that I had said too much.

"You would have made a great king, Evren."

Jorah's gaze slammed into mine as I spoke, and I feared that he could hear every word that was said between us.

"We should stop here." Jorah nodded to a cropping of trees that lay near a small brook. "The night will fall soon."

Evren nodded in agreement and led us over to the trees. He dismounted before helping me down, and I wrapped my arms around myself as I thought of what was to come. One more night. We had one more night before we were to make it to Nabál.

"We will arrive tomorrow?"

"We shall." Jorah nodded as he tied his mare near the water. "It's just another day's ride."

Evren pulled things from the saddlebags as he looked over at me. He knew what tomorrow meant as well. I could feel it like a bad omen against my marks.

I wasn't ready to face it, and neither was he.

"What did your word to Gavril say?"

"What?" Evren asked as he dropped a bedroll onto the ground.

"You said you sent word back to the palace. What did it say?"

"What does it matter, princess?" He cocked his head to the side as he watched me. "What did you want me to say?"

"I don't know." I shook my head, and Evren stepped toward me.

"Did you want me to tell them that you were captured by the vampyres? That I was going to have to go to the Blood Court and fight for you? That you may never be seen again?"

My heart raced harder the closer he got to me. "I don't know."

He wrapped his hand into my hair and angled my head until I had no choice but to look up at him. "Did you want me to tell him that I am more than willing to betray my family for you? That I'll give it all up for the girl who's supposed to be my brother's future?"

I swallowed hard as I stared at him. His gaze dropped to my mouth before he leaned forward and ran his nose along my jaw. I could feel his breath rushing out against my neck, and I melted against him.

"I could tell him those things, but he would never stop. He would hunt us down to the edges of the world to get you back."

"Gavril doesn't care about me."

"No." He shook his head against me. "But he cares about your power, and nothing else is more important to him. Nothing is more important to the queen. They would rather kill you than let me have you."

I bit down on my lip as I thought of what he was saying, and I knew that he was right. I shuddered. *They would never stop.* I didn't want to think about what they would do when they found me. When they found us.

"Let's get some rest." Evren pulled away from me slowly, and I hated the way he avoided my gaze as he did so. "I'll take first watch," he called out to Jorah. "Both of you get some rest."

He left me standing there as he went back to his horse and led him to the water. I quickly reached for the bedroll he left and unrolled it before slipping inside. Jorah moved near me, stacking wood for a small fire, and I clamped my eyes closed so he couldn't see the hurt and fear that lay there.

I listened to the sounds he made as he lit the fire and then laid his bedroll on the opposite side of the flames from mine. I shivered as I wrapped my arms around myself despite the warmth from the fire.

"Is she all right?" The sound of Jorah's voice startled me some moments later, but I kept myself perfectly still as I listened.

"I don't know." Evren sounded much closer than before. "She's not going to go back, Jorah. She'll run again before she does so."

"Then what's your plan?" Jorah hesitated for a long moment. "Do we tell her?"

They were silent for so long after his question that I almost drifted to sleep. "Not yet. I fear what she'll do when she finds out. I fear she may already know."

Know what? I could still hear their muffled voices, but the pull of sleep was too much to fight.

I fell asleep to thoughts of what he said running over and over in my mind. They haunted me until my dreams became worse. Thoughts of what would happen when we finally arrived preyed upon me in my sleep, and I awoke with a gasp as Gavril's mouth pressed against my new mark and my wrist burned as if I had been scorched.

I shot up in my bedroll and jerked my wrist into my chest. It had felt like I had only been asleep for a few moments, but the darkness had fallen over us and the only light left was that of the fire and the twin moons in the sky.

"Are you all right?" Evren stepped out of the trees at my side, and I jumped.

"Yes." I nodded even though I couldn't seem to drop my wrist. I looked toward Jorah, and his chest rose and fell peacefully where he lay on top of his bedroll.

"Are you sure?" Evren squatted down beside me, and I allowed myself to look up at him.

"I just had a bad dream."

"Do you want to talk about it?"

"No." I shook my head. I didn't want to talk about it or think about it.

"Okay." He reached forward and took my hand in his before he lifted it to his mouth. He kept his eyes on me as he pressed his lips to my inner wrist just along my mark. "Try to get some more sleep. We only have a few more hours before we travel again."

"Shouldn't you be sleeping?"

Evren grinned at my concern. "Jorah needs the rest. I feel..." He hesitated as he searched my face. "I feel strong."

"Because you fed from me?"

"I believe so, yes." He nodded. "I haven't tired like I normally would."

"You still need rest." I pulled my arm back toward me, and he reluctantly dropped it. "I could keep watch for a while."

He chuckled softly. "Are you going to protect us if we're attacked?"

"I could." I pulled my dagger from my boot and held it to his neck before he could realize what I was doing. "I'm not completely useless, you know."

"I don't think anyone could ever find you useless, princess." Evren grinned even with my knife pressed to his neck. "I could find many uses for you and for your dagger."

"What?"

He moved so quickly that I didn't have time to react. He flipped my dagger from my hand and into his before he slowly ran the tip along my collarbone.

"Would you like me to show you?"

"No." My voice trembled with the lie on my tongue.

"If only you had more clothes with you." Ever so carefully, he moved the dagger down my chest until it met the top button of my shirt. "I would cut through every bit of fabric that's standing between us."

He slid the dagger lower and cut through the first button. "I would cut the world down to keep it from getting between us."

"You confuse me." I shook my head and pressed my hand against his to stop my dagger. "You say things like that, but you're willing to hand me straight to them."

"What do you want me to do, princess?" He let my dagger

fall to the ground beside us. "Tell me what you want, and I'll give it to you."

"I don't know." I shook my head because I was more confused than ever. I didn't know what I was asking of Evren, but either way, I knew it wasn't fair. Gavril was his family. Citlali his kingdom.

And I was nothing more than the Starblessed he was meant to protect.

Evren pressed his hand to my chest, his fingers digging into my skin, as if he was searching for his control, and he felt as desperate as I did inside.

"If I knew how to do this, I would. If I knew how to love you without getting you hurt, I would never allow them to touch you again."

"Your family?"

"Your enemies." His hand slid up my chest and around my neck. My pulse raced beneath the tips of his fingers, and I knew he could feel the fear that ran through my veins.

"I don't want to go back." My voice cracked, and I hated how easily my fear was taking over. I had spent my whole life knowing what lay ahead for me, preparing for it, but it hadn't been enough.

"I know." He nodded and pressed his forehead to mine. "I won't make you."

"What?" I jerked back to look at him, but his hands held me firmly in place.

"I would rather leave this world than to watch my brother take from you again. I will give up everything for you, princess."

I searched his gaze, and I could see the truth that lay there.

"What do we do?" I rose to my knees to pull myself closer to him, and his breath rushed out against my lips.

"I don't know." He shook his head against me. "But we'll figure it out with the rise of the sun. Tonight, you need to rest."

He started to pull away, but I held him against me. I couldn't let him go. Not now. Not ever. "Tonight, I need you."

Evren looked over to where Jorah was sleeping only a few feet away from us, but I didn't care. I couldn't go another moment without touching him, without feeling alive in a way that only he could make me feel.

"Please, Evren." I pressed my lips to his, and he didn't fight me. Instead, he groaned against my mouth before he sucked my bottom lip between his. He bit down gently, teasingly, and pleasure coursed through me.

I reached forward before he could stop me and pulled his shirt from his trousers before I fumbled with the buttons. I was only halfway done when he reached behind him and pulled his shirt over his head.

He searched my gaze for a moment before he wrapped his hand back around the nape of my neck and forced my mouth to his once again. He kissed me with a desperation that I had never felt before. Tonight was different.

It felt like more.

More than what we had ever allowed ourselves to feel for one another. More than I ever allowed myself to admit.

Evren kissed me hard as his hand pressed against my breast and kneaded my flesh through my thin shirt. I moaned against him, and he bit down against my tongue before slowly sucking it into his mouth.

"Gods, you possess me." He pulled away and jerked my shirt over my head. "You make me feel like a man gone mad."

"I'm not doing anything." I shook my head, but the reality was that I felt the same. I couldn't think clearly when I was around him. I couldn't breathe.

"You most certainly fucking are." He gripped my hips in his hands and lifted me until I was fully on my knees. His deft fingers made quick work of my trousers, and I shivered even with the lick of the flames at my back. "You are sin, princess, and I need to taste it. I need the reminder on my tongue while you ride my face."

I whimpered as Evren pushed me down on the bedroll and jerked my boots from my feet before my trousers followed. I was left completely bare in front of him. He lifted his fingers, pressing them against my lips before he slowly ran them down my body. He caressed my neck before his palm met my sternum, slow and calculating. His touch dropped lower and lower until he slid a finger through my sex, and I cried out at his touch.

Evren dropped to his back beside me just as his thumb traced over the mark on my thigh. I trembled as I watched him touch me, and I yelped when his fingers dug into my thighs and pulled me up over his chest.

"Evren." My voice shook with the uncertainty that raced in my mind.

"I've got you, Adara." He lifted me farther until my knees were situated on either side of his head.

I pressed my hands to my thighs as I held myself above him, but Evren dug his fingers into my backside and tugged me down.

"Evren, I don't think…"

"I'm dying to taste you, princess." He lifted forward and rolled his tongue through my sex. "I've never tasted anything more perfect in all my life."

He jerked me down lower until I was practically sitting on his face, and I moaned as he hummed against me. "That's it. Sit on my face and fuck your pleasure from my mouth."

"Oh gods." I clamped my eyes closed as his words alone pulled pleasure from my body. Then he used his mouth.

He wasn't gentle or patient. He was frantic as he dove into my flesh, and I could barely hold myself up as he used his tongue and lips and teeth against me.

I slammed my hands back against his abdomen as I began rocking against him, and when I looked down and saw him staring up at me, a deep ache began in my stomach.

"Evren," I said his name as I rolled my hips, and he hummed his encouragement against me.

He sucked my sex into his mouth, and I squeezed my thighs against his head.

My pleasure soared through me quickly, stealing the air from my lungs, and I bit down on my lip to muffle my cries.

Evren didn't give me a chance to recover. He gripped my backside in his hands and slid me down his body until my hips met his.

He kissed me then, his lips brushing against my skin, and every bit of air left my lungs.

"I can't get enough of you, princess. I'll never be able to part from you."

He dug his fingers in my hair and pulled me away from him. He stared up at me, and his gaze ran over every inch of my face.

"My brother will fight for you, but so will I."

My chest ached, and I didn't know if it was from what he was confessing or from fear of what he'd be willing to do. "I…" The urge to tell him that I loved him was on the tip of my tongue, but I bit down against it to stop myself.

"I will fight through hell to keep you from him, Adara." His mouth was possessive as it ran down my body and caused spark after spark of pleasure to run through me.

He lifted me onto my knees, and I watched as he unbuttoned his pants and pulled out his rigid cock. It pressed against me, and I tensed with my hands on his shoulders.

"I want to watch you." He held his cock against my entrance and guided me until I slowly lowered myself fully against him. I pressed my eyes closed as the fullness of him overwhelmed me, and Evren nipped his teeth just along my sternum.

"Move, princess. You've spent far too much of your life being told what you want, but I want to see it from your eyes. Show me what it is you desire most."

You.

It was the only thing I could think as I rolled my hips against him. I used to dream of what life would be like if I ran, if I could be anyone other than who I was, but that dream had shifted.

It had become centered around a man that I shouldn't want. That I shouldn't need.

But it was him just the same.

He ran his fingers along my spine, urging me on, and something stirred inside me. Something that felt like it had been sleeping for a long time, and I pushed to my knees before dropping back down against him.

Over and over, the feeling built, and my body moved. I chased that sensation that flowed through me physically and somehow more.

I stared down at Evren and the way he was looking at me. His hands caressed my body, but they weren't demanding. This was about me, and my stomach fluttered as I thought about how easily he knew I needed this.

I was the Starblessed, the savior of his kingdom, but I was also Adara. And right now, I felt lost beyond who I was fated to be.

"Look, Adara." Evren rubbed his fingers over my thigh, and I tracked his movement. My star mark danced along my skin, and the slightest glow unlike anything I had ever seen radiated from it.

"What?" I shook my head as I tried to make sense of what was happening, but Evren pressed his thumb roughly against my mark, and my sex spasmed against him.

"You were fucking meant for me." He wrapped his arms around my back and helped me as I lifted and dropped against him. Harder and harder, his arms carrying my weight as he slammed up into me. "Your fate is wrong."

My pleasure raced through my body as if it were chasing his words like an oath.

"You are the firstborn son of King Riven," I whimpered as he slammed into me once more.

His forehead pressed against my neck, and his rough breath rushed out against my skin.

"I was fated for you, Evren." My spine burned like a million fires along my skin, and I knew I wouldn't be able to handle much more.

Evren's hands tightened around me as if he feared I would disappear, and when his fingers stroked over my spine once more, I fell apart with a cry on my lips.

I clung to him as he thrust into me again, drawing his own pleasure from my body, and I watched as the starlight along my wrist glowed against his skin.

I wasn't sure of anything in this life, but one thing I knew for certain was that Evren was my destiny.

TWENTY

I squatted down near the brook and dipped my fingers into the cold water. Evren and Jorah were packing up our camp and stamping out what was left of the coals in our fire.

I rubbed my wet fingers over my face and tried to clear my racing thoughts. Water dripped down my neck, and I grazed my fingers over the sensitive skin as memories of what Evren had done to me last night flashed through my mind.

There was a snap of movement across the water, and my eyes shot open as I searched the trees and my marks burned against my skin. I didn't see anything, but somehow I knew something was there.

"Evren," I said his name softly as I stood, but I didn't take my gaze away from the trees.

"Yeah?" he called out to me as he laughed at something Jorah was saying. "What is it, princess?"

A dagger flew through the air before I could answer him, and I cried in pain as it sliced through the outside of my left arm before lodging perfectly in the tree behind me.

"Princess!" This time Evren was screaming for me, but I was too busy staring ahead. A group of ten men rose from where they hid beyond the trees, and each one had a weapon raised in their hands.

"Princess has a nice ring to it, doesn't it?" The one who threw the dagger cocked his head to the side as he spoke, and I didn't know if he was talking to me or someone else.

I stumbled backward before reaching down and pulled my dagger from my boot.

"A fighting princess as well. Even better."

"What the fuck are you doing?" Evren roared from behind me before he jerked me backward and shielded my body with his own.

"The queen would like to meet her."

The queen?

"That's not fucking happening." Evren shook his head, and I noted the black smoke that swirled around his fingers. "Not today."

"I don't answer to you, prince." The man looked beyond Evren, and his gaze connected with mine. "I will be taking her whether it's willingly or not."

I looked behind me for Jorah, but he was nowhere to be seen. I didn't know these men, but they didn't wear the colors of the Citlali guard. Instead, they dressed similarly to Evren. Dark, inconspicuous, lethal.

"Is that what your other men were doing in the Onyx Forest? Coming to take the Starblessed?"

They were of the Blood Court then. The same court as Evren's mother.

"My men?" The man laughed as he ran his fingers over the blade in his hand. "If those were my men, we wouldn't be having this conversation right now."

"I won't let you take her, Calix." Evren squared his shoulders as if preparing himself for an attack, and I took a small step back.

"You don't have a choice." Calix didn't lift the blade from

his hand. Instead, power shot out of his fingers. Power like Evren's. Black as night and laced with doom, it came for Evren quicker than I could blink, but Evren matched his power with a wave of his own.

Their power slammed into one another, and a crack of sound echoed around us.

I stumbled backward, startled by the power that was flowing from both of them, and I noticed Jorah move through the trees across from us. He lifted his sword before running up behind one of the men who was watching what was happening in front of them, and I gasped when he sliced through his neck as if it was nothing.

The scene caught Calix's attention, distracting him momentarily, and Evren's power slammed into him.

"Jorah." Calix tsked, though his voice was now winded. "I see where your loyalty is buried."

Jorah chuckled, the sound crazed and cruel. "My loyalty has always been with the prince, Calix. The fact that you questioned that is a testament to your own lack of judgment."

Calix was still looking to Jorah when his power shot out again, and this time, Evren wasn't prepared. The magic hit him savagely as if aiming to kill, and Evren groaned in pain.

"Take Jorah," Calix commanded to the other guards, and they swarmed him so quickly that he didn't stand a chance. He held his sword in front of him, but he was far too outnumbered.

"Jorah!" Evren's voice boomed through the forest, and Calix took the opportunity to shoot another band of power in Evren's direction.

Evren stopped it with his own, and my marks burned like fire against my skin.

"You know she's coming with us, Evren. You're only fighting the inevitable."

"I will kill you before I allow you to take her." Evren bared his teeth, and fear coursed through my veins.

"You've become soft, prince." Calix shot his power in my direction and Evren dove for me. Panic filled his eyes as the power slammed into his back and knocked the breath from his lungs.

"Evren!" I charged for him as blood dripped from his lips, but Calix was faster.

I could see the defeat in Evren's eyes as he tried to climb back to his knees. My marks were set afire across my skin, burning more than they ever had before, and I could feel a part of myself breaking.

"This is your mate." Calix laughed before he gripped Evren by the back of his hair and forced him to look at me. "The bastard prince stuck between two kingdoms."

He still spoke, but all I could concentrate on was the word mate. It echoed inside me, rolling through my veins, and when I stared into Evren's tired eyes, I knew it to be true.

This man that was on his knees before me, the one fighting for my life with his own, was my mate. Flames formed in my gut, and my marks felt like they were charring my skin.

"Let him go," I demanded of him with a growl.

Calix laughed and only tightened his hold on Evren. "This one will be taken back to my queen just as you will, princess." He spat the name like a slur.

I didn't know his queen or what she wanted with either of us, but I knew I refused to allow them to take him.

I reached inside of myself, and I held on to that blaze that raged. "I said to let him go."

Evren shook his head, barely able to manage the movement with his hair still inside Calix's hand, but I was beyond taking orders.

The power inside of me built, the anger and rage rising and rising until I could feel it along my fingertips.

"You're lucky I don't kill the bastard." Calix laughed, and power shot from within me.

I didn't know where it came from, and I had no control, but power slammed into Calix unexpectedly. His gaze hit mine as the breath was knocked from his chest, and his hand loosened on Evren's head. I let my magic loose once more.

This time when it slammed into Calix, he was more prepared, but it still knocked him to his back. His men shifted around him, but not a single one approached me.

"Don't touch him again." I stepped closer to Evren, and I saw the fear in Calix's eyes as he watched me.

"The queen wants him back in the Blood Court."

"I don't give a damn about your queen," I growled at him, and another wave of black power shot from me. Some of his men fell to the ground, but I kept my eyes on him.

"You should." My gaze snapped up at the sound of a woman's voice, and I quickly put myself between her and Evren.

She moved around the tree in which she was hidden, and her long fingernails trailed over its bark lazily. She was beautiful with eyes that reminded me of the sea and my father. She wore black boots that went to her knees and covered her trousers that were tucked beneath.

She didn't look like a queen, but I knew in my bones that this was her.

Evren groaned as he reached out for me, but his hand trembled as he wrapped it around my shin.

"Queen Veda, I presume?"

"In the flesh." She cocked her head to the side and stared at the way Evren reached for me. "And here I thought you didn't give a damn about me."

"I don't." My fingertips buzzed with my power, and I gritted my teeth as I tried to keep control.

"Yet you protect my son as if you care very deeply."

Her words choked me, and I felt like I couldn't breathe. Evren's hand tightened against me, and my marks begged me to let my power flow through me.

"What?" It was the only word I could manage as I tried to make sense of what she was saying.

"He may be the bastard son of King Riven, but he is the first-born son of the Blood Court. He is our future and our destiny."

I jerked out of Evren's hold as she spoke, and I stumbled backward.

"He is an excellent spy and traitor to the fae crown. Apparently, he became an excellent betrayer to his mate as well."

"Adara," he said my name, and my gaze snapped to meet his. This man who I thought I loved.

"You lied to me." The truth shook through me.

"I didn't." He shook his head frantically as he tried to climb to his knees. "I told you I was born of both magic and blood. I told you my mother was a vampyre."

"But not the queen!" I shouted, and my magic surged through me.

Every eye was trained on me as a dim glow gleaned from my star marks.

"I couldn't tell you the truth, princess. I didn't know where your loyalty lay."

Tears flooded my eyes, and a sob escaped my throat. "Is that what you were telling yourself when you were between my thighs? Were you searching for my loyalty?"

Evren rose on shaky legs, but when he took a step toward me, I took an equal one back. "Adara, please."

"Don't." I held out my hand and my magic dripped from my fingers in a dark smoke that was so perfectly matched to his. "Don't you dare touch me."

Queen Veda laughed, the sound grated down my spine, and I clenched my teeth so hard that I feared they would break. "It would appear that the two of you have some things to work out, but the Starblessed will make a wonderful queen."

I jerked back at her words, and my gaze slammed back into Evren. He was pleading with me with his eyes, and we continued to stand there, watching each other while the others watched us.

"Princess," he whispered, and it almost broke me.

"I will never marry you, Evren," I said sharply, my conviction sliding between us like a promise.

He took a small step forward, and it somehow seemed to suck all the air from my lungs. His gaze was no longer pleading, no longer begging me to understand. Instead, his eyes darkened and the grimace on his face overwhelmed me. "You will."

"You'll have to tie me up. You'll have to force my hand, just as your brother did before you."

Evren's power shot out of him, the black smoke wrapping around me like a lover's touch. I wasn't prepared or skilled enough to fight back with my own, but still I glowed, brighter and more intense with every inch he touched.

He moved toward me then when I didn't stand a chance of moving out of his hold, and he leaned in, testing me as his power thrummed against my skin. "That can be arranged, princess."

His power strummed across my wrist, and I clamped my eyes closed to force myself to ignore the pleasure that ached under his touch.

No. Evren was not the man I thought I knew. He was as much my enemy as he had convinced me his brother to be, and I was a fool.

"Calix, get up!" Queen Veda barked at her guard, and he stood with a groan as he rubbed his chest. Right where my power had hit him. "We must move before Queen Kaida finds out of Evren's treason."

"He's fed from her," Evren spoke to his mother, and my back went rigid under his words. "Before he ordered her away, he fed."

"And what of his powers?"

"I don't know." Evren shook his head, and his magic trembled around me, holding my arms at my sides.

"And you?" The queen nodded toward him. "Have you fed from your mate?"

Evren hesitated for a long moment, and I hated how easily they were discussing something that had been so intimate between us. "I have."

"And?"

"She's powerful." Evren looked back toward me, and for the first time since I laid eyes on him in Starless, he looked like he saw nothing but my mark. "I could feel her power the moment I tasted her blood on my tongue."

"Get the Starblessed." The queen nodded toward her guards and two of them started toward me. I struggled in Evren's magic, but he didn't seem to notice. "We must keep her safe until we cross the border."

The guards moved closer, and my heart hammered in my chest. I looked to Jorah, but he watched me as closely as every other guard of the Blood queen. He was every bit one of them as Evren was.

"Don't fucking touch her," Evren growled, his power slamming into me. "The Starblessed belongs to me."

But the prince who belonged to two kingdoms was wrong. I belonged to no one.

Want more from the Stars and Shadows Series? Pre-order A Kingdom of Blood and Betrayal coming November 3rd.

MORE FROM HOLLY RENEE

Stars and Shadows Series:

A Kingdom of Stars and Shadows

A Kingdom of Blood and Betrayal

The Good Girls Series:

Where Good Girls Go to Die

Where Bad Girls Go to Fall

Where Bad Boys are Ruined

The Boys of Clermont Bay Series:

The Touch of a Villain

The Fall of a God

The Taste of an Enemy

The Deceit of a Devil

The Seduction of Pretty Lies

The Temptation of Dirty Secrets

The Rock Bottom Series:

Trouble with the Guy Next Door

Trouble with the Hotshot Boss

Trouble with the Fake Boyfriend

The Wrong Prince Charming

THANK YOU

Thank you so much for taking a chance on A Kingdom of Stars and Shadows! I hope you loved this world as much as I did creating it.

Ready to fall in love with another world that I have created? The Touch of a Villain is an angsty, enemies-to-lovers romance that will have you begging for more!

I would love for you to join my reader group, Hollywood, so we can connect and talk about all of your thoughts on A Kingdom of Stars and Shadows! This group is the first place to find out about cover reveals, book news, and new releases!

Again, thank you for going on this journey with me.

Xo,

Holly Renee
www.authorhollyrenee.com

Before You Go

Please consider leaving an honest review.

ACKNOWLEDGMENTS

Honestly, I find this acknowledgment hard to write because this book was such a labor of love. So many people believed in me when I wasn't sure that I could venture into this world.

Thank you to my husband, Hubie. No one will ever support or love me more than you. Thank you for always proving to me that true love exists.

Thank you to all the readers and bloggers for taking a chance on this book of mine. I poured my heart into these pages, and I am beyond grateful that you chose to spend your time reading it. I will never be able to truly show you my gratitude.

Thank you to Christina, for always believing in me no matter what crazy idea I throw your way.

Thank you to my entire team who I couldn't do this without. Amanda, Ellie, Rumi, Cynthia, Becca, and Savannah: thank you, thank you, thank you.